THE BUCHAN

J.D.F. JONES was until recently Lite   ......
Financial Times, where he was previously also Foreign Editor,
Managing Editor and founder-editor of the *Weekend F.T.* He is the
author of *Through Fortress and Rock* (1995), the story of Gencor,
one of South Africa's biggest corporations. His first novel was
entitled *Freeland* (1994).

J.D.F. Jones

THE BUCHAN PAPERS

THE HARVILL PRESS
LONDON

First published in 1996 by
The Harvill Press
84 Thornhill Road
London N1 1RD

2 4 6 8 10 9 7 5 3 1

© J.D.F. Jones 1996

J.D.F. Jones asserts the moral right to be
identified as the author of this work

A CIP catalogue record for this book
is available from the British Library

ISBN 1 86046 180 8

Designed and typeset in Bulmer at
Libanus Press, Marlborough, Wiltshire

Printed and bound in Great Britain by Butler & Tanner
at Selwood Printing, Burgess Hill

For Jules, without whom . . .

Eastern Transvaal

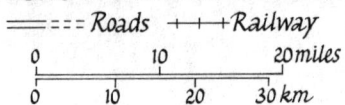

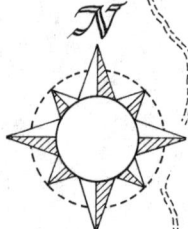

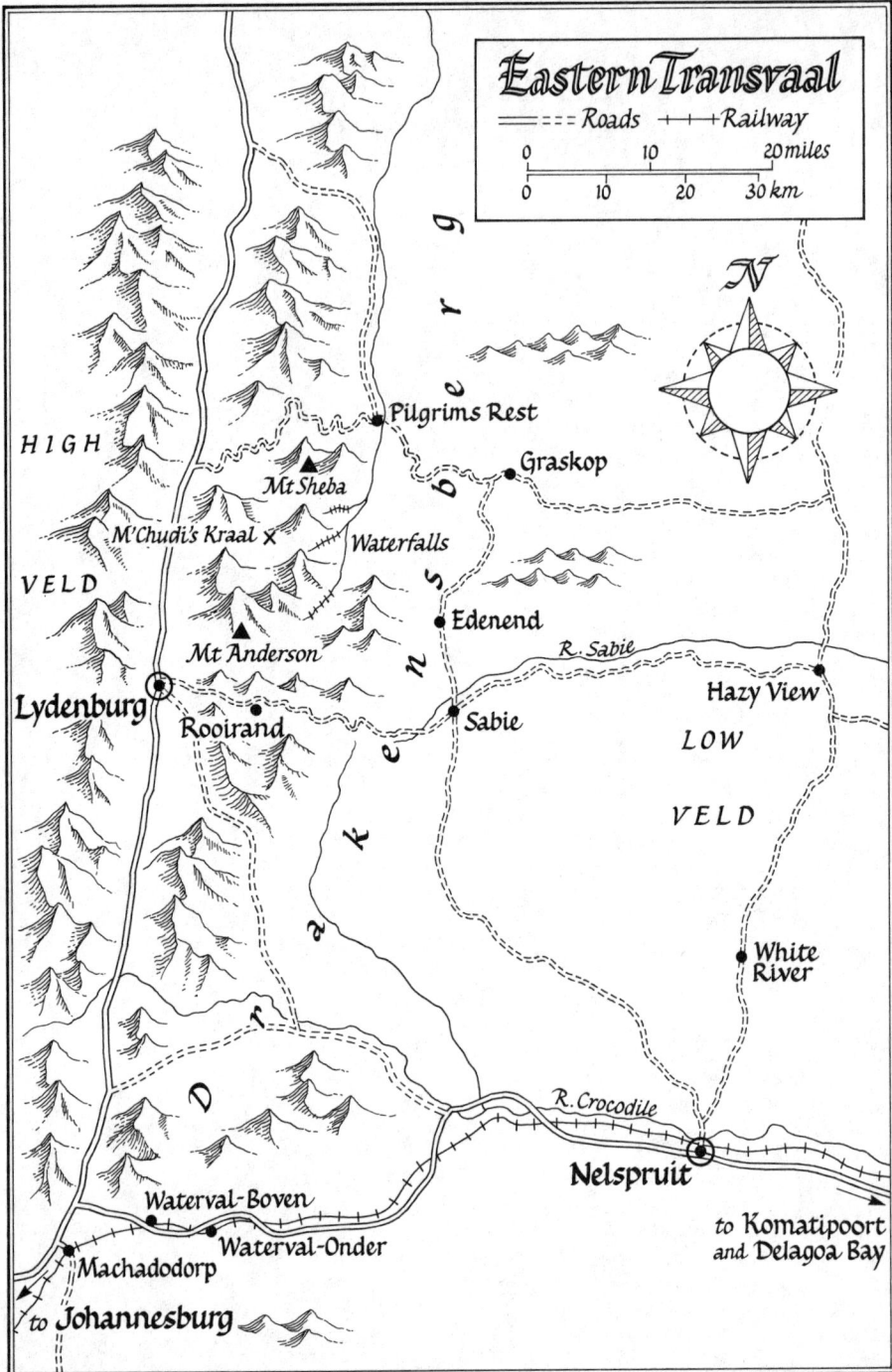

Roads   Railway

0   10   20 miles
0   10   20   30 km

N

HIGH

Pilgrims Rest

Mt Sheba

Graskop

M'Chudi's Kraal ×

Waterfalls

VELD

Edenend

R. Sabie

Mt Anderson

Hazy View

Lydenburg

Sabie

LOW

Rooirand

VELD

White River

R. Crocodile

Nelspruit

Waterval-Boven

Waterval-Onder

to Komatipoort
and Delagoa Bay

Machadodorp

to Johannesburg

THE BUCHAN PAPERS

Foreword

". . . I came over the Berg as the moon was rising behind the Lebombo. They were gaining on me with every stride, I could hear their steady breathing and the slap of their bare feet on the turf. I snatched a glance over my shoulder and they saw it and hallooed again, almost cheerfully, and several of them brandished their spears at me as though to make promises. I had a deathly dread that I was within their range and in these next seconds would be skewered in the back. That terror must have given me a last infusion of energy, because briefly I seemed to gain on them, and now I could see the brink of the cliff face like a trapdoor opening ahead of me. I was far beyond thought, I must have abandoned my life at that moment, because I measured those last yards and I launched myself out over the Berg and into the blackness, spreadeagled into space . . ."

A word of explanation may be in order. These are the lines, inscribed in crabbed and only slightly faded longhand, that first caught my attention as I shuffled through the contents of a box-file of the personal papers of Sir Lionel Phillips, marked simply "PP/LP" on the spine and dated 1904–07. I had spent longer than I could spare searching for the memoranda relating to the Dutoitspan takeover by General Mining and this bundle of foolscap, tied in the red ribbon beloved of London lawyers, evidently had nothing at all to do with the obscure but necessary detail of Mandelstam's option on one hundred thousand shares which I had been looking for all morning.

If the above implies criticism of the efficiency, or for that matter the courtesy, of the Barlow Rand archivists, I have been unfair. Barlows is of course one of South Africa's largest industrial and mining conglomerates. It has its headquarters in a custom-designed complex in the Northern Johannesburg suburb of Sandton, conveniently situated in a pleasant environment of walled gardens adjoining the motorway to Pretoria. I acknowl-edge that the head librarian of Barlows has something of a reputation for difficulty in my profession: she is famous for forbidding access to historians whom she suspects of a radical inclination, but – and it is perhaps a comment on my reputation, or perhaps my political complexion – I must emphasise that I was made entirely welcome when I wrote from my university in East Anglia to explain that I was working on a book tentatively entitled *Class, Gold and Race: the Role of the Randlords in the South African Reconstruction, 1902–05*.

I emphasise, therefore, that I have been given unrestricted access to the Barlow Rand archives, and indeed have spent many fruitful weeks working there. Barlows' mining division was orig-inally called Rand Mines, which was taken over by Barlows in 1971. The founder of Rand Mines, or rather a central figure in the group, was Sir Lionel Phillips, one of the "Randlords", as they have been called. Sir Lionel is largely forgotten today, though he had a dramatic career deserving of a new professional biography; I have it in mind as a future project if I can raise the research funds. The highlight, if it can be called that, in Sir Lionel's life was his arrest in connection with the Jameson Raid of 1895, and his death sentence, which was subsequently commuted to a prison term and a large fine. As I say, I had been pursuing the detail of the absorption of Dutoitspan by General Mining and had called for the Phillips private papers for the period because I thought they might explain Mandelstam's *volte-face* at the decisive board meeting. There was nothing in the contents to add to what I already knew from the General Mining records and the Mines Inspector's report; I had already scanned the latter at the Johannesburg City Library. There remained this unlabelled bundle of handwritten manuscript.

I read the first paragraph I turned to at random – I have quoted from it above. It meant nothing to me. I flicked through the pages only slightly curious (I was conscious that my sabbatical leave had a mere seven weeks to run and I was beginning to worry about my capacity to complete my research) when I discovered a slip of unheaded paper, apparently torn from a yellow memo pad. In the same hand as the manuscript, it read:

My Dear Lionel,

Again, so many thanks for Hampshire. Susan and I will never forget your kindness. So splendid to be a married man!

I thought you might be amused by the attached. You remember those delicate days when J.C. visited Lord M. in '03? I must confess that I played a rather larger role than you and your friends may have realised at the time. Obviously it is a tale which can never be told – which I regret because it seems to me to make rather a good yarn – but I jotted it down soon afterwards and thought it would be fun to show it to somebody who will understand, and be discreet, now that all is on the mend.

(You may be a touch startled by my new Style!

Well, as I think I once mentioned in an unguarded moment, I have it in mind to develop my undergraduate role as a Romancer. I thought I'd try my hand with this first-person and unpublishable tale – anything rather than another Memorandum! Tell me what you think . . .)

Best love from Susan,

Yours ever, JB.

This letter, I confess, diverted me from my wearisome pursuit of Mandelstam's share-rigging machinations. It was undated yet had been filed in the 1907 Papers: that might or might not have been a mistake – even the best archivists do silly things. But who was "JB"? I sought permission, which was granted, and ventured out into the sunshine and the gardens, where I opened my sandwiches and began to browse, first rapidly, then with fast-growing fascination, through this tale of the dramatic months following the end of the Boer War.

The protagonist could only be John Buchan, the novelist and statesman. Furthermore, the *author*, indeed, is John Buchan. I read on into the afternoon because – I would not confess this in my Senior Common Room – I have all my life been an admirer of Buchan, a devotee, by which I mean that I read him secretly, for private pleasure, and – this is nothing to do with my professional role as an academic specialising in the economic history of the years preceding the First World War, with particular reference to the processes of colonial development – I suppose I am familiar with the broad outlines of the man's biography. Born in 1875 in Scotland; Oxford; journalism and the Bar; to South Africa at the end of the Boer War as one of Milner's "Kindergarten" – the ambitious "high-flyers", as we would call them today, who joined the High Commissioner and helped him lead the divided country

6

to peace and (after his and their time) to Union; politics; publishing; authorship – *Prester John*, the famous sequence of "shockers" starting with *The Thirty-nine Steps*; the Great War; Parliament; the Governor-Generalship of Canada; etc., etc.

But I had assumed that the young Buchan was a fairly junior member of the Kindergarten. I knew that he had only been in South Africa for a comparatively brief period (I have since checked; the dates were 1901–03, when he served as one of Lord Milner's private secretaries). The pages I was now reading told me that I had been wrong, and that we historians had utterly missed out on the most extraordinary story of the months after the war, the months that set South Africa on to a clearly recognisable path to her dubious twentieth-century destiny. Here, in what I was reading, bewildered and astonished, in the harsh winter sunlight of North Johannesburg, was the truth at last of the mystery of "Kruger's Gold" – the fate of the bullion that vanished from Pretoria in June 1900: the funds that sustained the Boers' defiance of their British conquerors for years after President Kruger's lonely death in exile in Switzerland in 1904. And that story cannot be separated from the tale of the Afrikaners' slow and tentative revival in the years that followed, a revival which eventually led to their winning the election of 1948, and all that followed and is even today following from that.

I do not doubt that the author of this manuscript is John Buchan. The circumstances of his own movements in the Transvaal, as I have since checked them out from his published memoirs and from the official histories of the period, seem to indicate that his involvement – as described in these pages, if they are genuine – is indeed feasible, though he took pains to make not the slightest mention of these events, in effect to erase them, in all his subsequent writings. According to his own autobiographical chapters on his time in South Africa (*The African Colony*, 1903 – a volume which has since fallen into obscurity) he was travelling in the North-Eastern Transvaal in December 1902. His official biographer, Janet Adam Smith, records that he met the British Colonial Secretary, Joseph Chamberlain, several times in Johannesburg in January 1903. Buchan in his autobiography (*Memory Hold-The-Door*, 1940) reminisced about his impressions of Chamberlain and of his own chief, the British High Commissioner, Lord Milner. He added a curious passage on which, to my knowledge, no historian has offered a gloss. I looked it up in the University of the Witwatersrand Library the next day and my memory was confirmed:

> "Once I was involved in an unpleasant and rather dangerous business, for which I was not to blame but the burden of which I was compelled to shoulder. I consulted Milner and he gave me the advice which he would have given himself, to go through with it whatever happened; it was the highest compliment I have ever been paid . . ."
> (*Memory Hold-The-Door* 1940, ch. 5/I).

The manuscript which I had accidentally discovered at Barlows was certainly illuminated by that paragraph, written by Buchan, then Lord Tweedsmuir, nearly forty years later and shortly before his death in Canada. My reaction to the manuscript was also influenced by the brief letter attached to it, addressed to "Lionel" and signed "JB", offering "thanks for Hampshire"; Buchan married Susan Grosvenor on July 15, 1907, and his biographer records that the honeymoon was spent at the country house of Lionel Phillips, Tylney Hall, Hants.

At this point I found myself in something of a dilemma. I could not abandon my own research project, in which I had by now invested five sober years; on the other hand, while I studied the manuscript – already and prematurely catalogued in my mind as *The Buchan Papers* – I became more and more convinced, as I struggled to decipher the fast-flowing pen, that I had stumbled upon a major contribution to the history of the years immediately following the Anglo-Boer war. But some of the implications of what I was reading were provocative, and indeed some – in such matters as the portrait of President Kruger – would fan controversy even today. It was possible that Barlows, delicately placed on the front line in South Africa's financial and industrial affairs, might be nervous about the publication of a manuscript which appeared, after all, to belong to the private papers of one of their founders. I could of course seek the permission of the chairman of the company, who in my short meeting with him had been courteous and helpful: he might agree – or he might not, in which case I would be effectively silenced.

I decided to give myself longer to think through this professional and ethical dilemma, and so felt justified in photo-copying the manuscript (I admit that I took care to do this over several weeks so that my friend the librarian would not neces-sarily realise what I was doing). When I left Johannesburg to return to the new term in East Anglia I therefore carried with me a copy of *The Buchan Papers*, leaving the original manu-script (with some reluctance) in the same box-file where I had first found it. (I confess that I placed it inside a dozen of the 1907 company accounts of the more obscure mines owned by the group: there was no need to force this manuscript's existence upon the next researcher to venture into the archive.)

An important and indeed essential reason for having a copy of the document in my English study was that I then had access to my personal library of Buchan's complete published works, something which would probably have been hard to find in the Republic. I was then able to "edit" the Papers in the sense that I could check the historical background to the events they describe, cross-reference the characters as they appear, analyse Buchan's turn of phrase, and by dint of footnote and exegesis investigate, with my scholar's professional apparatus, the fundamental questions which had been on my mind since that first moment of discovery. These must surely be the experiences of the young John Buchan in January 1903. Here was his own telling of that tale. Was it possible that here – after nearly one hundred years – was the answer to the mystery of Kruger's Gold, that romantic myth which has lurked in the corridors of South African history ever since?

I must repeat that I can prove the truth neither of the authorship nor of the tale. But I urge my readers to follow my advocacy, through my editorial comments, and to form their own conclusion.

Editor's Note
1. I have to apologise for the word "kaffir" which appears frequently in this manuscript. I assure my readers that at the turn of the century the word was not considered offensive, and I have therefore chosen not to bowdlerise a contemporary document.
2. I also need to apologise for the inadequate Footnotes. Since literally hundreds of editions of JB's books have been published throughout the world and there is no definitive Collected Edition, I have been unable to provide precise page references.
3. JB's Dutch (Afrikaans) in this manuscript is very approximate (as it is in *Prester John*). I have updated it to present-day spelling wherever possible.

Chapter One

A S I RODE BACK across the high Transvaal plateau from our jaunt in the Wood Bush I was, I remember, in contented mood. The journey had been an indulgence, I would not deny it, but I had been weary from too many months of hard labour, and the landscape in these parts was of a sweetness that recalled my Scottish glens and soothed my spirit.[1] Our task had been to look into certain of the less technical aspects of land settlement in that distant and potentially fertile region. My responsibilities committed me to spend many hours in the saddle but I welcomed my release from an earlier role in this country, where I had had to suffer the misery of Boer mothers in the camps to which their menfolk's recalcitrance had consigned them. With that behind, I could respond in good faith to the invigorating challenge of this strange and bewitching country. I had picked up a little of the Boer language, the *taal*, and I flattered myself that as a Scot, a Presbyterian and a country-man, I was not too far from being a kinsman of these infuriating yet honest and companionable people; as one old farmer in Krugersdorp had lately conceded to me, while he

1 JB made a semi-official trek to the North-Eastern Transvaal, in the remote area between the Soutpansberg mountains and the border of Portuguese Mozambique, in December–January 1902–03. He would afterwards write lyrically about the region in his book about South Africa, *The African Colony* (1903).

proffered his *mampoer* brandy, I scarcely qualified as an *Engelsman.*[2]

There were moments when I could imagine how in other circumstances my loyalties might have been strained. Now that Kruger and his gang were out of it – the old rogue safely in European exile where his great age and declining health would certainly bury him – the last battle of the defeated Boer had a tragic appeal. Perhaps we might have given more credence to the more liberal elements in the Transvaal, to Joubert, for instance, and Louis Botha. Perhaps such men, with others, like Smuts, might yet signal us the way ahead.

These were my traitorous thoughts, provoked by youthful energy and good spirits, as my wagon clattered across the stony tracks of the northern Transvaal. I had left the crags and virgin forest of the Berg far behind me by now and the mules made good speed because the dust of the open plateau was kept down by the evening showers of the high summer. I had left myself no space to dawdle, for Lord Milner himself had specified that I was to be returned to Sunnyside, our mansion headquarters to the north of Johannesburg, in time for the arrival of the Chamberlains when, he was kind enough to intimate, I could expect to be introduced to my master. That, he seemed to suggest, might be no bad idea, which I took to mean that I had now been on his staff for nearly eighteen months and, as we all knew the path of reconciliation and reconstruction would be a long one, we should consider – in the great man's company – whether or not my own career need delay

2 JB's first job on arriving to join Lord Milner's team in October 1901 had been to help re-organise the notorious "concentration camps" into which Boer women and children had been gathered in the latter part of the Anglo-Boer War; the death of more than 20,000 civilians in these camps has overshadowed Anglo-Boer relations to this day. Milner then made JB responsible for post-war land settlement.

me much longer in southern climes. It was not my business to speculate whether Lord Milner might have similar thoughts on his mind. He had already carried immense burdens and those of us in intimate daily contact with him were aware of the rumours that he was anxious to retire. No doubt these matters were to feature in their weeks in Sunnyside.[3]

It was hot as Hades in Johannesburg and I was reminded that I did not care for this quondam mining camp. The local rags were full of Chamberlain's speech in the *Volksraad* parliament in Pretoria where, so far as I could read between the lines, the Secretary of State had given an uncompromising response to the Boers' demand for an amnesty, and nevertheless been cheered by them for it.[4] We dined that evening at Sunnyside, a big party, but the ladies were present – Mrs Chamberlain perfectly charming to me – and, as I had anticipated, there was no serious talk even as we passed Lord Milner's best port. I had warmed to the Minister though I could not see any great qualities of leadership in him. He was dapper and businesslike, no doubt an excellent General Manager of the British Empire, but he seemed, I felt, to lack vision. Nor was he impressed by my story of meeting the Boer general De La Rey, which Milner insisted that I tell. The villain had taken to me and had offered to have me on his staff in the next war, which would, he said, be fought by the British

3 Lord Milner was the British High Commissioner in South Africa (and also Governor of the Transvaal and the Orange River Colony). Joseph Chamberlain was the British Secretary of State for the Colonies, who arrived in South Africa on an official visit on December 26, 1902 to discuss unity and reconciliation (the war had ended on May 31, 1902).

4 Chamberlain travelled to the Transvaal and made major speeches in Pretoria to Boer leaders on January 6 and 8. He and his wife were Lord Milner's guests in Johannesburg from January 8–22, 1903, when they certainly met Buchan. They left South Africa on February 25.

and the Dutch against the Jews! Chamberlain did not seem to share the table's amusement at this tale and we rejoined the ladies shortly afterwards.[5]

The next morning my confidence was quickly restored. A group of us – we now accepted with pride the public appellation of "Lord Milner's Kindergarten", originally given us in jest by a local politician – lunched with the great man from London. Milner stopped me as I was joining the general exodus. He looked at me in that quizzical, languid style of his, which so often concealed his true feelings, and said, "Spare us a moment, if you please, Buchan, the Minister has something he wants to discuss with you . . ." I confess that my heart missed a beat, but I composed myself and, after a short wait, my friend and colleague Ironside ushered me into Lord Milner's study on the cool south side of the house where I found that the host had settled himself on an ottoman to one side and surrendered his desk to our visitor. After the courtesies I noticed that Ironside was told to permit no interruptions. The fellow had the cheek to give me the shade of a wink as he withdrew.[6]

Lord Milner may, I fear, have noticed Ironside's indiscretion for he stirred in the shadows – the room was heavily louvred against the glare of the Transvaal midsummer – and apologised for his intervention. "This discussion will be taken by the Secretary of State. But I suggest to you, Buchan, that this meeting does not exist, if you take my point. Ironside will be instructed

5 This passage, with others in this chapter, is echoed in some of JB's letters home at the time.
6 Edmund Ironside was another member of Milner's "Kindergarten", a friend of JB, a professional soldier, a giant of a man known to his familiars as "Tiny". It has frequently been suggested that he was the model for Richard Hannay, Buchan's best-known fictional hero; I have never been wholly persuaded of this.

accordingly, and your colleagues at Sunnyside will be told that you have returned at once to the North."

In that sentence my mood was transformed. I had been expecting to be required to brief our visitor on land transfers, child mortality in the camps – that sort of business. I suspect my jaw may have dropped: certainly I forgot all sense of nervousness. Our visitor, I realised, had been observing me coolly, without evident enthusiasm, rather as my tutor at Oxford used to respond to a jejune Greek verse. He wore a flower in his buttonhole: I remembered that he was celebrated for favouring orchids from his own Birmingham hothouses, though heaven knows he wouldn't find an orchid in this uncivilised town. He stared at me through that famous monocle, and then I began to see a benevolence in the old gent, and so to feel more at ease.

"Mr Buchan," he said at last, "I have had good reports of your work since you came out here – what? – more than a year ago? –" I was careful to look modestly at the carpet, though my heart began to sing. "But I do not want to talk to you about your present responsibilities, admirably though I am sure you fulfil them . . . I have in mind less orthodox business. By which I mean a small, and very confidential, problem which demands a solution."

Again he paused: the dust shimmered in the slatted sunlight; his lordship was silent as a footman.

"I have in mind a task which I agree ought not to belong to the High Commissioner's private office. But the military mind is so limited, in my experience, and the Constabulary scarcely exists at present . . . So I am looking for a man of imagination and initiative – You are not afraid of danger, I trust? – But believe me, you are under no obligation to accept this assignment. Feel at liberty to decline, it will not be held against you . . ." I stammered something which allowed him to gather his thoughts.

15

"If you will give me your attention I shall start with a question. Namely: would you agree that we have not fought a long and costly war in order to permit, through an oversight, a minuscule group of Boer exiles to persist with their miserable cause?"

This was clearly a rhetorical question, so I nodded discreetly, which was apparently acceptable since he repeated the phrase "through an oversight . . ." and lapsed into meditation. Lord Milner had turned his attention to his polished brogues. The great fan was turning languidly: I would have preferred to go to the switch and increase its velocity but I did not dare seem so bold.

"Young man . . ." the Secretary of State resumed, and he leaned back in his chair and gazed up at the broad beams in the ceiling, "I am going to tell you a sordid tale and then I am going to place the matter in your hands." And after that preamble, which would have taken away the breath of the least impressionable young patriot, he told me the history of Kruger's Gold.

He reminded me how, as the war entered its final phase, the Boers took the painful but realistic decision that their ancient President, *Oom* Paul Kruger, should leave the country for Holland in order to evade capture and to attempt to keep the *Vierkleur* flag flying in Europe.[7] He departed Pretoria in May 1900 and eventually left South Africa in September. The State Treasure of the Transvaal Republic was despatched after him in the week that followed his departure from his capital. "We have discovered the records," said the Minister, and referred to an *aide memoire* on the desk in front of him. "The State Mint and the National Bank in Pretoria sent gold bars and coin valued at £800,000 to the Pretoria Railway Station, from where

7 The *Vierkleur* was the standard of the Transvaal Republic.

it was despatched to Machadodorp on the rail route to the Indian Ocean. The High Commissioner" – he glanced at the silent Lord Milner – "has taken particular pains to clarify these matters since they have already become the subject of unhelpful speculation . . ."

My attention could hardly have been greater if I had been listening to a judge pronouncing my fate. There was adventure in this tale, I knew it, and also advancement: this was why I had deserted the Inns of Court to sail to the colonies, this would make up for those heart-breaking months arguing the exact total of dead infants in those wretched camps where we had so foolishly herded the Boer families.

He paused, and carefully replaced the memorandum in the file before turning back to me.

"However, the true situation turns out to be more complex even than public gossip imagines. In addition, as must be perfectly obvious, the rebels' State Treasure would also have embraced a quantity of gold which had been mined in the areas controlled by the Boers during the war. This, of course, was seized by Kruger's officials." He raised a hand in acknowledgment: "Yes, I agree, no doubt a good part of it was subsequently embezzled by those same officials, but the fact remains that we have had great difficulty in estimating the true volume and value of the missing gold . . ."[8]

I said, "We brought a test case in the German courts and . . ." I stumbled to a halt.

---

8 The true value of "Kruger's Gold" has never been established and has been the subject of argument ever since. Chamberlain's references here to the despatch of the gold reserves from Pretoria and the court case brought by the UK authorities in Germany are historically accurate, as is his public promise to use this gold for local charity work.

"Yes, we lost. But we were only able to document a claim for fifty-one boxes of bar gold shipped from Lourenço Marques to Hamburg in September 1900. We believe that a considerably larger treasure – for that is the word – has never been accounted for."

I said, greatly daring, "Sir, I understand your concern to wind up this matter, as a part of the processes of peace, but even at the most generous estimate these funds are not going to be fundamental to our plans for Reconstruction. The scale of that is far bigger than a few boxes of pilfered gold bars."

Mr Chamberlain did not look best pleased, but I could see him make the effort to explain himself. That meant, I reckoned, that he needed my enthusiasm, however junior I might be, for some scheme he and my immediate master must have worked up.

"You are right," he granted. "That is why our High Commissioner here has repeatedly emphasised that the whole of these – alleged and so-called – 'Kruger Millions', once recovered, will be used for the relief of poverty among the burghers. No, what is much more important has all along been to expose Kruger and his court-in-exile, as you might say. How can they continue to claim the sympathy of Europe once they are shown to be sitting on millions of stolen pounds? Nothing would settle their game more conveniently!"

I sat there in a stiff stinkwood chair feeling pretty nonplussed. I could see my masters' dilemma, but it seemed to me a long day's trek from my appointed task of restoring the mechanisms of the local administration of the Transvaal. Were they going to suggest that I return to Europe to pursue the gold through the courts?

Then I realised that the Minister was grinning at me – that is the only word I can summon for the mirthless rictus that passed across his features. He looked at Lord Milner and said, "You agree, Alfred?" Lord Milner inclined his head, still silent.

"I am leaving out of this narrative just one element. Yes, fifty-one boxes of gold travelled aboard the *Styria* to Europe in September 1900. Yes, they have been the subject of a court action and Dr Leyds, the self-styled ambassador of the Transvaal Republic in Brussels, is welcome to them. But as you will gather from what I have just said, a significantly larger consignment of gold was despatched across the eastern Reef later in September."

The Secretary of State paused, whether to yield to the drama of his tale or merely to refresh his memory from his note.

"That gold, we now know, was seized from its Boer escort. Not by our own forces, I fear – General Buller had not reached Pilgrims Rest at that time – but by an unidentified force of Natives. The gold has vanished. The Boer has kept quiet about its loss for obvious reasons. He would be as disturbed as we if the Natives were to start acquiring weapons on a dangerous scale. That danger I do not take too seriously. But for us there is a second danger, and a very real one – which is that these last Boer fanatics – I am told they are dubbed the *Bittereinders*, which is a word which even I can understand – are determined to fight on and to track down the bullion, wherever it may be hidden. We need to find that gold first – 'Kruger's Gold' I am happy to call it if *hoi polloi* insist!" He paused, then added, very quietly: "Or rather, young man, *you* are to find it."

No honest fellow could have failed to respond to such a commission. I felt exhilarated, honoured and apprehensive at the same time. Promotion surely beckoned, and, I imagined there was a gleam of sympathy in Lord Milner's silent features. I also had the presence of mind to admit a degree of bewilderment.

I tried to explain some of this. I blathered for a bit – they must have thought it was a boy's excitement – but I took care to put a precise point. What was the evidence for this story? What corroboration did we have to go on? How on earth (I didn't use those words, of course) was I supposed to proceed? Kruger's Gold had vanished off God's earth two and a half years ago. In that time those Native brigands would surely have scattered it across the continent – unless the Boers, whom I never underestimated, had not quietly caught up with it in the meantime, *sjamboked* the kaffir thieves and whisked it off with Portuguese connivance to Kruger, in Switzerland or Holland or wherever he was hiding.

These things I managed to put in a civil way to the great man, who appeared to take no exception. Indeed, he nodded. So I guessed there was something still to be told.

"Yes, we have of course pursued our enquiries. That area of operation does not relate to your present duties. Believe me, our calculations show that the consignment which was shipped to Europe represented only a portion of the total seized by the Boers. We are certain that the rest of the gold has not left this country."

He looked up at me from his notes. "You do not need to know the detail of our investigations . . . I believe that there was a brave man in Delagoa Bay who clarified some of these matters before his violent death. And there was an Indian trader who reports to us from Sabie, not to speak of some quick thinking by Wheatcroft in Komatipoort when he discovered a Hollander in the location. Before all that there had been a passage of arms in –" he looked again at the notes in front of him "– a place called Bosbokrand, where there is apparently an insubordinate Chief. And the Germans have been very helpful, for a change. No! Believe me, the gold has not crossed the border. We suspect that it probably sits today in the territory very close to where it was first seized. But as we all know, this is an immense country. We could not seek such a needle in a haystack without first discovering a point of human contact – a contact with the abduction."

He added as an afterthought, almost to himself, "And the Boers will have the same problem."

I said, "I imagine, sir, that you are telling me that you have found that contact." My career was looking promising but my spirits were curiously subdued all of a sudden.

"Yes, we found him," nodded the Secretary of State, and he too seemed unelated. There was a silence. It was not my task, I judged, to break it.

"We found a young Native carrying what they call –" he checked his note "– a *veldpond*. As you may know, that is apparently a coinage that was issued by the rebel government in the Eastern Transvaal in the later period of the conflict. The gold mines in the Lydenburg area kept on operating for most of the time. A month ago a platoon of our men in Pilgrims Rest came across this Native by chance and the Major there had the wit to interrogate him with a particular view to the gold coin."

"And?"

"The black fellow confirmed he knew about the ambush of Kruger's Gold. Described it. Said he knew that the gold had not been moved since it was taken and hidden by his compatriots. Said he knew where it was hidden."

Joseph Chamberlain – "Honest Joe" is his soubriquet at home, I believe – was no longer looking me in the eye, and his narrative had become brusque, almost disjointed.

"So if I may ask, sir – if you want me to go and get it, as I think you are instructing me – where is it?"

"That we do not know."

Neither Lord Milner nor I said anything.

"The Native prisoner didn't exactly tell us . . . not precisely," said Chamberlain, and Lord Milner and I continued to hold our silence. I could see through the shutters that the sky over Johannesburg was darkening. A summer storm would break in cascades of blessed water within the half-hour, but until then we waited, perspiring, uneasy.

Chamberlain said, "He left a sort of message."

"What do you mean, sir – 'left a message'?"

"He was very sick."

"And getting sicker all the time!"

The words burst unbidden from the ottoman in the corner: they were the first that my master had uttered and Chamberlain gazed across at him, not angry, I realised at once, at this intervention, but not protesting against this statement of humanity. Milner made a gesture of silent apology and for a moment the two of them ignored my presence. "You are thinking," said Chamberlain quietly, and he was no longer talking to me, "Is it for this that we won the war? So that we can torture the local population with the same impunity as the Boers have always done? Is this to be the future of South Africa?" The two men looked at each other silently: I had the sense that these were issues they debated privately into the night and that later historians would give them little credit for.[9]

I made myself interrupt them. "Sir, we have a clue drawn from the interrogation of a Native prisoner. May I ask what it says?"

Mr Chamberlain grimaced at me, as though relieved to have been called back from this dangerous territory. "The clue, as you

9 Milner this month agreed with Chamberlain that he would serve another year and in fact did not leave South Africa until 1905. (If the account of Lord Milner in this chapter sometimes suggests a cold character, it may be noted that recent biographers have discovered a certain Cécile who was for years maintained by the Proconsul in a house in south London.)

put it, is minimal. The man has since died, which I regret. He said that the gold had not been moved. It was after the waterfall."

There was a long pause.

I said, "And?"

"That is the entirety of it."

"After the waterfall?"

"Just so."

The expression on my face must have betrayed my confusion. I was saying to myself, "After the blasted waterfall . . ." and thinking that there must have been a hundred waterfalls up in the Wood Bush last month and there would be countless thousands dotted across this region . . . My brain would have skidded into helpless expostulation if I had not been recalled to duty.

The Minister allowed himself to raise his voice. He was requiring my attention and my obedience. "Consider, if you will, that this is the first contact we have had with the bullion. Let me add that I attach great importance to its recovery. The High Commissioner has told me that he values none of his staff more highly than he does you. My instruction therefore is that you take yourself at once – and covertly – to the Eastern Transvaal and discover whatever you can. I shall personally esteem your best efforts."

He had risen to his feet and was shaking my hand, presumably in dismissal but also, I could feel, in encouragement and approbation so that my spirits were intended to be revived.

My own master had also risen and at last allowed himself a contribution. "I suggest you go down to Pilgrims Rest," he offered. "Examine the commanding officer, there may be more details to be had. But for your own contact with me rely on Colonel Wheatcroft at White River – he has been briefed on the whole matter. And finally –" he looked across at Chamberlain, who inclined his head benevolently – "you will be assisted by a Boer friend of ours whom you have not had occasion to meet before. His name is Schalk Minnaar. Trust him with your life."

"Who would he be, sir?"

"A friend of ours, as you will gather. I believe he comes from one of the grand old Free State families who have a grievance with Kruger, but he is with us for the best of reasons."

"Was he under cover for us in the war?"

"No, he spent the war in East Africa on certain other business. He has proved himself many times."

"Where do I find him?"

"I have no idea. He comes and goes. He will find you."

They both insisted on shaking my hand again, very cordially.[10]

I was living in Pretoria at the time but continued to have use of quarters at Sunnyside when I was in town. I walked across the grounds through the beginnings of the afternoon storm and by the time I had passed the second tier of sentries (we were still under pretty stiff security) I was drenched to the skin and ready to join the Anarchists. I had, I reckoned, been doing pretty well in Milner's private office – yes, so well that he had given me this

10 Buchan in his novels was to refer three times to Kruger's Gold. First, in *The Island of Sheep* (ch. 4) (". . . the Kruger Treasure business . . ."), secondly, and more substantially, in *The Green Wildebeest* (see *The Runagates Club*, 1928) – "You remember the wild yarns after the Boer War about a treasure of gold which Kruger in his flight to the coast had buried somewhere in the Selati country. That, of course, was all nonsense: the wily ex-President had long before seen the funds safe in a European bank. But I dare say some officials had got away with Treasury balances, and there may have been bullion cached in the Bushveld. Anyhow, every scallywag south of the Zambesi was agog about the business and there were no end of expeditions which never found a single Transvaal sovereign . . ." Thirdly, this is taken up briefly in *Mr Standfast* (ch. 12) – "I [Hannay] contributed a yarn about the men who went to look for Kruger's treasure in the Bushveld and got scared by a green wildebeest . . ."

poisoned chalice, nothing less than nomination to sort out the country's biggest unsolved mystery since Dingaan's parentage.[11] I was as willing as any of Milner's youngsters to tackle a conundrum for the State, but all they had given me was the screams of a dying kaffir, who might – I guessed – have still been trying to mislead, but whose racked body did not allow him to risk too great a licence. There was something in this commission that stuck in my gullet – I believe I must have grunted like a bad-tempered brute when Ironside hailed me outside the study door; I had remembered myself and muttered something hypocritical about having to repack all my kit and get back on the road to the North, so that he must have assumed that I was exasperated by my instructions from the Big Man; indeed, it might be helpful if my tone of voice betrayed a filthy mood. I needed to get away before my pals could cross-examine me about my afternoon with the Chief.

So I changed my wet clothes and hastened to clear my desk to be ready for an early start, while the summer storm lashed down over the Ridge and moved on south, thunder and lightning and all the works, to flood the empty streets of the new town as dusk came down over the Highveld.

By the time the sky had cleared my temper was restored and I could begin to plan in my head the route down over the Berg to Nelspruit and White River. I went out through the wet grass and across to the stables to warn Japie, my Coloured boy, that he would be back on the road in the morning but would be able to follow me with just the pack horses, not the mule team, and in that fierce early moonlight that I can never get used to in these southern climes I made my way back to my quarters, my imagination afire.

11 Dingaan was the notoriously bloodthirsty Zulu king, half-brother of and successor to Shaka, who slaughtered Boer trekkers at Blood River in 1838.

They had put me not in the main house but in a *rondavel* just beyond the distant gate of the compound, which was kept available for any fellow who came in from the bush for a few nights. It was a civil set-up; we had a sort of common room where we could smoke and rag, a couple of boys to care for us, and, I suppose, a sense of escape from the formalities of the big house where his lordship did not permit his minions to relax any more than he did himself. There were sentries in the grounds of course, but they knew us all, and a salute and a greeting from a brawny Highlander were all I had encountered.

The oil lamps had not yet been lit so I fumbled for a whisky-soda on the butler's tray and ambled back down the *stoep* to my own room. My mind was full. I had recovered my composure; fortune must be taken at the flood. I also thought to write to my mother before I left: there were dangers in this commission, no doubt of it, though the thought did not discomfort me, and I wondered whether I should look to my modest armoury. By now it was almost entirely dark save for the moonlight, and I was thinking to shout for the boy, but first to take a long draught from my glass, when I smelt the stink of coarse tobacco. And then – my nerves are no worse than the next man's, but the hair stood up on my neck, I swear it – I realised that I was not alone. I must have frozen as solid as Lot's wife. I had no weapon, of course; I remember cursing the sentries for delivering me to – what? To the enemy? Even in these early days of peace?

The voice came from behind me, from the battered rocking-chair in the corner of the *stoep*, where we kept the month-old London newspapers.

"*Meneer*," said a gentle, almost apologetic voice, "I was looking for the Plough, but the lights of that *dorp* down there make daytime out of night." (He must have meant the first flickering flambards of Johannesburg, scarcely visible in the moonlight.) As he spoke he scratched a match to rekindle a dying pipe, and in the brief moment I caught a glimpse of the man.

Since he is an important presence in my tale I ought to describe him. He was small, I guessed, though by that I mean he was trim and light, built hard and fit so that no one would ever doubt his stamina. There was no elegance in his garb – on the contrary, he wore a battered bush shirt and villainous boots – but my attention was seized by his eyes. He was unshaven, he wore a classic Boer beard, pointed, neatly trimmed, and he was deeply tanned, his features etched deep by the elements. But the eyes (I later found they were the palest dove grey) were gentle, reassuring, sweet, almost sleepy. They smiled at me – sweetly, I repeat the word – in that brief splutter of flame, and I discovered that my heart had stopped pounding and that I welcomed a new friend, whoever he might be.

"You must be known to the sentries."

He laughed softly. In the accent of the deepest Free State he said, "They did not see me."

"Then why are you here?"

"My name is Schalk Minnaar. We have bad business ahead of us."[12]

The boy brought lamps and Minnaar and I scrutinised each

12 There can be no shadow of doubt that this is the model for one of Buchan's most memorable fictional characters, Peter Pienaar, the African hunter who appears as Richard Hannay's old friend from the bush in *The Thirty-nine Steps* (briefly), *The Island of Sheep* (in one chapter), *Greenmantle* and, most memorably, *Mr Standfast*, where he sacrifices his life for the British cause. If this present manuscript can be relied on, it will become apparent that JB's relationship with Minnaar/Pienaar was more complex than has previously been imagined.

other. I guessed that he was surprised to see a mere youngster. For my part I had formed an affection for the Boer people and reckoned I saw here a classic example of the African frontiersman, with the redeeming feature in this case of his authenticated loyalty to the Crown. He left me in no doubt of that from the beginning. "Yon Smuts," he volunteered at some point – we had sent the boy for more whisky and I had found my own cigarettes – "is a bad devil. We – and by that, *Meneer*, I mean us – must not trust him an inch. He means to play the *jakkals* on our country."

I realise now that Schalk must have determined to set me at ease. He told me, volunteering it in his shy, stumbling way, that he had a patchwork past. He spoke of *skelms* – rogues – he had known (I wondered whether he himself had seen the inside of the *tronk* – I must remember to check it in the morning, but why bother since he was approved by my masters?) – and of adventures deep in the Kalahari. Rhodesia he knew, he volunteered, like the palm of his hand, particularly the Zambesi Valley down towards Tete; Portuguese East was another of his territories, across to Mozambique Island. But none of these traveller's tales was told for effect. I offered him a few of my own experiences, in Swaziland and up beyond Zeerust, and he reminisced about elephant-hunting north of the Limpopo and a disagreement with the law on a trek beyond Groot-Marico. He had never, he confirmed when I taxed him, travelled outside Africa, and he protested he had never felt the wish to do so.

At last we stirred ourselves to business. "*Basie*," he said – I noted it as an affectionate term of acceptance, and also, which gave me pause, an apparent acknowledgment of my seniority in the venture ahead – "*Basie*, there has been dirty work in the Lowveld."

"You know what we have to find, Schalk?"

"I know it."

"So what do you suggest?"

I could not deny my sense of helplessness, of ignorance, of inexperience – of my youth.

Schalk Minnaar tapped out his pipe for the second time in the hour, cracking the ash on to the murram floor, scorning the ashtray. He smiled, ever sweetly, at me.

"*Ons sal 'n plan maak,*" he said.[13]

---

13 *Ons sal 'n plan maak* is an Afrikaans expression which means, literally, "We shall make a plan," but is closer in sense to "We'll fix it" (the phrase has today moved back into South African English with that latter meaning). For JB it became – I am convinced – some sort of talismanic phrase. To take just a number of examples, it occurs in *The African Colony* (ch. 8), *Prester John* (ch. 21), *Greenmantle* passim (chs. 7, 9, 15, 20), *Mr Standfast* (chs. 14 and 17), *The Free Fishers* (ch. 10), *The House of the Four Winds* (ch. 21).

In *Mr Standfast* Buchan illustrates the prime meaning of the phrase – "'Never mind, Dick,' [Pienaar] said. 'It will all come right. *Ons sal 'n plan maak.*'" In *The African Colony* (ch. 8) he tells the joke which may have fixed it in his memory: "Once upon a time, as the story goes, a Dutchman talked with a *predikant* about the welfare of his soul. 'You will assuredly be damned,' said the *predikant*, 'and burn in hell.' 'Not so,' said the Dutchman. 'If I am so unfortunate as to get there, I shall certainly get out again.' 'But that is folly and an impossibility,' said the *predikant*. 'Ah,' said the other with confidence. 'Wait and see. I shall make a plan . . .'"

Buchan uses the phrase usually in English, sometimes in Afrikaans. Since the words can have meant nothing to the enormous majority of his readers I am tempted to argue that it was one of those secret messages which all of us allow ourselves. Perhaps it was a private superstition, arising out of some youthful experience in South Africa, that it should so often be smuggled into his books. Perhaps it was a private joke from the same period – with himself or whoever. My suggestion is entirely serious since I can see no other explanation for the recurrence of these particular words.

Chapter Two

I SET OFF ON MY MISSION not on my favourite pony, Alan Breck,[14] nor even with my trekker team of Cape-cart and mules, but in the slow comfort of a railway carriage. My first destination was Pilgrims Rest, where Ironside, after much use of the telegraph, had located the officer who had interrogated our deceased Native informant. It would have wasted precious days to ride the tedious miles across the Transvaal Highveld to the eastern lowlands beyond the Berg, so I told my Coloured foreman to follow after me by road while I packed the simplest kit and reserved a carriage to Machadodorp. From there I would pick up horses from the Constabulary and make my own way up the coach route to Lydenburg and on over the Berg to the mining villages in the canyons beyond. There was, I reckoned, only a small risk of indiscretion, but I prepared a tale that I was en route to examine the smallholdings at White River, where we had set up many of our own troops from the war who had no wish to return home after their victory. Schalk Minnaar – I was delighted that we had straightway become firm allies – had gone about his own business, assuring me that he would catch up with me in the Lowveld. Chamberlain, I saw from the local journals, was

14 "Alan Breck" was JB's own horse in Johannesburg, the name a tribute to Stevenson and *Kidnapped*.

said to be preparing a statesman's speech for the banquet in Johannesburg in a week's time.

It was by this same line of rail, I reflected, that the gold had also travelled before me. In the first days of June 1900, our agents had reported that dozens of cabs had arrived at Pretoria railway station from the State Mint and the National Bank, loaded with gold bars and coin. The gold had arrived at Machadodorp – which I was presently approaching – and there the story faded. I knew of the energy Lord Milner had put into the matter. Some of the gold had been shipped from Lourenço Marques to Hamburg that September; some had been employed in the war chest of Kruger's successor, President Steyn. My master had come to believe that, contrary to popular speculation, very little of it had then been taken away by Kruger himself, who had fled the country via the Komatipoort border post in the same September. (He had been granted his salary, in silver for some reason rather than gold, by the weeping members of his *Volksraad*.)

However, it was not at all clear how much gold had been confiscated by the Boers from the mines of the Rand in the early weeks of the war, nor how much they had scraped from the plates in the treatment plants – the magnates in exile in Cape Town had great difficulty in establishing the detail. Our official calculations had also had to leave out of account the bullion which had been seized or diverted from the Eastern Transvaal gold mines – and the fighting had never entered that territory between Pilgrims Rest and Sabie, so that the Boers had been free to use it not just as sanctuary but also as exchequer. Therefore not only did no one know where the treasure lay hidden; no one could be certain of its value. I had recovered from my first irritation. I remember thinking as I lounged in that railway carriage that I was the luckiest man in the Kindergarten.

31

Even in this height of summer, there was a chill in the dawn air when we arrived at Belfast. It claims to be the highest township in the country, but soon the plateau breaks away and plunges thousands of feet down to the tropical delights and diseases of the Lowveld and Portuguese East Africa. The rail line was a masterpiece of engineering as it swooped down the Berg from Waterval Boven to Waterval Onder. I recalled that *Oom* Paul Kruger had tarried in Waterval Onder on his slow route into exile, before he was persuaded that it was necessary he take passage for Europe, knowing he would never return, in the vessel the Dutch queen had sent for him. But I had been counselled to leave the train at Machadodorp and strike north through the foothills to Lydenburg and thence to descend more directly on Pilgrims Rest. Horses were awaiting me as Sunnyside had commanded and word was waiting too from Wheatcroft – who was much trusted by Milner – to confirm his presence at White River and his plan to move up shortly to Sabie, where he trusted I would make contact. I assumed that he would bring with him a force equal to any emergency. So, pausing only to buy some few provisions for my journey to add to my kit, modest enough for a saddle-bag, I was off in the mid-morning glare into the maze of wagon tracks that were the rough and earlier engineering of the transport-riders of the Bushveld.

The great yellow-grey plains of the Transvaal Highveld rise imperceptibly to a rim of mountains the like of which can have no parallel in the world. From the Rhodesian scarp, hundreds of miles down to the Drakensberg of Natal and Swaziland, the Berg sweeps north to south, sometimes a rampart of cliff, sometimes a line of rocky crags, and everywhere there is a confusion of wild *kloofs* and gentler glens as the land plunges to the plain. Up on the Highveld you have the clearest sensation that you are on the roof of the world, for the land seems to slope away from you on every side. The mountain rim is like the edge of a pie-dish from which the slow, sluggish streams of the plateau are hurled eastward in torrents and cataracts, thousands of feet into the steaming mists of the Lowveld. Machadodorp is the easterly outpost of the Highveld; the Delagoa Bay railway is there forced to dive into the Elands River canyon. I turned away from it, north into rough hill country, where a stony road climbed and descended, climbed and twisted again, for mile upon mile to Lydenburg. I had a lively Basotho pony who would have given Alan Breck a chase, but for all our efforts I could make no great speed. The track was littered with the debris of the transport-riders, who had earned a hard living dragging the miners' supplies from the railhead. Some of it, I could see, was the detritus of the war. There were rusted cartwheels in the ditch, broken crates stencilled with the names of patent foodstuffs, the skeletons of oxen whose hearts had burst as they toiled between the shafts, their carcases picked clean by carrion. But the air had the freshness of the hilltops still and I pressed on, through the straggling village of Lydenburg in its amphitheatre of soft green slopes, and climbed again to the higher peaks.

Now I was on the knife edge of the mountain range, the peaks of Formosa, Anderson, Sheba around me; the yellow grass of summer was springy in tufts beneath our hooves, there were no bushes or trees, just the sudden clumps of granite boulders, and everywhere the African aroma of sun-dried herbs, a scattering of frail flowers, the humming of a million insects, the sudden gusting of mountain breezes. I observed how the geology of the typical eastward scarp face reminded me of my boyhood days on the Scottish hills: there would be a near-vertical scree for the first hundred feet or so, and then a precipitous grassy slope, sometimes speeded by a sheer precipice, and then far, far below, the smoke of Africa in the valley. Beyond one of these valleys, I knew, would be Sabie, beyond the Devil's Knuckles, the Staircase and the Old Harbour Road (a famous South African route much debated by the generals two years before).

I had no wagon to hinder me so I set my pony on the tangled paths that led towards the Blyde River. It was a scene of wild and perfect beauty and I gloried in it until, as I pressed on into the late afternoon, a heap of cloud pulled like a blanket across the sun and the golden landscape turned grey and the hilltop breeze grew chill. Thousands of feet beneath, the valleys vanished into a surly mist and for the first time since my heady departure from Johannesburg I felt a tremble of apprehension. I was accustomed to trekking for weeks by myself in the veld, and thought I had come to relish the solitude, but here, without the cheerful chatter of my boys and the rhythmic squeak of the wagon shafts, I felt alone. I wished I had a better plan, I regretted the absence of Schalk, and at that moment I would have preferred to have been laughing with my fellow Kindergarteners on the lawns of Sunnyside. I found that I had no great desire to know the truth of the death of a Native at the hands of my fellow country-man, and my resolution wavered mightily until I cursed myself out loud, told myself that I was a white man, and spurred my stumbling pony down the tortured descent into the goldminers' camp of Pilgrims Rest.[15]

There have never been true pilgrims in that narrow valley. It was the first diggers who named it jestingly after themselves a

15 Curiously, JB gave the name *Pilgrims Rest* to a book about fishing which he was working on at the time of his death 37 years later.

couple of decades before. Today it was a well-established, not untidy, little settlement, much of an improvement on the usual run of squalid and diseased mining camps. There were trim houses and shops, a church and a clutch of saloons, all in the dark grey stone of the locality, and, stretching down the stream, as neat as a mile of fish traps, were the sieves and dredges of the miners. When the Boer commanders had retreated at the end of the war they had left the panning operations un-damaged and at Sunnyside we had reckoned there need be no great delay in resuming a successful industry, though its value paled into insignificance beside the later discoveries on the Reef.

This, I remembered, was where De La Rey had set up his Mint – the *Staatsmund te Velde* – to strike specie from the gold that had been trans-shipped from Pretoria. Here, too, they had struck the *veldponde* coins, one of which was the occasion of my visit. As I clambered, stiff and weary, from my pony, I again discovered in myself that I was not relishing this errand as I should have. No doubt, I told myself, it was the strain of a hard journey, not to speak of a ravenous hunger. With that excuse I resolved to put off my official business until the morning. I sought out the more respectable of the village hostelries, devoured a discreet supper, and set myself to sleep.

The morning began in a Scottish mist, as I suspected was not uncommon in these grim valleys, but the sun of high summer could not be denied and by the time I ventured out into the one and only village street the sky was blue as a July in the Highlands of my own Scotland and my courage was restored. To the south, through a gap above the valley, could be seen tiers of broken blue hills rising towards Swaziland. The S.A. Constabulary, which

Baden-Powell, my celebrated countryman,[16] was in process of creating, was flying its flag above a simple *rondavel* beyond the Dutch Reformed church, so I made my way there and asked for the military commanding officer.

There were Native sentries at the wicker fence, smart-looking fellows, and a gloomy young sergeant of about my age with an accent that hailed from west of Bristol, who was perfectly courteous but asked me to wait while he sent in my name. I assumed that a telegram from Sunnyside would guarantee me rapid access, but the minutes passed until, as I took my second turn on the *stoep*, I heard a mutter of voices and two men emerged, apparently in conference. The shorter one came briskly from the door and brushed past me rudely on the plank steps. I murmured an unnecessary apology, received a grunt for my pains, and caught a glimpse of a yellow complexion, dark moustaches and a work-manlike kit of stained white bush shirt and slacks: he was not, I thought, a white man. But I forgot him at once because I found myself looking up at a giant of a man, six-and-a-half feet if he was an inch and built as wide as the mountain behind me. He was glaring down on me without the warmth, let alone the deference, that I suppose I had been expecting for the Secretary of State's emissary. And when he opened his mouth I was further discoun-tenanced because no one had seen fit to warn me that Major S. was not only no Englishman (which I might have guessed from his name) but, to judge from his accent, had only recently arrived from somewhere east of the Elbe. As I followed him into his office

16 A disrespectful reference, interesting because it was widely felt in the Army at the time that Baden-Powell's defence of Mafeking in the first stage of the Boer War had been excessively applauded by British public opinion. The popular hero, and the future founder of the Boy Scouts and Girl Guides movement, was currently engaged in setting up a national police force for South Africa.

I could see how his tunic was wrinkled and strained across his massive torso. His neck bulged over his collar, his head hinted at the proportions of an inverted pear, as in a *Punch* caricature of the classic Prussian, and when he turned to face me again I saw that his eyes were bright and angry and, I thought, contemptuous of my youth. He and I would never be fellow souls.[17]

"This is your first visit? I am honoured . . ." He made a ridiculous inclination of the close-cropped head, and I reckoned he was mocking me.

"My first to this sector, Major."

"You will find that all is very damn quiet here."

"So I see. I shall of course be calling on Colonel Wheatcroft."

"He will agree. I have been in this Lowveld longer than any of you."

I asked, "And before that?"

"I was in South-West. I learn my trade in the Herero territory. There we allow no nonsense."

Why hadn't you stayed there, I was wondering, in a war in which our German friends were butchering a whole tribe?[18] Why on earth did we need to use a character like this? He must be

17 "Major S.", as these Papers always refer to him, was probably Colonel Steinacker, a German professional soldier – we would today call him a mercenary – who played a shadowy role during the Boer War, based on the Mozambique border at Komatipoort. He raised a mobile force called "Steinacker's Horse" and harried the Boers on behalf of the British, but his loyalty was always tenuous and his methods alarmed the British command. He continued to serve in the army after the Vereeniging peace treaty but at some point fell out of favour. I suspect this narrative may explain why, but I have been unable to confirm from the military records in Pretoria or the Ministry of Defence in London that a Major or Colonel Steinacker was stationed in Pilgrims Rest in early 1903.
18 The Herero tribe in South-West Africa (today Namibia) was to be savagely put down by the German colonial authorities in 1904 after a decade of tension and oppression.

valued for something – was it efficiency, or simple ruthlessness? I would ask Wheatcroft when I saw him.

"Where do you find your main problems, Major? With the Boer commandos as we resettle them, or with the Natives?"

The Prussian favoured me with a crude expletive. "The Boers are thickheaded peasants. They should have been hunted down like pig dogs if your generals had had the sense. No, they are too stupid to make trouble. As for the kaffirs, I can deal with them – and they all know it." He guffawed, abruptly, very loud, and slapped a mighty paw on his desk, raising a great cloud of dust that cast doubt either on his command of his paperwork or on the competence of his domestic staff. "You will have coffee – sir?"

We were sitting in a room which, I saw to my surprise, was crammed with the impedimenta of a Native *kraal* – rusty spears of every shape and size, wooden masks and leather shields, dusty bowls overflowing with beads and trinkets, and the floor was cluttered with clay pots gaudy with a hundred patterns and glazes. What nonsense was this, I wondered? I could understand that he might have been confiscating Native weapons but most of this jumble belonged rather to a museum – the Major could only be a Collector, I had found him out in his Germanic hobby. He prided himself on holding down the Native even as he valued and acquired his simple artifacts. However, I made no mention of it.

Instead, he shouted for coffee and we talked uneasily about the redevelopment of the Valley and of the mining operations. My civil servant's interests were unlikely to enlist the sympathy of a professional soldier like this, and his patience gave out before mine. He reached for a clip of flimsies in a tray on his desk and flicked through them as though to remind himself whether Wheatcroft's telegram had betrayed why I had come down all the way from headquarters. I had given some thought to my tactics, though I had assumed I would be speaking to more of a fellow soul.

"We are a little worried –" I began, and tried to allow the "we" to signal all the majesty of the Empire – "we would not want any Native trouble at this delicate stage in the Reconstruction."

Major S. shook his head as vigorously as his thick neck permitted. "I have told you, I permit no impertinences from the kaffirs. They do not forget it."

"So what of the fellow you caught the other day, the one with the gold?"

"That is what I tell you. I catch him. No more problem."

"Is that all there was to it?"

"What else do you civilians want?" The Major was contemptuous rather than angry. "My men stopped him at a road block. He tried to run but – no use. They search him and find the gold coins. Then I talk to him."

"And?"

"Nothing. The damn idiot did not talk."

"Not at all?"

I was getting to the bit I didn't like.

"Young sir, I promise you I am very good at asking questions of these dumb kaffirs. Perhaps he does not know what to say. Perhaps he is stupid. I asked him questions for three days . . ."

"Did you tell Wheatcroft that you had arrested him?"

The Prussian waved me aside. "I run my own show, as you people say. First in Windhoek. Then on the border, through all the war. Now here. I do not need to bother White River with just one kaffir."

"Yet with all your experience, Major, you failed to find an explanation of what the Native was up to."

A gleam of triumphant justification flickered in the Major's protuberant eyes. "Yes I did! In the end, he spoke."

"You mean he said 'After the waterfall'?"

A nod.

"But what did he mean?"

My colleague did not seem to think that that was his concern. Let us civilians do the decoding. He shrugged.

I protested, "And is that all, Major? Nothing more at all? Before he . . ."

Perhaps for the first time the Major may have realised that he might be subject to censure for the failure of his interrogation, if not for the death of an obscure black youth. To my surprise his face blotched red, flushed as a young girl. For the first time he averted his glare. I tried to press home. "Nothing at all?" I repeated.

He seemed to make a heaving effort to remember, then slowly – I believe he made a true effort – he shook his head. "He also said 'Near Pilgrims Rest' . . . Yes, he said 'After the waterfall, near Pilgrims Rest'."

"But which waterfall?" There must be thousands, I was thinking, especially near Pilgrims Rest.

"There are thousands of waterfalls in this damn country." He had recovered himself.

"Don't we even know who the man was? Which is his *kraal*?"

"That, above all, he would not tell me. I tried very hard, believe me, on that point."

"And the name of his Chief?"

The Major shrugged again.

I did not think it my place to discuss the detail of the man's death, nor did I wish to dwell on the Major's favoured techniques of interrogation. I remembered Lord M.'s expostulation, his civilian protest in that shaded room in Sunnyside.

Perhaps it was as well that I had gone no farther and abstained from protestation, because when I was leaving the soldier called me back. He said, "The kaffir was carrying this with the gold. It was important to him. He wept like a baby when I took it away."

He tossed a slim length of a heavy fabric to me. I looked at it, bewildered: it was a patch of cheap native cotton, grubby and stained, and heavy because it was covered with embroidered beadwork arranged in a crude but not unattractive pattern. "I kept it for my collection," said Major S. "But I have plenty of the rubbish. It will help you maybe."

I wondered if it was his gesture of apology.[19]

---

19 Colonel Steinacker – if it is he – appears to be something of a model for Buchan's Colonel von Stumm in *Greenmantle*, though Buchan developed that character to include patriotism (and a strong hint of the effete – "the queer other side", as Hannay described it (ch. 6)) as well as cruelty. It was Colonel von Stumm who in *Greenmantle* (ch. 4) agreed with Pienaar that he had cut off the head of a Herero chief and sent it on tour in South-West Africa in a pickle jar.

Chapter Three

I SHALL PASS OVER the detail of the next two days. They were neither happy nor comfortable. I realise now that a part of my problem was that I did not know *who I was*, by which I mean that I had not adequately thought about the personality I should have assumed for my mission. Schalk Minnaar would explain this to me later. I understood that I could not wander around the Bushveld as one of the Milner Kindergarten in an undisguised search for Kruger's Gold. Nor could I profitably call up a platoon of Wheatcroft's horse and crash around the country-side requiring to know the identity and the business of a dead Native; that would get me nowhere. But what to do? Should I wait for my boy Japie and my mule train to join me? And who would I then become? A sportsman? A rich young traveller? A mining engineer? In the end I let the people I encountered draw their own conclusions. The fact that I had no escort seemed to confirm that I could not be on government business, and I was soon dishevelled and dusty enough to pass as one of the flotsam of odd types that were always wandering, with no apparent purpose, through this frontierland. As for the Natives – they would not think to wonder what a white man was up to.

There, however, was the rub. The answer to my quest lay in some Native *kraal*. In one of these simple beehives that dotted every hillside, someone was mourning a vigorous young man, whether he had been a son, a husband or a lover. So was I to comb every mountain in search of a bereavement? I knew it was hopeless, for I had the *taal* but none of the Native tongues. Nor could I recruit assistants better equipped than I, because secrecy was of the essence. I racked my brains, but nothing in my experience offered an answer. All I could do was to cling to a frail instinct that, if I loosened the reins on my pony and gave him his head, the Fates would provide. That alone kept my sense of futility at bay.

I wandered up and down the grassy glens of this enchanted landscape and, as the day went on, I edged my pony higher up the scarp, above the foothills where the miners had stripped the bush for their fires and their props, up into the remaining clumps of indigenous forest. I kept a sharp eye out for Natives, and greeted enough of them, but mostly they were surly and ignored my salutation; there might be mischief brewing, I thought, and remembered Major S. and his crass confidence in the power of the gun and the *sjambok*. Thinking on that, I resolved again to speak my mind to Wheatcroft about the man.

That first night I begged a bunk from a weary old storekeeper on the banks of a noisy mountain stream at the confluence of two dark valleys. He was lonely for a white man's company, but had evidently forgotten the obligations of society for he overindulged his bottle and fell into a stupor before I could properly cross-examine him about the Native *kraals* in the vicinity. In the morning, after I had endured a restless, chilly night under his corrugated iron roof, he was summoned to the store and I had lost my chance of a private conference. Conceding that Japie could not now catch up with me – the lazy beggar would no doubt be happy to wait for me in Pilgrims Rest – I restocked with provisions for my saddle-bag and turned uphill again, towards the passes over the Berg, where the morning mists were swirling and the air had such a northern zest to it that it gave me fresh heart. That same morning I came upon a couple of ragged frontier prospectors, smoking their pipes in a secret glade above the great valley and taking their ease as though they were grandees surveying their ancient estates. They had a villainous appearance and I hesitated to dismount, but they greeted me cheerfully and turned out to be splendid chaps, pressing tobacco on me and plying me with bold tales of the fortunes they had made and lost. They spoke of gold, but not of *veldponde*, and I took care to keep my business to myself.

Then I was off again, wandering from *kraal* to *kraal*, noting the squalor and the hunger, remarking too that there were few able-bodied men to be seen, hailing everyone I saw with false joviality, knowing that I had no way of interrogating them and that, even if I had an interpreter, I could not hope for the truth, let alone the truth about a murdered man and a cache of stolen Boer gold. That second evening, in the fragrance of a meadow of aromatic herbs – wormwood, southernwood, bog-myrtle, musk and peppermint – nestling under a Berg which stood like a great ship above the dark green sea of the bush,[20] I came upon a lonely Boer farm where, with the hospitality of the race, they insisted that I stay the night and share their modest *bobotie* curry and mealie porridge, with a taste of their own apricot *konfyt*. The house had been stripped to the walls two years ago by our English troops, who to my embarrassment had used every scrap of woodwork for fuel, but the old folk did not hold this against me, nor even that my host had spent a year as guest of Her Majesty in Ceylon,[21] whence he had only recently returned

20 This phrase was later to appear in *Prester John*.
21 Some Boer prisoners of war were shipped by the British to camps in Ceylon.

to reclaim his womenfolk from one of our concentration camps and return to this vandalised homestead and broken-down domain. I set myself to be as pleasant as my knowledge of the *taal* allowed, and with the bitter coffee they brought out a tot of *mampoer* that made my head sing. When the *vrou* showed me to the loft, where they had found a thin mattress, she saw my exiguous baggage and, with the new confidence that came from a happy evening, asked why I was carrying kaffir crafts with me; she had noticed the piece of fabric that was my gift from Major S. I fumbled for an answer and failed to find anything plausible, so to cover my confusion I showed her the beadwork, only to see her seize it and peruse it carefully, tracing the pattern from one end to the other and holding it closer to the lamp so as to scrutinise the colours of the cheap glass ornament.

"It is a pretty enough nonsense," I proffered. "I may take it to Johannesburg."

Mevrou du Plessis nodded impatiently. Then, to my astonishment, she looked up at me and said, "You know that this is a message?"

I must have appeared thunderstruck because she laughed sweetly as though to reassure me that there was nothing unusual in what she had said.

"You didn't know that the kaffir girls have a language of the beads? They put together a pattern – and certain colours – and make a secret message . . ."

"A message to whom?"

She smiled, a dumpy little farmer's wife, innocent of the dramas and the violence of this land. "Sometimes to the man they love. Sometimes to their betrothed. I do not know – I cannot read the beads, it is a secret they keep from us."

My head was in a turmoil, but I must be careful not to betray too keen an interest. "Never mind, it is a pleasant bauble," I said. "Tell me, can you discover, from the beads, where it comes from? Does it indicate a local clan, or a *kraal*? I found it not far from here . . ."

She shook her head. "It is a pattern which the local girls often wear, I can see that, but I cannot tell who made it. If I could, it would not be a secret, would it?"

"Or who it was sent to?"

She shook her head again, handed the cloth back to me, gave me one of the lamps, and bade me "'*Nag, Meneer*".

I was awake before sunrise on a crisp morning, the clouds still a heavy blanket draped over the surrounding peaks. The brief exhilaration of the previous night's discovery had vanished and my head was heavy, whether from the *mampoer* or from a sensible depression as to my prospects. I stuck my head into a bucket of freezing water and forced myself to take an educated man's view of my situation. The "waterfall" was as unhelpful as ever – I could see half a dozen if I looked out from my host's *stoep*. The Major's addition, that it was "behind Pilgrims Rest", did not necessarily mean any more than that it was somewhere within a circumference of, say, a day's journey from here. As for last night's conversation with my hostess, that at least was new. Major S. had spoken of the Native lad clinging to the beads, so they may have had a meaning for him, but I could not see how a piece of cloth was going to find me the one *kraal* of the thousands that dotted these hills where I might find a clue to my Grail. So this particular knight rode out that morning with a queasy sense of approaching failure: how long before he must return to Camelot at Sunnyside and confess defeat?

46

Once more, I set the pony to follow its own path as we continued to climb ever upwards, and so we made our slow progress through many steep vales, along clumsy tracks that sometimes climbed through tangled forest, yet always steering towards the line of crag that hung high above our heads. This morning I had tied the bead-cloth loosely to the strap of my saddle so that any of the Natives I passed might see it and, perhaps, recognise its provenance; but it was a hopeless project and I knew it too well as I braced myself to leave the path wherever I saw a *kraal* and to ride amongst the beehive huts, cursing the yapping mongrels, making greeting to the elders, smiling down on the hordes of boisterous childen. Heaven knows what they made of me as they discovered that I did not know a word of their tongue and proposed no apparent business or command for them.

This went on all morning and by noon I had climbed near to the head of a great valley where the breezes were pleasant and the traveller could look out on the distant Lebombo hills to the east.[22] Discovering I was hungry, I dismounted in the shade of a stack of great yellow-wood, centuries-old, and lay down to eat the stick of dried *biltong* and a scone that the good *Mevrou* had forced on me. The wind kept the insects away and I was relieved to have this solitude after the stink and the hubbub of the *kraal*s, when I saw, to my irritation, that an ancient kaffir was hobbling eagerly towards me from a *kopje* on the other side of the rough road. He was a very old man, bent almost double, and I could hear him

22 The Lebomboberg is a mountain range running north-south on the border of the Transvaal and Mozambique, south of Komatipoort. See: "The ground rose so that we had a sight of the distant Lebombo hills to the east . . .", *The Green Wildebeest*. This short story, collected by Buchan in *The Runagates Club*, purports to be an autobiographical tale told by Hannay about an adventure just after the end of the Anglo-Boer War: ". . . I was on a prospecting job in the north-eastern Transvaal . . ."

wheezing and muttering to himself; to my regret, it was clear that he had spotted me and intended to make my acquaintance. As he approached, wiping his hands in some sort of respectful tribal greeting, I could see that his clothes hung in tatters, and indeed I could savour the stench of him as he passed upwind. On his back he carried an old iron cooking pot, the sort with three legs that you find everywhere in these parts, and in his hand he brandished a short spear that could hardly have protected him even if he had the strength to wield it. Mixed up in his rags I spotted a Native version of a kitbag which no doubt contained his worldly goods. He coughed, and spat behind his hand in the Native fashion, and greeted me with a long rigmarole of some dialect which was double Dutch to me. I gave him a civil word in both of our European languages and (he was still upwind) tossed him a twist of tobacco and waved him away. He caught it neatly and launched into another litany, which I judged to be in gratitude, then stuck the plug straight into his mouth and, retiring by at most a dozen yards, squatted on the ground and chewed loudly, pausing every few minutes to squirt tobacco juice between his dusty toes. I gestured angrily at him several times, but he beamed and cackled and clearly was determined to join me.

We all know how our rest can be hopelessly disturbed by the presence of an uninvited observer. After half an hour of this I had had enough and remounted, wheeling my pony back on to the steep track, only to find to my irritation that the old man was determined to accompany me. It was still slow going and he was surprisingly agile on his pins, and for the life of me I could not see how to shake him off without resorting to violence. All the time, too, he kept up a meaningless chatter which, as we came round a bend in the valley revealing the saddle over the main ridge of the Berg, rose to a crescendo of urgency. He was trying to tell me something and, when he hobbled ahead and made urgent gestures insisting I follow him off the track in the direction of a stand of ancient, wind-blasted timber, I shook my head, but his entreaties intensified, and then it occurred to me that there might be an emergency for which my help was needed. There seemed no danger in it, so I signalled that I would follow. He scurried up a beaten path, yelping with something like delight; we were approaching yet another *kraal*. There were more huts than usual, and more people too – more young men, I reckoned, and had the impression that this place was cleaner, in that sense more civilised, than those of earlier in the day. I also observed that many of the young men were carrying spears, as though they had been hunting. And as I rode into the central clearing, it occurred to me that the old man, all of a sudden, had vanished.

Waiting for me was an imposing person who could only be the Chief. He was not old, as most chiefs are, but he exuded a palpable authority and confidence as he stepped forward to examine me. Nor did he wear tribal dress but, presumably as a sign of his sophistication, not to say his superiority over his fellows, he sported a white shirt, not of the cleanest, and a threadbare pair of khaki trousers which I suspected might once have formed part of the wardrobe of a British trooper. He did not at all resemble the Native headmen I was accustomed to: he looked me straight in the eye, he made no effort at the fawning greetings and compliments normally offered to the white visitor and, most surprising of all, he addressed me in English. It was a careful, occasionally hesitant, mission school English, and it was not welcoming. I didn't understand why, after the old man had led me here, I should be greeted in so hostile a manner.

"The *baas* is looking for something?"

That was true enough, but I began with a few words of salutation and introduction, only to be cut short.

"We do not welcome strangers to our *kraal*."

Since the day I arrived in this country I had never been spoken to like that by a Native and I was on the point of giving the kaffir a piece of my mind when my wiser self told me that a touch of caution might be politic. The Chief was a well-built man, I saw, and apart from a blemish in one eye – a "wall eye" I think we call it – a not-unhandsome figure of a man. His confidence was evident, which made his hostility even more perplexing. It was not as if I had ridden into his private kingdom unannounced and with a detachment of soldiery. I noticed, with a first whiff of apprehension, that the young men were bunching behind him: their faces were blank; none of them had responded to my greetings. On either side there was a subdued rustle of activity and I saw that the women and children had emerged from the huts and come running in from the veld to form a silent circle around me. I looked around for my horse, but it must have been led away; I knew that my rifle was strapped to the saddle-bag, though a lot of good that would do me, I realised, if we got to a scrap. Diplomacy was evidently called for.

"What welcome is this for a passing traveller?" I asked, my voice bolder than my morale justified. "I came to see if you had sickness in your *kraal*." The old man had definitely vanished, and I cursed him for diverting me.

The Chief repeated, "What are you looking for?"

The thought came to my mind to reply, as in the child's game, "So what are you hiding?", and the phrase choked in my mouth and I began to think very fast.

"Chief, I think there are strange things to be found in these mountains . . ."

He said nothing. Two of the youths jabbered at him and he silenced them with a brisk order. I tried again.

"I have friends in high places who will reward you if you assist me."

"We do not want the white man's gifts."

"Your people are poor. Your children are hungry."

"Who are you, *Mister*? And why do you come?"

The impertinence was unmistakable and the longer I tolerated it the more he would know his mastery over me. Major S. would never have got himself into this situation, I reflected, and, defying my beating heart, I raised my voice in what I hoped would sound a masterful command.

"Be wise, O Chief, and take care not to speak in that manner."

He laughed in my face and, on his prompting, the young warriors shrieked in derision. I felt the sweat start out on my brow.

"I see that I am not welcome," I said lamely. "So I shall leave you," and half turned to see where I might best hope to break through the circle that surrounded us.

At that moment there was an eldritch shriek and a figure burst through the crowd, almost knocking me aside as she rushed up to the Chief. It was a woman, or rather a girl, slim, impassioned, and I could see at once that by the Native style of these things she was beautiful. She was on her knees in front of the Chief, pouring out a jumble of protest and exclamation, and in her hands she held – proffered to him – a wretched strip of kaffir blanket, stained and dirty and coloured in a distinctive pattern of reds and ochre. The Chief was listening to her intently, as indeed was the entire *kraal*, for they set up a hubbub which he impatiently silenced with a word of command; then he looked at me and his expression seemed to have changed – not, I hazarded, for the better. I could have sworn he was seized with a deep emotion, and I wondered whether it was not just anger but also – was it fear?

"You will not leave us yet," he managed to say, and recovered his composure.

It was clear that I had no chance of breaking through the throng, which had tightened around me so closely that, whenever they wished, those in the front could have reached out to touch me or strike me.

The Chief addressed me, and again I thought I detected a shadow of some secret emotion in his one clear eye. "You will tell me – why do you bring the blanket?"

I was dumbfounded. "I've never seen it in my life before," I managed to say.

The Chief shook his head. "It was on the saddle of your horse, as you must know."

I began to protest at this nonsense. I wanted to say, "The only kaffir cloth I'm carrying is the piece of bead-cloth . . ." but out of some instinct I stifled the words and looked across at the girl. She was glaring at me, her black eyes enormous; she was panting furiously, as though her hatred for me could not be contained. I held her gaze and, for a second, I wondered if there was a message in those wonderful eyes.

"I have never seen that blanket," I repeated, and when the Chief snorted angrily, and my words were translated by him to the crowd so that his warriors growled in harmony, I added, "Why? Who does it belong to?"

The Chief said, "You will be sorry for what you have done," and added a burst of instruction in his own tongue. Then the young men charged at me, and forced me to the ground while I struggled and cursed, and I think the women shrieked and spat at me, and as I drowned beneath the rancid stink of black bodies and felt my senses fading, my last thought was that, if I was to die, I would have wished to know the crime of which I was guilty.

Chapter Four

WHEN I RETURNED to consciousness, with a moment of waking panic and then instant recollection of the day, I was lying in near-darkness on the smooth earth of what I slowly realised must be a beehive hut. My hands and feet were bound with grass thongs and I had been laid on my side; they cannot have been too violent with me because I could check that no bones were broken and my head, though throbbing, seemed clear enough. A little sunlight came filtering through the grass thatch, which must mean that I had not been there long. I heard a rat – or a snake? – rustle above me. I strained my ears but could hear no sound of human voices; perhaps I had been imprisoned in a hut on the perimeter of the *kraal*. It was a situation requiring my deepest and most concentrated reflection, but I can now confess that my first concern was that I was damnably hungry and had a thirst to go with it.

As though in answer to an unvoiced prayer, I heard soft footsteps padding towards the hut and a rattle at the rough door, felt a blast of hot daylight, and saw the silhouette of a slim figure approaching me cautiously. They had sent me the girl, my accuser, and she carried a gourd and a clay bowl, which she set to one side of me. There was no hint of sympathy for me in her face. She stood for a moment, looking down on my manacles, and scowled in what I now realise might have been perplexity rather than anger, and hissed a long question at me, *sotto voce*, but I understood not a word, so she scowled again and dropped the gourd on the ground beside my head. I smelt the food first, and then I saw it to be a mess of white tripe in a bed of native porridge – *putu* – and my stomach had begun to heave even before she leaned forward and spat, a heavy gobbet, into the bowl. That seemed to settle the matter. She left, darkness resumed, and I knew I could live with my hunger.

I lay there for an hour or so, striving to flex my stiff muscles and shift my position to keep the blood flowing to my limbs, and thinking with the cool intensity that comes, I was discovering for the first time in my short life, with the most desperate danger. My first decision was to summon the Chief – to demand his presence – and tell him who I was. As an educated man he would know of Lord Milner and I would be able to prove to him my authority. But when I thought further I knew that that must surely seal my death warrant. The Chief had insulted me and laid hands on me on the understanding that I was a lone traveller who, somehow, had done him wrong. Once he discovered that he had abused the representative of the Empire his fear of the consequences must be such that he would surely decide that his best course must be to cut my throat and bury me in a ravine, trusting that my disappearance could not be traced by the soldiers to this distant place.

I paused at that point. The Chief's reception of me had been untypical of his people as I had experienced them everywhere. Why should he fear that I was seeking something? Why for that matter had the verminous old man brought me to this *kraal* and so delivered me to this pretty mess? What – as I had almost asked – did the Chief have to hide from innocent visitors like myself? There was a mystery here that would repay investigation, but the more urgent mystery was the invention of the wretched blanket: what was the girl playing at? Why had she produced this blanket – and not the beads? What did this blanket signify? And indeed – it came to me – what might the beads have signified?

The hut was stuffy and I must have dozed for a time, for when I was next conscious the light was fading fast and I may have been woken by the rat in the thatch. It was certainly a rat, not an insect, I reckoned, because the rustling became louder, and bits of dry grass fell near my head, and as I twisted around and looked up I saw, and my tormented nerves shrieked again, that a whole section of the roof had fallen aside. Then, with a quick scuffle and a gasp, a silhouette darkened the twilit sky and a figure dropped through the rafters and landed at my side.

He was familiar by his stench. I saw it was the old man – the same who had brought me to this strait – and I groaned with exasperation and made as if to roll aside. But the old man would have none of it: he scrambled after me and, to my horror, clamped a grubby hand tight over my mouth so that I almost retched, and put his mouth to my ear and whispered –

"*Basie*! Not a word or we are done for . . ."

Then I looked closer, and saw the blue eyes, and felt against me the lean body, no longer bent, and knew that it was Schalk Minnaar.

He had taken a knife from out of his rags and was sawing urgently at my bonds. After my hands were free he passed me the gourd of water and paused, listening, before he tackled the ropes on my feet. "We must hurry, my friend," he whispered. "This is Chief M'Chudi's *kraal* and it is too hot for you. They think you tortured and killed their man in Pilgrims Rest. Now they are deciding how they are going to do the same to you." He paused again to listen and must have caught something beyond my hearing because he flung aside the bindings and rubbed my calves fiercely as though he feared that I would be cramped.

I managed to haul myself to my feet. I was stiff, but I found that I could walk. Schalk muttered, "You must move fast. The edge of the Berg is only half a mile to the east. There is a *kloof* with a trail. You must find it and get down the mountain."

"Where's my horse?"

"No, you will be seen. I'll try to bring it later. Quickly! You must get out of this place . . ."

He bent down, seized me at the knees, and hoisted me up through the hole in the thatch. I took a quick glance around me. The dusk was coming down with a vengeance. We were on the edge of the *kraal*; the other huts were behind us and there was a clump of pine twenty yards away. I whispered, "All clear!", and Schalk gave an almighty heave and I tumbled through the straw and pitched on my head on the turf. "Run like hell!" commanded my rescuer.

From the brief safety of the pine copse I took my bearings. The *kraal*, as I remembered, nestled in a narrow fold in the mountain slope, protected from the winds. Beyond the outer huts the hillside rose again, smooth as the Sussex downs, empty of any bush to give me cover, but beyond the horizon I knew the slope would plunge down again to the cliffs and *krantzes* of the great descent into the valleys to the east. The alternative was the narrow defile that broke away to the north, but I did not trust myself to a dense thicket of thorn and creeper where I could so easily become trapped in the dark. This world seemed to float in a hazy twilight, under the first shy stars, and I knew that only minutes of this mulberry light were left to me. Should I wait for the darkness before cutting across the open meadow? No, Schalk had insisted that those minutes might bring my discovery. No less compelling, I needed to see what lay over the edge of the Berg, the nature of the terrain through which I would have to attempt my escape in darkness.

I commended myself to my Maker, breathed deep of the cool, sweet air, and hared across the open ground. Four hundred yards, I had reckoned, and slightly uphill, but the mountain light was deceptive and the minutes went by, the breath rasping in my lungs, and I knew I was naked to any piccaninn who might glance up from his toys. By the grace of God I nearly did it. I realise now that I must have been in wild silhouette against the line of the hill when a banshee cry went up behind me. I hurled myself on and then had the wit to fling myself to the ground and crawl the last yards, but it was too late, the damage was done and a great hubbub went up, a screaming and a babble and then a deep bass command as the Chief required silence. In that brief respite I found that I had breasted their horizon and was looking down, deep down, on a long soft slope that led to emptiness – and beyond and below that emptiness there was the dark cavern which was the Bushveld thousands of feet below. Above, there were wisps of cloud against an indigo sky.

I had forgotten Schalk's order to aim for the *kloof*, and anyway it was too late. I had heard a clatter and another order – I knew by some instinct that they were seizing their weapons – and I put down my head and sprinted.

The turf was not so smooth as it appeared. Again, the evening light must have been misleading. There seemed to be shadows everywhere, which was strange because the sun had gone down long ago, the starlight was still faint and the moon had not risen, but shadows there were and I measured my length in two of them; I could hear myself sobbing. After the second fall, half-winded,

I paused and looked back, and there I saw a sight to make a man's blood run cold. Just emerging from the far side of the slope, climbing smoothly into view as though riding on some new-fangled elevator, were a score of warriors; they were bare-chested and they loped gracefully, without any of my frantic effort, their spears held high in their right hands. They saw me, saw me looking back, and cheered, as though in salutation. I pounded on, praying for the cliff, yet I had no sense of what I was to do, whereas they would be familiar with every inch of this hillside, and my youthful scrambling on the Scottish crags, when I would innocently glissade down the screes, seemed an age away. Yet that memory struck at me even as I ran. I remembered how I had recently noted that the geology of these mountain formations was so consistent: the cliff edge, then the scree, and then the grassy precipice. I held on to the image of it.

I came over the Berg as the moon was rising behind the Lebombo. They were gaining on me with every stride, I could hear their steady breathing and the slap of their feet on the turf. I snatched a glance over my shoulder and they saw it and hallooed again, almost cheerfully, and several of them brandished their spears at me as though to make promises. I had a deathly dread that I was within their range and in these next seconds would be skewered in the back. That terror must have given me a last infusion of energy, because briefly I seemed to gain on them, and now I could see the brink of the cliff face like a trapdoor opening ahead of me. I was far beyond thought, I must have abandoned my life at that moment, because I measured those last yards and I launched myself out over the Berg and into the blackness, spreadeagled into space, and even as I flew through the air I heard their exclamations of astonishment and may have felt the whisper of an iron shaft as it was hurled after me.

59

I landed with a colossal crash, still upright for a brief moment but staggering as I hit a promontory which promptly collapsed in fragments under my impact. It was indeed, as I had gambled, a slope of scree: the stones were jagged but – that was my salvation – they were small. I tumbled over and over from the momentum of my death's leap and felt my clothes rip, my flesh tear, and then I was perilously upright again and, remembering those days on the peaks beyond Tweeddale, I set myself to ski down the scree. There was an almighty din because I had set many tons of granite into motion, so that I could hear no more of the voices above and I almost forgot about my enemies in the concentration to keep some sort of balance. The dangerous bit, I remember thinking, was yet to come: what lay at the foot of the scree – a grassy slope or a fatal precipice?

The good Lord was watching over me that night. I hit solid ground – which flung me down again, and immediately fell away under me so that I rolled, helpless, buffeted, head over heels, like a sack flung down a slag heap, crashing through clumps of brush and bush, absurdly aware of the aromatic herbs that were crushing around me, trying to shield my head between my arms, over and over until I was dizzy as a child who rolls down the family lawn. It went on without end.

Long, long afterwards, I came to rest in a thorn bush. I lay there for unheeded minutes, oblivious of my wounds. Eventually, I managed to push aside a branch and looked out. The cliff towered above me but I could just see, far, far above, the line of the Berg across the dark sky. I listened to the night. Behind the clamour of cicadas, there was nothing – which surely meant that they had not dared to follow me over the edge.

There must be other paths and by now they would be hard on their way. I staggered to my feet and began to run. I did not know where I was going, nor where I might find shelter, but I knew I must devote every ounce of strength to escape from the Berg.

Looking back on that night I suspect that I was unhinged. I cannot now report with certainty that M'Chudi's warriors pursued me across the night as I then believed. My only thought was to set many miles between myself and my new-won enemies, and to do that I knew I must somehow hold an eastward course, down through the corries and glens, past the *kopjes* and the forests, until I found safe haven. Eventually I would reach White River and Wheatcroft's cantonment, but for that I would need to find a horse: my plans did not extend beyond the next hours and I kept stopping, freezing in my tracks, to strain my ears for sound of my pursuers.[23]

The sky had brightened with the stars of Africa, and this starlight gave me a dim shadowy glow by which I could pick my stumbling way. The bush was mysterious around me, the shadows a deepest dark tinged with green, the trees looming taller and threatening. My route had to be downwards, always down-hill, away from the massive Berg wall; that was just as well because my limbs were heavy and stiff and I did not know how far they would carry me. Only the secret menaces of the bush – the rustling of a shrub, the bark of a wild dog, the startled scamper of a buck or a warthog – were warning to me not to slacken my pace. I must have covered several miles in this fashion when the moon came out again from behind a deep ridge of cloud and suddenly the whole landscape was swimming in its silver light. I remember

23 Some of the phrases in this chapter echo passages in Buchan's *The Watcher by the Threshold*, which is curious because the latter was published in 1902, before this journal was written. Perhaps JB subconsciously remembered his earlier turn of phrase.

worrying that it would help M'Chudi's men to track my spoor. It was because of that sudden fear that I looked for the next river, to ford it and hide my tracks, and I was halfway across the shallow sandbanks when I thought of crocodile and, panicking, scrambled through the reeds and up the bank and plunged back into the bush. Once, looking back, I saw the flicker of a lantern. Once, I heard voices – the deep grumble of Natives. I knew that I could not trust any *kraal* that night so on I staggered, lightheaded with hunger, faltering with a terrible fatigue. I had lost all sense of time and of distance, but I could tell that the country was levelling out: there seemed to be fewer *kopjes*, the bare turf was yielding to grass and fern, and on the hillsides I could see the silhouetted stands of yellow-wood and stinkwood. There was a sense that man might put his stamp on this landscape. And so my flight continued, for time beyond my measuring.

Then I saw, half a mile below me, a gleam of light, a pinpoint in dense blackness. For the first time I slowed to a very cautious walk. I lingered, hugging the clumps of shadow, listening always for pursuit, prospecting for dangers ahead. I stumbled on a fence and allowed myself to topple over it. I weaved my way, half crouching, across an open field, towards a block of darkness and, I now saw, a corrugated iron roof which shimmered in the rays of the moon. The light seemed to have vanished.

Now I found I was in a kitchen garden, scrambling through pumpkins and a screen of mealies; then a lawn, and a thin barrier of shrubs. Ahead of me the house was clearly visible. In the glare of the moon I saw windows, low gables, a long *stoep*; I thought I could see empty chairs, a table strewn with familiar things. I had a gasping sense that I had found sanctuary, that I had come home.

Then, just behind me, I heard the low, spine-freezing growl

of a dog who has found an intruder: I swung round and saw a great ridgeback, teeth drawn back in a vicious snarl. High above him, outlined against the stars, was the silhouette of a man and the glitter of a shotgun levelled at my eyes.

Chapter Five

"LORD! IT'S A WHITE MAN," exclaimed a cheerful voice, and the barrel dropped and the idiot dog hurriedly began to fawn. "Some character has been crashing around out there for ten minutes. You were making so much din I thought it was a hippo."

We had turned towards the house and my new host was fiddling with matches and with the lamp on the *stoep*, which he must have dowsed when he heard me. The wick caught and the soft light flickered over my torn and tattered presence.

"Great heavens, what's happened to you? You look as if you've been trampled by buffalo."

I found I was shaking uncontrollably, and I had a great urge to lie down on the rush matting. Instead I managed to say, "I came down from the Berg. Over the top! They're after me – M'Chudi's men, they'll be here any minute . . ."

Yes, I thought, I would lie down on the matting.

"We'll see about that!" declared the stranger in a tone that did me good. "I don't stand any kaffir nonsense on this homestead and they all know it. Now! You're in no state to argue – do you realise how many miles you must have covered? Sit yourself down on that couch, pour yourself a stiff tonic from that bottle, and give me a couple of minutes."

He strode out into the night, followed by the hound, and vanished immediately into the trees. I heard him whistling up his boys from the compound, and then there was a barrage of cries and orders as though a platoon was departing in the direction from which I had come. I drained a tall glass of water and then risked a slug of neat brandy. It hit me like a blow in the stomach and I nearly vomited, and then I felt the tension go out of me like air escaping from a punctured balloon. I may have slept a brief sleep of utter exhaustion.

When I opened my eyes my host was sitting opposite me, puffing at his pipe and nursing his own glass. He grinned at me cheerfully, as though this was a normal episode in his evening routine. "You can relax," he said. "There's no one out there, but I've posted watchmen for the night. You're safe in Edenend. Now we'd better get those scratches cleaned up . . ."

"They can wait," I interrupted. "I must get on to White River. I need to find Colonel Wheatcroft."[24]

"You're in no state to go anywhere tonight. The Colonel can wait till the morning when we'll be able to see what's going on. First we clean you up. Then we feed you. And before all that, we both need another brandy."

Douglas Green was his name and fortune had led me to a splendid fellow. He was a tall, well-standing chap, about my age or perhaps a little older. He told me he was a mining engineer by profession who started off on the copper concessions in South-West, where

24 Wheatcroft, who was at this time the senior officer in the Eastern Transvaal, with his headquarters at White River, seems to be the model for Captain Jim Arcoll, the police officer who plays an important role in *Prester John*. One of his tricks in that book is to disguise himself as an ancient Native and totally deceive David Crawfurd, the young hero. Incidentally, Arcoll is the only character in the Buchan canon who links *Prester John* with the Richard Hannay books; he appears – rather as Wheatcroft does here – in the self-contained African chapter in *The Island of Sheep* (there is also a fleeting reference to him in *Greenmantle*).

he got a bellyful of the Germans so he moved across to Rhodesia, only to get caught up in the Matabele business, where I guessed he had played a sterling role.[25] "I made my pile in Rhodesia," he told me in his candid way, "but I never liked the way Cecil Rhodes and his Company were running things, so when I saw you chaps had taken the measure of the Boer, I moved down here and bought a place of my own. I always wanted to farm, and down here in the Bushveld there's a bonus: I can get all the hunting I want."

Edenend was a low-built, sprawling lodge, modest enough, but appropriate to the needs of a bachelor more at home in the bush than the drawing-room, and with a style all its own. There were two wings, newly whitewashed, containing bedrooms, a library and a gunroom, all set under the wide, corrugated-iron roof, but the heart of the house was a giant *stoep*, scattered with low rattan chairs with extendable arms on which to drape your dirty boots, a trio of tables strewn with faded picture magazines, a kneehole desk pushed behind a door and stacked with a collection of bottles and pipes, a parrot in a cage, enveloped at this late hour under a ragged old bush shirt but nevertheless protesting at the interruption, boxes of seedlings on the step and, balanced on the rail, a tray of cold beef and chutneys. Add to that a couple of decent eland heads above the doors, old Portuguese prints on the walls, a dozen glass jars of geological specimens, the ridge-back who had decided that I was his oldest ally – and I decided that I envied Douglas Green his remote life. Most especially his plate of cold meats. But the man was a Trojan and without any hint from me one of his boys brought a double portion to set on my knee, with a foaming flagon to wash it down. There was no sense nor sight of a female hand.

25 In 1897 in what was to become Rhodesia (now Zimbabwe) the Ndebele tribe rose in major revolt, followed by the Shona.

I liked the look of the man. He was, I thought, a man to trust. It was time to put my cards on the table. I needed help, and my host was going to be the chosen one.

"Mr Green," I said, "you have saved my life tonight and in return I am going to tell you a tale which might cost you your own . . ."

He was standing on the upper step, looking out over the lawns, gleaming platinum in the moonlight, that ran down from a line of turpentine trees into the shadows of the surrounding bush. He looked back at me, perfectly serious. "I don't usually admit it," he replied, "but I was getting just a spot bored with the farmer's life. You begin to interest me. And my name is Douglas, if you can manage it . . ."

First, I told him who I was, my commission and my masters. I swore him to secrecy, which I felt I had to do, but pressed on quickly because I saw that this irritated his sense of his own honour. Then I changed my tune and, not least to help myself, I spoke to him as though I were briefing Lord Milner on my recent misadventures: that is to say, I described the events since I had left Johannesburg and then I posed the questions which seemed to me to arise out of my travels. What was the meaning of the dying Native's words at Pilgrims Rest? Did the bead-cloth signify anything? Had Schalk deliberately led me to M'Chudi's *kraal*? Who was the girl? Finally, and not least, where should I turn next? To Wheatcroft? Or back to Sunnyside to admit failure to my masters, even as Chamberlain was delivering to a Boer audience the key speech of his visit in which he would promise South Africa a new beginning?

It was late by the time I finished and my muscles were reminding me of the rigours of the day. Green was plunged into a silence of the fiercest concentration, though I noticed he had punctuated my narrative with frequent sorties to the brandy decanter. I had the sense to realise that I had been staving off blind exhaustion and sustaining my monologue with the help of that same medicine, and knew I would have to sleep.

"But Douglas," I demanded, "where do we turn next?" The "we" had slipped out unconsidered.

"That's easy," declared my new friend. "We go back, of course. We must go back, up on to the Berg! We'll leave as soon as you are rested."

I protested: indeed, I was horrified and, I must confess, literally terrified. I reminded him of M'Chudi and his warriors and our need of Wheatcroft's troopers.

"Heavens, man! There's no point in sitting down here, hiding in the tobacco sheds. We must go back on the mountain. That's where the gold is – why else do you think they were trying to kill you?"[26]

I slept the sleep of the just and woke in mid-morning with a passionate ambition for a trencher of ham and eggs. That was

26 Not the least interesting aspect of these Papers is that here we surely have the true model for "Richard Hannay", who was to be Buchan's best-known and, in various ways, most successful "hero". Hannay in Buchan's *œuvre* rose with remarkable speed from his arrival in pre-war London as a rich colonial outsider of Scottish ancestry (*The Thirty-nine Steps*), through the heaviest battles of 1914–18, with dramatic episodes on the side (*Greenmantle; Mr Standfast*) to emerge as a Major-General and an English country gentleman secure in possession of a knighthood, a Cotswold estate, a teenage society bride and, after a suitable interval, a beloved son who is sent to Eton (see *The Three Hostages*, *The Island of Sheep*, various short stories, and references throughout the corpus). Buchan's model for Hannay – as has already been footnoted – has usually been given as Edmund Ironside, JB's colleague at Sunnyside. The argument is based on Ironside having been a military man (he became the youngest Major-General in the British army), an Africa hand – he knew South-West Africa in particular – and a remarkable linguist. But Ironside was highly intelligent (which Hannay – and Douglas Green – do not appear to be); he was not a mining engineer; he was not *nouveau riche*; and above all he was not an outsider in the eyes of the British establishment. Of course, novelists do not draw their characters from life alone.

assured me by my friend, who had evidently been awake for hours to judge by the paraphernalia he had assembled in front of the *stoep*, including, I noted, a minor armoury. But first I was made to wallow in a gigantic tank at the end of the orchard, where his boys had been boiling water all morning. It was a painful experience and I found I was hideously bruised and torn, but by a miracle nothing was broken; Green smeared me with a foul-smelling unguent, which I imagine he obtained from the local witch doctor, and pronounced me fit for our venture.

With eggs and bacon sizzling before us, my courage stiffened and I managed to ask how he thought it possible, let alone sensible, for me to return to M'Chudi's den.

"You will," said Douglas, "be disguised."[27]

I must have looked unconvinced because he became

27 Disguise is important in Buchan's novels. In *Prester John* Captain Arcoll, the Wheatcroft figure, passes as an elderly Native. In *The Thirty-nine Steps* the doomed Scudder plays a Gurkha officer, Hannay goes through a variety of successful disguises from London milkman to Scottish road labourer, while the villains impersonate, with equal success, the First Sea Lord, suburban English tennis players, etc. In *Greenmantle* Sandy Arbuthnot begins an extraordinary career of *alter egos* (he eventually *is* Greenmantle) while Hannay plays a Boer rebel. In *Mr Standfast* the evil Ivery is admitted to be "the most amazing actor in the world", switching effortlessly from garden-city philanthropist to French staff officer to Kansas City newspaperman, and Hannay carries conviction first as a Borders travelling salesman and then as a Swiss peasant. Hannay's Mary plays a dance-hall hostess so well in *The Three Hostages* that her husband does not recognise her, and Sandy is (once more) an Oriental mystic. In *The Courts of the Morning* Sandy is at it again. The hero of *A Prince of the Captivity* spends a good part of the book, as a Great War spy, pretending to be someone else. In *John Macnab* the distinguished Sir Edward Leithen passes successfully as a tramp, despite forgetting to take off his Etonian medallion. As for the Dickson McCunn books, let me simply record that they finish with the Glaswegian grocer impersonating a king (*The House of the Four Winds*).

There is no need to list here the entire register of disguises. The point is that they are invariably successful, whether by hero or villain, and it is therefore implied that they are not difficult to carry off. The analysis of, and explanation for, Buchan's obsession with disguise in his fiction are not, I think, the proper task of this volume; my psychoanalyst friends would I am sure have much to say.

unusually eloquent on the theme. He told yarns of his own adventures in Mashonaland and South-West. He reminded me that Schalk Minnaar's achievement in accosting me as a stinking old kaffir confirmed his point. He was very insistent about his theory, no doubt shared by Schalk, that you have to think yourself deeply into a part; more than that, you have to *become* that part. You can then appear before people who know you in a different context and you will not need extravagant disguise for them to fail to recognise you. But it is imperative to take up the new personality completely – witness Schalk's identification with his role when he led me to the *kraal*.[28]

I was relieved to hear that I would not be required to become a great actor, and asked what he had in mind.

"Chief M'Chudi knows me and has a clear sense of who I am and what I do," Douglas explained. "He knows that I sometimes go up on the Berg to recruit labour – I've sometimes hired men from his own *kraal*. He does not associate me with the British authorities in Johannesburg. He will not be interested to see that I am travelling on this occasion with a business colleague. So – once you have a new haircut, and an entirely different wardrobe, something, for example, that would be worn by a young businessman just out from Jo'burg on a brief visit – there's no reason why he should give you a second glance. But you'd better keep quiet and leave the talking to me."

I didn't like the sound of this. "You're not going to paint my face?" I asked.

"Just a slight change to the complexion. I learned how to do it when my pals were teasing the Hun in Windhoek."

28 cf. *A Prince of the Captivity* (ch. 2/1): "'You must think yourself into it,' he was told, 'and imagine that you have never been otherwise. That is the only real disguise.'" See also *Greenmantle* (ch. 3) and *The Thirty-nine Steps* (chs. 5 and 10).

"So who am I to become?"

Douglas Green had evidently thought it all out while I was sleeping. "I reckon you could be – let's say, Ari Goldstein from Sherman Friedman, the Jo'burg broking house. You are travelling with me to check out a possible gold prospect this side of Lydenburg. We knew each other in Bulawayo and now I'm doing you a favour in my new territory."

There may have been a momentary silence as I digested the news. Douglas Green looked worried and I remembered that I had little alternative if I was not going to retreat to Sunnyside in disgrace.

"So be it!" I said. "If Schalk Minnaar can be a kaffir, then I can be a Jew."[29]

The history of my new friend's exploits in South-West and Rhodesia was at this time a mystery to me, but I began to realise that Green was more than a simple mining engineer when he sat me on the higher of the stools on the *stoep* and produced what he called his Amateur Theatricals kit from Bulawayo, which included various small bottles and brushes and a razor. I urged restraint upon him, but when he insisted on developing an imagined conversation with Ari Goldstein and required me to

29 Buchan has frequently been accused by enemies and critics of being anti-Semitic. The charge is not fair and should be rejected, but it remains true that his books are littered – far more frequently than his defenders admit – with references that are derogatory of Jews, especially of Jewish businessmen. It is offered in Buchan's defence (a) that he does not personally share, or accept, the attitudes of his fictional characters, and (b) that he was echoing the idiom of his time. Nevertheless it is curious to find here this previously unknown description of JB himself having to pretend to be a Jewish South African financier. The extra curiosity – which may be a further point behind this text – is that JB was sending the tale to one of his best friends, the man to whom he would later dedicate *Prester John* – Lionel Phillips, who was a South African Jew! Maybe they both enjoyed the joke . . .

respond in the appropriate accent, thereby immersing myself in my role, we both succumbed to the absurdity of the situation. By this time my hair had been sleeked and shaped and, against my protests, darkened with the help of one of the bottles; my eyebrows had been redesigned by the cut-throat, my eyeballs had been rendered ghastly with the application of a touch of kohl, my healthy tan had been persuaded to turn sallow, and we were arguing over the advisability of a new moustache. I was insisting that it might peel off in the heat of the moment, when there was a sudden agitation outside, a rattle of heels on the path and, before we could think what to do with ourselves, a woman's voice.

"Why, Douglas!" it cried. "Are you playing charades?"

"Damn!" said Douglas, though *sotto voce* so only I heard him. Then, turning to the newcomer, he said – and it sounded to me less courteous than a lady might expect – "Oh, Helga, I didn't hear you coming. How good of you to call."

At this point I need to confess that women had never come much my way and that, when I turned from the stool to acknowledge the new arrival, I assumed I would see the *vrou* from a neighbouring homestead, or perhaps the bashful daughter. Green's voice should have warned me; it was suddenly nervous, almost, to use an absurd word for so masterful a man, shy. So I was unprepared, to say nothing of my understandable self-consciousness that I had a towel pinned to my shoulders and paint on my face, when I swung around to see, to my astonishment, a veritable vision of a goddess.

She was tall – that was the first thing I realised because Douglas was shaking her hand and she yielded little to him – and she was slim and lithe as a boy. Her hair was a cloud of the palest gold. Her costume was a parody of our usual bush rig-out, tailored and pleated in a cool beige. She held in one hand a floppy contraption of a hat, but her face was brown enough to suggest that she had no truck with the local convention that the sun is an enemy to all womanly complexions. She was looking at me, seemingly half-amused at my disarray, half-curious, and I saw that her eyes were the palest grey-blue.

"Introduce me to your friend," she murmured to the evidently confused Green, and I noticed that her accent was heavy, I suspected German, though not unseductive.

I was presented, rather more formally and correctly than I would have wished: either Green had learned his manners in an old-fashioned school or he was trying to conceal his irritation at the lady's arrival. Helga Ingeburg,[30] he explained, a traveller – with her friends – in the district. They had a splendid house in the highlands, but were down here in the Lowveld on a hunting trek. To his relief he was distracted by one of the boys with a question about supplies.

She turned her back on him and favoured me with an entrancing smile. Her beauty surpassed anything I had encountered in my limited experience of European society, it reached out to me and swayed my senses. I noted at the same time, and was conscious of the discourtesy, that she was older than I, as she surveyed my manicured features with an expression part-amused, part-engaged. She was enchanting, I could not deny it, but some deep well-spring of instinct cautioned me against her.[31]

She said, in her soft, accented tones so that I had to strain

30 The name occurs once, fleetingly, in Buchan's *œuvre* – in *Greenmantle*, ch. 8: (of German names starting with I – "I had made a list of about 70 at the British Museum before I left London . . .")
31 There might be a model here for Hilda von Einem in *Greenmantle*, though Buchan's description of her in that book (chs. 14 and 15), like the descriptions of all the female characters in his novels, is minimal.

to hear her, "Am I permitted to ask why Douglas is painting your face?"

I didn't have an immediate answer to that. I did not want to explain that I was assuming the role of Ari Goldstein in order to visit M'Chudi's *kraal* without his knowing it. I doubted whether the lady would be familiar with Lord Milner's latest efforts to achieve National Reconstruction, but without getting into such matters it would be hard to explain to a beautiful German visitor why a Rhodesian mining engineer turned farmer had been applying kohl to my eyes. I stumbled, she waited patiently, and Douglas, breaking aside from his conversation with his foreman, said, "Please, Helga, you mustn't ask questions. My guest – no, I can't explain . . . We have to get back on the Berg on urgent official business. So you must forgive us – I'll call on your uncle as soon as I can . . ."

Douglas Green, it occurred to me, was a splendid fellow, but sometimes a very stupid man.

Later that day, as we rode westward again and into the setting sun, I said to Douglas, "Why did you tell that woman we were travelling on government business?"

He shuddered in apology. "I can't stand the girl. She terrifies me, I admit it – and she seems to have set her cap at me . . ."

I was wondering whether she gave that impression to every man she encountered.

"I'm damnably sorry," he went on, "but I can't see it will matter. She and her uncle have been in the district for months. He must be comfortably off, they've taken a house on the mountain which was built by one of your Randlords before the war. Don't worry about her. You'll be back in Jo'burg before she thinks about Edenend again."

"At least you didn't introduce me as Ari Goldstein."

"No, there's a relief for you . . ." He stopped, then turned red with embarrassment as he remembered the formality with which he had made the introduction. "Oh, hell! You mean that because of me she now knows your proper name. But will that matter? Will she know what that means?"

"Only if she is very well-informed."

"Or if her uncle is."

I did not distress him by labouring the point. If Helga Ingeburg chose to think of it, the sight of one of the High Commissioner's private secretaries making up like a theatrical mountebank before riding off with a couple of rifles into the heights of the Berg would give her a tale on which she could dine out for a month. But as Douglas would say, where was the harm in that?

We climbed quickly towards Sabie. Behind us we left the sleepy haze and malarial dangers of the Lowveld; to the left, in the far distance, we spotted the peaks of Swaziland. We were riding through successive plateaux strewn with a confusion of granite *kopjes*. Before us there were range after range of dove-grey and blue mountains, stacked one over the other like firewood against a barn wall. There was smoke rising from the valleys below the track. A new breeze cheered us, then faltered. The dust of the road, thick and ochre, hung in the air for whole minutes after our passage – if we were pursued in this terrain, there would be no concealing the plumes of our route. When the sun dropped suddenly behind the line of the Berg and the easterly plains faltered into deep shadow, we encamped in a maze of massive boulders, weathered and deformed and grouped in a pattern that helped us build a rough *skerm* screen of thorns for the horses; there had been talk of lion in the vicinity, so Douglas reported. We also built a massive fire and Douglas produced whisky-sodas as though we were snug in some lodge after a day's stalking on the Scottish hills.

With a speed that spoke of long experience he produced a *braaivleis* of chops and *boerewors* and – he seemed to be relishing the expedition more than his companion Goldstein – he told his tales of youthful days in Etosha and Okavango. I reckoned the farmer's life would be too quiet for him, and told him so, but he protested that he had great plans for the future. He had made a start with timber – "I guess I'm still young enough to plant for the next generation and my friends in the mining houses tell me this country will never have enough wood for its pit props" – at which I chided him that he was merely trying to recreate my native Scotland in these tropics. He had been starved of company and wanted to talk shop.

"I have it in mind to try coffee. I reckon it's about the right elevation at Edenend, though I'm told it's a difficult crop."[32]

I felt warm to the man. "Come home!" I said. "You've made your pile. You can do your farming in the Old Country."

Douglas leaned forward to kick a smouldering log back into the centre of the flames. We were high enough on the scarp to welcome the heat of the fire. "Yes. I'll be coming home one day – when I'm ready. I dream of it sometimes, it's like the Arabian Nights for me.[33] But I'll always miss Africa, I've learned its ways . . ." and, to my astonishment, he seized a heavy knife

32 Douglas Green was correct in his planning for the future. Timber plantations now cover the Eastern Transvaal, distorting its natural landscape, and coffee grows well at a certain altitude. I have been unable to discover records of a Douglas Green at Edenend, but if my researches are correct I have located the farm which today houses an hotel. It is possible that for reasons of security JB used pseudonyms for both "Douglas Green" and "Edenend".

33 This curious simile was later to appear on Hannay's lips on the first page of *The Thirty-nine Steps*. It was to be used again after JB's 1910 visit to Constantinople (see Janet Adam Smith: *John Buchan*, ch. 10.)

from his belt, tossed it, twirling, above his head, and caught the blade, clean and unbloodied, between his lips.[34] "There!" he said. "The Shona taught me that trick. I must try it out on your friend Mr Minnaar."

"So why don't you do just that, Mister *Engelsman*?" came a voice from the shadows scarcely three feet behind us, and as Douglas swung around in consternation I recognised a familiar accent and rolled back on the ground, shaking with honest laughter.

"Schalk, you scoundrel!" I managed to say. "I was beginning to wonder where you were. Now – on condition you've had a bath since I last saw you – you can come and say hello to our new colleague."

---

34 Hannay performs this improbable feat in *The Thirty-nine Steps* (ch. 4).

Chapter Six

SCHALK MINNAAR HAD RESUMED the appearance of a white man, and also the white man's kit, which was just a little less tattered than his kaffir rig. He squatted at the fire, relaxed as though he had not a care in the world, his body as trim and taut as an athlete's, his face as gentle as a child's. He had requested two bottles of beer, which I was to learn was a habit of his, one to quench a thirst, the second because he always said you could never be sure when you would next have a drink. Douglas had fallen silent, his expression that of a man trying to remember whether and when he had met this newcomer. Schalk looked across at him and recognised the condition: he smiled mischievously. "You will be thinking, Mr Green, that someone salted your Manica concession back in '99 . . . It was not me, I promise you, and one day I will tell you the *skelm*'s name."[35]

Douglas nodded slowly, as though an old and nagging problem had been resolved. He grinned, leaned over and extended his hand. "I seem to have been recruited to your team, Mr Minnaar. I hope you have some idea of where we go from here because

35 To "salt" a mine prospect you introduce to the site minerals or stones which do not belong to it in order to exaggerate its value. Many of the references in these pages to Schalk Minnaar are echoed in Buchan's later descriptions of "Peter Pienaar", particularly in *Greenmantle*. See also (of Peter Pienaar): "Then he took to working off bogus gold propositions on Kimberley and Johannesburg magnates, and what he didn't know about salting a mine wasn't knowledge . . ." *Greenmantle*, ch. 3.

the *baas* – we call him Mr Goldstein, by the way – is not too keen on paying a second call on your friend Chief M'Chudi."

Schalk said, suddenly as serious as a *dominee*, "Believe me, we must go back to that *kraal*. That is where the secrets come together. It took hard labour to find M'Chudi."

He responded only slowly and hesitantly to my questions as we sat before the flames and waited for our supper to cook. There had been a delay in leaving Johannesburg, he admitted, because he was making enquiries of an IDB[36] merchant in Troy Street when the Constabulary had interrupted their conversation. He had diverted himself to Pretoria to take coffee and rusks with the grandson of his old *Tante*, a sickly lad who, he remembered, used to work as a clerk in the *Staatsbank*, but that had taken time, too, because Schalk wasn't popular in Pretoria and also the young man had shown an unfamilial reluctance to remember the old days when the gold reserves had left town. At Belfast Schalk had been fortunate to run into an Indian trader who owed him a favour, which was repaid with a briefing on the true situation in the East. In Lydenburg he tracked down an old Shangaan servant who had told him alarming tales of Major S.

"I prefer not to meet this Major," murmured Schalk. "If you don't mind, *basie*. He and I once had a disagreement in Swakopmund and I think he still carries the scar . . . To make things worse, I bumped into him after the battle at Modder River in December '99 and he remembered me."

I said, "I thought you were in East Africa throughout the war."

"Who told you that?"

"Our master."

36 Illicit Diamond Buying, the combating of which was then, and still is, an obvious preoccupation of the South African police.

Schalk said, "He must have forgotten the detail. I shipped out in July, I had no choice." Strange, I thought, Lord Milner was usually very strong on detail.

To resume Schalk's tale, he had visited Pilgrims Rest, discreetly, where he had resumed acquaintance with old pals from the pre-war days of the transport-riders. He said, "The trails are still there, all the way from Delagoa Bay. But the railway has killed the business and now my comrades sit in the sun drinking brandy and telling tall stories." These stories had somehow taken Schalk back on to the Berg with a line on a particular Chief, and so into a change of garments. Then I had turned up in all innocence, the perfect instrument to unnerve M'Chudi.

Unamused, I said, "You might have warned me. That girl was almost the death of me."

"Yes, the girl knows something. She is M'Chudi's junior wife and she is very frightened of what the Chief might discover. Your arrival was very good, it startled the herd."

I interrupted. "When you dressed up as a stinking old kaffir and dragged me into that *kraal* you nearly settled my account, as well you know. The girl produced that blanket – which everyone recognised, I imagine, because it used to belong to the wretched chap who fell foul of the Major. But why didn't she show them the beads?"

Schalk looked baffled, as well he might, so I had to explain.

"The Major gave me a piece of bead-cloth which came from the fellow he interrogated. I was carrying it on my saddle. I never saw the blanket that the girl produced in the *kraal*."

"I managed to find your horse that evening," said Schalk. He spat into the fire in the local way that betrays deep concentration, "There was no sign of any beads. And no one had touched your kit – not even your gun."

80

"So the girl must have rescued the beads, but first dreamed up the blanket."

"The blanket was intended by her to link you with the death of the man in Pilgrims Rest. The bead-cloth on your saddle also connected you with that death – but the little *meisie* particularly did not want the rest of the *kraal* to know about the beads."

"You mean, her husband in particular."

"So she produced an old blanket and hid the piece of cloth."

"And very nearly succeeded in disposing of me. So why?"

"Because the beads are a clue . . ."

"A clue to what?"

Schalk said, "Let us guess, to the gold –"

"But how?"

We had lapsed into a baffled silence, tranquil enough in the cosy warmth of the fire, when Douglas interrupted for the first time. He had been puffing on his pipe and frequently recharging his glass. "I've got it! These beads were something personal between the girl and the man. The beads were private between them, don't you see? The blanket didn't matter because everyone in the *kraal* knew it used to belong to *him*. Then you arrived, obviously the big white man, with the bead-cloth flapping on your saddle for anyone to see, and the girl took fright. So she decides she has to have the beads, and grabs them and hides them. I've no idea why – but it certainly signifies something." Douglas was looking rather pleased with himself.

"Surely!" I exclaimed, with a sudden inspiration, "There's a message in them."

My head was full of the words of the Boer farmer's wife those few days ago on the meadow above Pilgrims Rest, and I began to explain what she had told me, but I saw that Schalk was shaking his head.

"You English!" he said. "You don't know this country from Ancient Egypt and you'll believe any old wife's tale. You like to believe these pretty stories – that a few beads can be sewn together and tell a story. Don't you?"

I nodded and nobly refrained from pointing out that the story had come from the faithful wife of a good Boer whose family had probably arrived with Van Riebeeck.

Schalk kept on shaking his head. "I am sorry to have to say this but the beads do not tell stories. They cannot. They can only make very vague, imprecise, statements. They can say 'I love you.' At the very most they can say –" he rolled his eyes and attempted a falsetto – " 'Please pay ten cows *lobola* – bride price – for me' or 'I want a big house like this picture.' That's fine. But they cannot communicate things like 'The treasure is hidden in a hut in the *kraal* five miles to the north' . . . So I am afraid the beads are not going to help us so much, my friends."

It was Douglas who exploded in his honest way. "*But it doesn't matter*, Schalk. It doesn't matter what the beads did or did not say. The girl had to hide them because they were a message *from* her *to* him. They must have meant *something*, however vague, because the Major said the kaffir boy was so upset about them. And she is frightened that someone else should know that."

I said, "Douglas may be right. She is probably terrified lest M'Chudi discover she sent her bead message to the boy."

Schalk was thinking it through carefully, with much assistance from his black, wide-bowled pipe.[37] We had the wisdom to leave him in silence. Then he nodded, as though that much was

37 It is explained in *The Island of Sheep* (ch. 4) that Pienaar had a pipe matching this description which had been carved for him by a certain cousin who had been imprisoned in Ceylon. In *Mr Standfast* (ch. 15) he has a pipe which has been made for him by Jannie Grobelaar in St Helena (another p.o.w. base). Perhaps he had two.

accepted. "As I told you," he allowed himself to say in concession, "the girl is at the heart of this."

"So?"

"We need to talk to the *meisie*. She may have been a naughty girl. If we are not to tell her husband, as a good Christian surely should do, she will have to tell us more about her deceased friend."

The word "deceased" somehow sounds more sinister in a Boer accent.

I confess that I was dreading the return to M'Chudi's *kraal*, the very thought gave me the shakes. Douglas read me a lesson about being a white man and so on, and, more helpfully, pointed out that the three of us would be armed; I was to be allowed to carry a Lee Enfield as well as a pistol secreted on my person. My disguise, they both told me, was masterly. As I knew, Schalk turned out to be a fellow-believer with Douglas in the importance of thinking yourself "into" a role. They insisted on discussing with me such matters as the recent rise in share prices on the Johannesburg stock exchange in the conviction that this would improve my cover, until I told them in no uncertain terms to stow it.

Sabie sits tight under Mount Anderson and the Berg wall. We decided not to waste time attempting to find if Wheatcroft had arrived at the cantonment. Our party made an early start and was clattering through the town – more a village – before seven, and attacking the Long Tom Pass, only recently dubbed so after the dramas of the war. The route started with a long haul westwards, then we pulled higher, struggling to keep our pace, up the so-called Staircase and the Devil's Knuckles – the old names speak their own story – and onto the Old Harbour Road and its wagon-width of rough stones. In late afternoon we broke out onto the plateau, at what must have been at least 7000 feet. The air was fresh and clean and it was glorious to be out in the open again after the steaming discomforts of the Lowveld. A breeze sprang up to buffet us and we stretched our muscles and breathed deep of those great windy spaces. We scarcely bothered to look back into the mists of the tropics far below. After the tangle of bush and *kopje* we relished the empty hillsides, the grass springing, tufted, yellow not green, the spare granite of the boulders, the rare midsummer flowers; there were no bushes, and no trees except the indigenous timber clinging to the narrow gorges that plunged down into the plains. It was, offered Douglas, a somewhat Scottish scene – a reflection which seemed to startle Schalk.

We were approaching M'Chudi from a very different angle from my last arrival and departure. "On with your topcoat, Mr Goldstein," said Douglas, and took the lead. Schalk, we knew, was unrecognisable to anyone in the *kraal*. I had my fears for myself but suppressed them by dint of keeping a tight grip on the pistol in my pocket.

"I remember," said Schalk, who had his people's fondness for an anecdote but may have been trying to divert me, "I was once in a scrap with your *Engelsman* friend Cecil John.[38] It was in '96 when you had that trouble with the Matabele up north, and then the Mashona joined in, which none of us had expected, the Shona being a sentimental and spiritual tribe, or so we thought. I was riding with Rhodes in his personal bodyguard as a scout. He needed us, I promise you, because he refused to carry a weapon, only his riding crop, and used to put himself into all manner of danger, if you think how important he was. I always said he

38 Cecil John Rhodes, the greatest of the South African mining "Randlords", creator of Rhodesia, Prime Minister of the Cape. He had died, aged only 48, in March 1902.

had a knowledge that the good Lord was not going to call him right then. It could wait – and we all know what happened. We went into a *kraal* – like this one – where we half-expected a stiff welcome. It was in the heart of the troubles that year and a missionary and his wife had been butchered the week before. So what happens? The old chief comes out to meet us, takes one look at Rhodes, and hugs his feet. 'I was your cookboy, *baas*, in Umtali when you arrived from Beira five years ago.[39] Do you remember me?' And Rhodes raised him up and shook his hand very warmly, in front of all of us, and said, 'The best breakfast scones I've ever had . . .' Afterwards he told me he didn't remember the kaffir from Adam. So, Douglas, try to remember if M'Chudi was ever your cookboy and we'll be home and dry."

"Are you trying to encourage me?" I asked.

So different were the circumstances that I would scarcely have recognised M'Chudi's *kraal*. It had become a huddle of mean huts. The children who ran to greet us were pot-bellied and fly-encrusted, the women no more than whining beggars. The young men – the warriors who had pursued me with their spears to my death – seemed to have turned into cowed and listless boys who surrounded us pathetically, querulous, in the hope that Douglas might offer them hire. M'Chudi, too, had lost much of his authority. Douglas, as had been planned, took him off to his hut to discuss some fiction of a project, and Schalk and I lounged, he to the manner born, I still uneasy, though it had been immediately evident that no one associated this urban swell with the dusty traveller they had chased over the cliff.

39 Rhodes visited his personal colony in the summer of 1891–92, trekking, with considerable difficulty, from Beira.

But the girl spotted me. I was playing with some piccaninns while Schalk practised the Native lingo with their giggling mothers when I looked up and saw her gazing at me. She was unmistakable, as I must have been to her. She was, I remembered, beautiful in her fashion and she was younger than I had thought, almost a child. I tried to evade her stare, but could not help myself looking up again and there she was, transfixed, her mouth agape, her complexion – I have to say it – grey with what could only be mortal terror. She must have thought me dead; she could hardly doubt that my resurrection might seal her own fate. I was all too conscious that she would again sound the alarm, yet I sensed a different concern in her and, almost instinctively, I caught her eyes and laid my finger, very fleetingly, on the temporary moustache on my lip. I was offering her discretion, though I did not know whether this simple maiden would understand her need of it. Her deep, dark eyes fluttered once and, when I next looked up from the children's entreaties, she had vanished.

Schalk, I saw, had followed the exchange. "I think now we can go and make camp, and Douglas will follow. Do you see that cliff?"

He pointed to a ledge of clear turf a mile or so to the south at about our altitude. "We can make our *laager* there," said the Boer, "and keep an eye on our friends."

And they on us, I thought, but I had lost my fear of them.

The girl came to us that evening, as Schalk poured the first sundowner in our new camp. There was a yelp from the ridgeback and Douglas emerged into the firelight pushing a terrified child before him, her arm doubled back. I shouted at him and she was flung on the turf at our feet. Schalk broke into a flurry of whatever Native tongue; he talked gently to her, not seeming to look at her directly, and as she began to follow his meaning – once, when he was searching for a phrase, they both giggled at his problem – she may have begun to overcome her terrors.

There is a grace and an enchantment in these Native women while they are still slender and childlike; all too soon they get with child and broaden in the hip and their youth is prematurely ended. This lass was sweet and fearful and clearly had much to hide. She would not have understood that we had guessed at most of her secrets. Schalk was soothing her, chattering away in a lingo incomprehensible to Douglas and to me mere gibberish, but she seemed to relax. Her eyes lost their panic fire. I saw Schalk make a joke about my revised appearance and she glanced at me out of the corner of her eye and giggled again. This, I remembered, was the virago who had driven me over the cliff. She would be nursing memories of her lover, I thought, and I felt compassion for the child; how young she was to suffer this bereavement, her heart must have been broken. And then into my Calvinist soul drifted the Biblical text: ". . . for where your *treasure* is, there will your *heart* be also." There was treasure in this tale, that was for sure. How did the text begin? In matters such as these my childhood memories never played me false: "Lay not up for yourselves treasures upon earth, where moth and rust doth corrupt." And where your heart still is – I played with words – there will your *treasure* . . . ? The girl was still chatting with the Boer in an incomprehensible dialect and I had an instinct to cut it short.

"Ask her, Schalk," I interrupted, as though I was suddenly impatient of this flirtation. "Ask her straight out: 'Where is the Waterfall?'"

The Boer paused and looked as if to question me, but I sensed we must seize this moment of her first relaxation from terror. "At once, Schalk! No more chit-chat. Challenge her on the waterfall – this is our chance. Tell her she is safe, promise her we won't say anything to her husband about her friend, but she must tell us about the waterfall."

He nodded. The sky was a mulberry gloaming behind his head and I could hear the meat sizzling on our fire. The girl's great eyes were staring at me; she might so easily panic again.

Schalk had resumed a long gabble of dialect, punctuated with clicks and hesitations. He seemed to struggle more than before to express himself; it was evident that she had to make an effort to understand him and in doing so perhaps lost her fear; he was palpably no threat to her, and I dare say she knew that he would protect her against the rest of us. So she would tell him the truth.

She queried something and he replied very firmly in what must be an affirmative, then smiled his sweetest smile at her. I took it that he had assured her of safety. He resumed his obscure inquisition and still she seemed to hesitate. I heard him repeat the same question, insistent. Abruptly she nodded and spat out her answer.

Schalk turned to us and said, very quiet, "Listen, you two. She says yes, she'll take us to the waterfall. At first light, in the morning."

Which waterfall would that be, I wondered, but I kept my doubts to myself.

She was true to her word. Dawn had just arrived, in a rush of gold and crimson, when she was waiting, shrouded in a blanket, beyond the *skerm* of thorns towards the slope where wraiths of mountain mist played tricks with our view. Schalk had been smoking his first pipe of the day. "We'll need rifles," he announced. "I don't trust M'Chudi."

But when we saw her, shaking with fear rather than the chill mountain air, we changed our mind. We could not believe that she was leading us into an ambush: we had required her to furnish what she thought of as "the" waterfall, and that she would do in order to protect her innocence in the eyes of her husband, the Chief. We all now assumed, without need for discussion, that the Major's victim had been her lover: he was also our only lead to Kruger's Gold.

There had been a healthy and invigorating breeze blowing across our belvedere, but we lost it as soon as she led us down into the gorge to the immediate south. We lost, too, the simplicity of meadowland. Suddenly we were plunged into thick bush, and there was scarce sign of a track. Schalk was audibly cursing the need for a panga until she looked back and reproached him with a phrase which we interpreted as requiring silence. It is true that there was a path but it was vertiginous. Soon we encountered a stream, flowing steep and vigorously, and she turned upwards, towards the mountain and the water's source. There began thirty minutes of suffering. We crossed that stream a dozen times, always struggling uphill, into the gorge. We fought our way past every variety of vegetation, including trees and shrubs of a beauty that would be exalted in the botanical societies of Cape Town, not to speak of London's Kew – assegai, yellow-wood, wild pear, and each of them tore at my clothing more savagely than the last. I am lean in build and not disposed to sweat, and thank heaven it was the coolest time of day, but I confess that my shirt was wringing wet (and Douglas was in similar condition) when we abruptly gained our delivery.

We found ourselves standing on a green lawn, trim as the front garden of an Edinburgh villa. Before us was a shingle beach and a slate-green pool of water. Above us was a torrent, a cataract, plunging a hundred feet to splash and tinkle at our feet. The spray gusted over us, a gossamer shower from a breeze that sprang up from nowhere. It was the ultimate secret place. We had entered a bosky retiring room – or do I mean a bedroom? – shielded on all sides and from all intrusion by dense forest screens, a precious and innocent sanctuary.

Douglas lay prostrate on the turf, his eyes closed, his breathing soothed. I wondered if he had fallen into a swift sleep but no, he was gazing up at me: "There's your waterfall!" he murmured, and we shared for that moment the *temenos* of the place.

The girl and Minnaar were not so content, they were disputing about something. I guessed she was saying that she had completed her contract, while he seemed to be asking for more. I said, "We'd better search the area," but I guessed that my words were empty. We poked around in the surrounding trees for half an hour, but there was nothing in this place beyond a trysting spot, a private greensward bed for secret lovers. Was this what the young Native had meant? In his agony had he been driven back by the Major to the site of his heart's ecstasies in this perfect place?

I said, "Schalk, ask her again, why here?" and Schalk replied indignantly, protectively, "She doesn't know anything. This is her waterfall. This is where he used to bring her. This is what M'Chudi must not know."

The girl heard the name of her husband and cast us a terrified glance. Douglas spotted it and made conciliatory, flapping gestures at her; he actually sat up and tried a few words of kitchen kaffir[40] on her.

"Be off with you, my dear," said Schalk, waving a hand to demonstrate that she was dismissed, and she was off in a flash,

40 A very primitive form of the local Native languages used by Europeans to address their servants.

darting back like a Nereid along the way we had come. At the edge of the clearing she paused, looked back at us just once for a brief second, uncomprehending, then vanished.

We searched again. I said, "That brute in Pilgrims Rest definitely said 'after' the waterfall. Perhaps the trail goes on."

Douglas said, "It doesn't go on. It's a dead end. This leads nowhere."

Chapter Seven

W<small>E GOT BACK TO CAMP</small> feeling pretty rotten. Not even a mighty breakfast of porridge and curried eggs could repair the damage. Douglas thereupon went off to shoot for the pot, as he put it; maybe he wanted to make himself scarce so that Schalk and I could talk affairs of state, but neither of us was in a mood for strategy. Shortly afterwards Schalk took himself off as well to see if he could pick up a spoor – I did not believe it in this landscape and guessed he might be trying M'Chudi's *kraal* again – and I sat there feeling sorry for myself, looking out on the finest panorama in Africa and finding no pleasure in it. After an hour of this *accidie*, I got out the maps to search for waterfalls. They were ten a penny in this stretch of the Berg and there would be hundreds more which our mapmakers had missed or not bothered to record. It was like looking for a particular pebble on a beach and when I thought again of trudging back to Sunnyside to confess failure I fell into a serious melancholy.

I was shaken out of it by the sound of a flurry of hooves. When I looked up I saw a rider galloping, graceful but foolhardy, across the rough sward that connected our promontory to the main rampart of the Berg. The newcomer reined to a halt in front of my tent, dropped lightly from the saddle, whipped off a hat and – my face must have betrayed me – revealed herself to be Helga Ingeburg, whom I had been assured was hunting in the Lowveld.

She wore some sort of baggy breeches above a nonsense of puttees and boots. She greeted me as if we were the oldest of friends, but then paused and said, "You look different . . ."

I had of course given up the kohl and, I now realised, I had forgotten my moustache. The charade was no longer needed, I reckoned. "I owe you an apology," I said. "We were playing a silly game. At least Douglas told you I wasn't called Ari Goldstein."

I saw she was laughing at me. "I am not Goldstein," I repeated. "I think you may know who I am."

"Then you must come to luncheon," she declared. "Now that I know you are entirely respectable, I can introduce you to my uncle. His house is only a few miles from here – just beyond M'Chudi's *kraal*. Do you know it?"

Imagine a wooded glen poised miles above the sunlit plains that lead to the Portuguese border. You enter that glen by a track that leads through a strip of evergreen forest matted with monkey creeper, huge ferns and the thickest undergrowth entwined around sneezewood and stinkwood, and then you emerge into paradise. We bridged a Highland stream, skirted a deep, dark pool, and came on to an expanse of parkland of a beauty that would put England to shame. It was a slim tongue of land, a true belvedere pushed out from the Berg and poised high above the valleys, hemmed and protected on either side by deep gorges, on the east by a sheer cliff. I had taken note of our route. We had circled round, a safe distance above and behind M'Chudi's place, and had resumed a position on the northern face of the Berg: M'Chudi therefore stood between our camp and the German lodge.

The house had the simplicity of true elegance: walls of whitewashed stone, a thatched roof, green shutters. Inside, the floors were stone and the fireplace wide – for the site was on top of the world and the evenings would be cold – and the walls were unplastered, covered with skins and horns, books and prints and pictures, but always of a luxurious simplicity. There was very little furniture, I noticed, by the European standards of our time – a few low chairs and tables, some Lamu chests, a cabinet of Native craft, a Cape Dutch desk, very fine, a stinkwood refectory table, and on the main wall a long sequence of Harris hunting scenes.[41]

There was also Douglas Green, nursing a glass on the *stoep* and looking rather shamefaced. The state of his wardrobe proved that he had had a strenuous morning.

"I found him slaughtering guinea fowl on the hill," declared Miss Ingeburg in a distinctly proprietorial manner. "So I sent him back here and rode over to ask you to make up the party."

"And our host?"

He entered on cue.

He was an old man, but his face was not an old face. It was clean-shaven and benevolent, fleshy but healthy, the cheeks rosy; it might have been the face of a wise and plump schoolboy had it not been for the skull, which was as bare as a glass bottle. His figure was full, almost portly, his gait was brisk and surprisingly lively, but it was the eyes that caught my attention, they were clear

41 For years JB seems to have been caught up in a fantasy of building a "Lodge in the Wilderness" (the title of a now near-forgotten early book of his); it was an image he derived from his experiences in South Africa. This is not the place to discuss the significance of this concept in his life and work, but it should be noted that here in this manuscript we have one of the earliest models for such a house, elements of which are found in *The African Colony* (1903) (ch. 8) ("Hereabouts, when my ship comes home, I shall have my country house . . ."), *The Lodge in the Wilderness* (1906) (passim), *The Grove of Ashtaroth* (*Blackwoods*, 1910 and *The Moon Endureth*, 1912), *The Green Wildebeest* (in *The Runagates Club*, 1928) and *Memory Hold-The-Door* (1940) (ch. 5/V)

and candid and horribly intelligent.[42] I found that I was instantly ill at ease with him. He was dressed in flannels and carried a leather-bound volume which he discarded as he crossed the wide room to greet me – Douglas he had acknowledged with a cool, almost dismissive wave of the hand.

It was not possible to attempt a pretence in this civilised household. I shook his hand and introduced myself by my own name and he welcomed me enthusiastically to what he called his "cottage". His accent was strong, but his command of English flawless.

"I have been working it out," said Miss Helga. "This gentleman must be one of the *kinder* in His Excellency's *garten*,"[43] and she laughed charmingly. I was discomfited and my host intervened swiftly. "I am honoured to have you as my guest. Would you be travelling on business?"

"I'm sure you should not ask, Uncle," said Helga, whose mood today seemed playful.

He reprimanded her for her levity and I hastened to set the record straight. I explained that my particular responsibilities had originally been for the reform of the so-called "concentration camps" in which the Boer families had been protected from the consequences of their leaders' folly, but I now specialised in implementing our land settlement policy. I had a trick of becoming very boring about land settlement and my host and his niece, I noticed with relief, were soon happy to change the subject.

---

42 cf. the old man in *The Thirty-nine Steps*, ch. 6.

43 Lord Milner's "Kindergarten", as has already been noted, was the name given to the team of bright young men who worked with him on the Reconstruction. The term was originally invented by the Cape politician J.X. Merriman to make fun of Lord Milner's Germanic earnestness (Milner's family background was German). JB would later say, modestly, that he was very junior, more a member of the "Creche".

We were by this time sitting on a terrace overlooking the Garden of Eden and contemplating a grilled trout and a hock the like of which I had not tasted since I last dined on High Table in my distant Oxford days. The Old Man, as I thought of him, assured me that he was a scholar, or rather, he corrected himself, a fortunate dilettante whose present interest lay in the study of the Great Zimbabwe culture of Monomotapa and its influence southwards into these present territories.

"Would you gentlemen be familiar with those ruins north of the Limpopo?" he asked, the very model of a scholar-innocent. Douglas hastened to assure him that he knew them well. "Then I have a heretical theory for you, Mr Green," said the Old Man, and cast his cold eye over my friend. "I shall wish to argue that those extraordinary edifices were created not by the Phoenicians, nor by the Greeks, nor even by the Portuguese – but by the kaffirs!"

Douglas was properly astonished, as I imagine he was intended to be, and offered a case for the defence.[44] They argued earnestly while I discovered that the lady insisted on knowing more of my simple life, and professed to be fascinated by the scraps of information I felt obliged to offer her. I now imagine that if I had been more of a connoisseur of these things I would have relished her company and her badinage. The fact is that she unnerved me. I stumbled and stuttered and knew myself for a thorough fool, it ruined the meal for me and sometimes I forgot to wonder why she persisted in flattering me so. I also forgot to ask why they had returned so rapidly and prematurely from their hunting. But I did not forget that our meal was supervised by a butler who served us with impeccable discretion and who also (it took me a while

44 Scholars would today agree that the Old Man was right. The Zimbabwe Ruins are in southern Zimbabwe near Fort Victoria, near a town now called Masvingo.

to pin down his swarthy features) bore a remarkable resemblance to the character who had been ensconced with the Major when I first called on police headquarters in Pilgrims Rest.

We seemed to have agreed to meet again very soon and there was much jollity and, it might have appeared, new-found friendship as we made our farewells. Douglas explained his good humour at once. "Thank God! I think the woman has transferred her affections to you, old chap. I really must congratulate you."

I did not tell Green that, as we had been waiting for him to collect his basket of fowl, I had seen the Old Man covertly place his hand upon her in a caress which, from an uncle to a niece, would be unspeakable. Yet she had not rebuffed him.

Schalk was waiting at the camp and showed no great interest in our news of our luncheon; these European delights, we gathered, were not for him. It emerged that he had spent the afternoon in M'Chudi's *kraal* where his latest role was to play a dissolute and often drunken transport-rider, nostalgic for the old times when the wagon route through the Bushveld was the lifeline of the entire region and the men who kept it open were the local heroes of white and black alike. He had taken care not to seek out the young wife – her role in this drama, he said, was ended – but he continued to wonder about M'Chudi's own involvement in our story. The man was a cut above his fellows. He was intelligent and confident, he was bold enough to argue with the Boer, and he had his mission school convictions concerning the future development of this country, convictions which Schalk characterised in several unrepeatable phrases. Above all, Schalk's hunter's instinct told him that the chief's spoor would lead to – what?

"Can we arrest him?" asked Douglas.

"And hand him over to the Prussian?" Schalk added a few more oaths for good measure.

"Then can you do a deal with him?"

"You can't make deals with these Natives."

Douglas said, in a tone of innocence which I thought might conceal irony, "The kaffirs may be *slim*, Schalk, but I'm sure you Boers are slimmer . . ."[45]

"For that matter, how *slim* are your German friends?" I put in. "They keep a civilised table, but I don't like the look of their butler." I explained where I had first seen him, though Lord knows, I added, it was no offense to call on the local constabulary.

"I know the man," nodded Douglas. "His name is Dorando, or something of the sort. He's a typical Portugoose from Beira way."

"Then he's a double-dyed traitor to his race, like all of them,"[46] avowed Schalk, and spat. Like many of the *Volk*, my colleague was not an admirer of the neighbours who had for centuries made a curious job of their responsibilities on the far side of the eastern horizon.

"Then why on earth does the respectable Miss Helga put up with the likes of Dorando?"

Schalk shook his head sadly. "Women are queer cattle,"[47] he offered, and spat again. Douglas snorted angrily. I didn't understand why he and Schalk were sniping at each other.

"So what do we conclude?" I asked, anxious to change the mood, in my formal voice rather as Lord Milner used to check his young men in Sunnyside.

45 *Slim* is Dutch (Afrikaans) for "clever" in the sense of "smart" or "sharp", even "sly". See the storekeeper Japp in *Prester John*, ch. 3 – "The Dutch about here are a slim lot and the kaffirs are slimmer . . ."
46 cf. "my fingers itched to get at the Portugoose – that double-dyed traitor to his race . . ." (*Prester John*, ch. 9).
47 cf. *Mr Standfast*, ch. 15.

98

No one answered. We were trapped, as the three of us would have hated to admit. "We'll make a plan," Schalk had said once, but I was miserably conscious that we had no plan. That evening, while we sat before the fire and drank our brandy as the African moon toppled gently over this frail encampment above a great precipice, our vulnerability frightened me. I began to wonder whether we were safe from M'Chudi's warriors. I spun fantasies involving a Portuguese manservant and a Hunnish lady. Douglas may have been in a similar state of mind.

"There's something I've been wondering about . . ." he began.

It had happened that morning, before I arrived at the lodge – indeed, before Helga had despatched herself to collect me. "I had gone to check that my pony would be properly watered. I came back to the house from the stables and the old boy and Helga were talking on the *stoep*. I wasn't eavesdropping, you see, but they didn't realise I was there, and anyway they must have been arguing. They were talking in German, which may have made them careless because they don't realise that I picked up that lingo when I was in South-West."[48]

The fellow seemed embarrassed lest he had broken the niceties of social etiquette. "Out with it!" said Schalk, who would not have worried about such things.

Douglas took another hefty swallow from his tumbler. "I distinctly heard her say to him, 'Leave the young one to me. He will find the waterfall for us.' Then they heard me coming."

"That's a peculiar remark coming from the niece of a scholar of archæology," said I, not too amused to be described in such dismissive terms.

---

48 Hannay in his youth did three years prospecting for copper in German Damaraland (in South-West Africa); his father had German partners, which helps explain why he spoke German. (*The Thirty-nine Steps*, ch. 2).

"Not to speak of a hunting party who are supposed to be on the flats," added Schalk.

I said, "Who told them about the waterfall?"

"Presumably the same person who told you," answered Schalk. "Another German . . ."

For the second time in this saga I resolved that I would see Major S. cashiered if it was the last thing I achieved in this country.

One last exchange remained, much later, before we drew the curtain on a miserable day. Schalk had retreated to his bivouac over at the foot of the *kopje* where, he said, the local lion wouldn't find him; it was, we thought and hoped, a jest. Douglas was knocking out his pipe, treading carefully on the ashes. A mist was coming down on us, drowning the moon which had swung in the direction of M'Chudi and his people. There are moments when the African night becomes sinister. A hyena barked, not so far away, and I would have welcomed my boisterous lodgings in Sunnyside. Douglas cleared his throat nervously and said, "While we're casting around like this, without a proper spoor, there's another thing that occurred to me . . ."

I must have encouraged him with a word or a gesture.

"You remember that story Schalk told the other night – the one about Rhodes and the cookboy . . ."

"Yes."

"He got it wrong. Not that it matters, of course . . . But I was there myself. It's years ago and it was a sad business. I often think we Rhodesians were lucky to survive. I was just a boy but I was in the thick of it. Actually, I was riding with Rhodes at the time Schalk mentioned."

"So you might have met him?"

"No! He wasn't there. I would have remembered him for sure. There were only a few of us. I can't see why he told it that way. Not that it matters, of course . . ."

"He was spinning a yarn," I said. "Schalk can't resist a yarn. Forget it. Go to sleep."

Douglas said, "Sorry. My memory must be playing odd games."

I came out of sleep reluctantly.

The moon had gone down and there was a bitter chill in the air. It was the hour before dawn when every sound of the bush is hushed; it is the hour, they tell me, when most of us can expect our death. I stumbled up from the camp bed to check that I had not been disturbed by intruders, but no, it was the cold that had awoken me, our fire had died down to glowing embers. A bank of cloud had come down in the night and the blaze of the stars had been snuffed out. My brain was suddenly in a fury. I anticipated my despatch to Lord Milner – to be copied, no doubt, for forwarding to Chamberlain himself: "I regret to report my inability to ascertain the location of the hiding place . . . difficulties of the terrain . . . hostility of the local tribes . . ." And so on and so forth. I shivered in the mountain chill and pulled the blanket tighter.

No, I must go back and take my medicine like a man. *Sunt lacrimæ rerum.*[49] I had been given the great opportunity of my career and I had ploughed it. At least I would bring down the Major with me. Douglas could return to his tobacco, Schalk would slip off on his dubious affairs in the bush, and I would ride across to the railway at Waterval-Boven. Or did I mean Waterval-Onder? My mind was confused after the dramas and

49 Virgil (literally, "these are the tears of things"). Buchan in his novels had a predilection for Latin tags, usually the more clichéd ones.

the journeying of this past week and it seemed a century since I had arrived on the train from Johannesburg. Which was it? Still fuddled with sleep, I forced myself to work out these confusing Dutch prepositions. *Boven, onder, agter* - above, under, behind. I must stay awake long enough to work it out, but my brain was skidding, my dreams kept intervening. Was there a railway station at Waterval-Agter? Below the point where the Elands River plunges - yes, like a waterfall? It sounded familiar. What had the Major said to me in his hideous accent, so long ago in Pilgrims Rest? Waterval-Agter? No, he had said "After the waterfall". He was a German, translating from Dutch into English. It sounded the same.

But it wasn't the same at all and I broke surface out of the ocean of sleep with a shock of understanding and forced myself to sit up vertically to absorb the point. "*Agter*" was the Dutch for "behind". So - I took it very slowly and deliberately, like a drunken Cape Coloured aiming for his shanty - there was a simple difference between "After the waterfall" and "Behind the waterfall". It was, I was thinking, a very big difference indeed, as one dead young Native would have agreed.

I was cold no longer, nor was I at all sleepy. I felt a little wind come up and knew that it would be the precursor of the dawn.[50] Looking out over the plains below, I saw the first pale glow stealing upwards, then the first tremors of light. Around me the detail of our camp began to emerge from the black shawl of the night ; above my head the jagged edge of the Berg took back its shape. I pulled on my *velskoen*, calculating that I was likely to take a tumble but that I must put my revelation to the test. First I must steal away from the camp without arousing the others –

50 Buchan was to use this bush knowledge in *Prester John* (ch. 14).

But no, I blundered straightway into a familiar figure. He stood erect, facing the east where the horizon was now flooded with bright streams of light. His head was bowed, I saw with sudden embarrassment, and his hands were folded together. Schalk Minnaar was addressing his Creator.

He had heard me and turned with the same sweet smile.

"You are up before the cockerel, my friend."

"Schalk!" I said. "It must be *agter* the waterfall – *behind* the waterfall . . ."

He gazed at me, very solemn, and I could see how, slowly, he understood me.

"*Kom!*" I said to him, and heard him chuckle as he replied, "*Ja, baas!*"

The sun was still below the horizon as as we thrashed our way through the age-old vegetation to the waterfall. Down in the gorge it was semi-night, unreal. We stumbled and cursed through a world that still belonged to our sleep and our dreams. We smote furiously at the thorn and the creeper that encumbered our path and we scarcely believed the evidence of blood and wounds on our limbs. The torrent was ice-black, turgid. We struggled across it again and again, skating on slippery granite, and both of us kept glancing up at the sky, impatient for the day.

The sun came up at the very moment we broke through to the green lawn before the pool and, by a chance of nature – by the dispensation of the surrounding yellow-wood trees – it burst through upon us, dazzling, as we flung ourselves, panting, on the turf. Here, suddenly was a scene out of Eden, primæval, enhancing. The space was not large – perhaps the proportions of a baronial hall – and the privacy, the secrecy of it, was overwhelming. It was hard to believe that we were not the first men to penetrate this corner of paradise.

Schalk muttered, his voice hushed as though awed by the sanctity of the place, "*Agter*, you tell me? Then let's try it like this . . ."

And the two of us scanned the cliff face down which the cascade plunged, shading our eyes against the glare of light. I said, "It's no good . . .", and stripped off my shirt and breeches to wade into the icy pool. Schalk said, "*Ach*, hell, man . . ." but with a Boer modesty waded after me in his bush kit.

Then there was a struggle, a freezing of the flesh, a long holding of breath as the spray thundered down upon us as though nature were still determined to force us back – and, abruptly, a sanctuary.

We were standing on a sandy shore, behind the waterfall, *inside* the waterfall, which now fell like nothing so much as a mighty crystal curtain, behind our backs. But here there was a blessed tranquillity, a peace beyond understanding as the Book puts it. We struggled to catch our breath and shake off the spray. The low rays of the sun could not reach us now, but a pure white light was refracted through the endless deluge of water and we looked around us at a cavern which was more secure than any bank vault in this world. There, in front of us, on a narrow beach of shingle, patiently stacked in neat piles, were scores of crates made of rough slats of unfinished timber. I knew before I saw it that one of them would be gaping open, and so it was, the one nearest to us; inside there was a glimpse of canvas and crumpled newspapers. Solemnly, and very wet, Schalk and I shook hands in an Anglo-Boer understanding.

"Now we can make a plan," said I, noting that I was rapidly drifting into the local dialect.

The British are famed for their stiff upper lip and I suppose that was what Schalk and I were pretending in that early-morning moment of high triumph. After we had re-emerged from the heavy wall of water and regained the lawn, we changed our minds and embraced, slapped each other on the back, protested lifelong affection. We did all this in front of the curtain of eternal water which fell, oblivious of our presence, as it had fallen, unrecorded and unobserved, since the beginning of time.

I would be off to Wheatcroft in White River, I was thinking. "We'll send a telegram to Sunnyside and get porters and wagons up here . . . First of all we'll need a platoon to establish security . . ." I was also conscious of a great and mighty hunger, and Schalk and I might shortly thereafter have been seen lurching back to our belvedere through the evergreen forest, arm in arm, and demanding sausages and bacon. We sang a few songs, I remember, as we stumbled up the gorge, sweating like horses, through the stinkwood to our belvedere.

Chapter Eight

IT WAS NOT to be so simple.

We saw Douglas, standing bare-headed, two hundred paces away. He was looking out for us as we emerged from the thick bush and we hailed him.

"We've found it!"

He waved back, but there was something cursory in it; he had turned his back on us as though he had not heard. Five minutes later as we toiled, jubilant, on to the grassy ridge, we began to understand. Miss Helga, elegant on her pony, was making conversation with him. Behind him were Domingo and a Cape associate; both, I noticed, were armed with rifles, and gazed at us without evident enthusiasm.

The lady was in cheerful mood. "I have been sent by my uncle to summon you for breakfast," she cried. "No objections! – I insist!" Her accent was entrancing.

Douglas said, "I'm sorry, you fellows, I didn't know where you had gone."

Helga directed a dazzling smile at me; her eyes today were the blue of sapphires. "You will be sure to be hungry after your walk," she said. "Did I hear you calling to Douglas that you had found something? How exciting – what can it be?"

Douglas was glaring at me, as though about to panic. I began to think very fast.

"That's right," I managed. "There's a big bull kudu down there – we were tracking him yesterday. Schalk's a genius, he picked up the spoor."

She looked down at me appraisingly. I was so purple with exertion that there was no danger of a liar's blush.

"And do you always find what you are looking for – you three musketeers? But no, we must hurry, Uncle demands that you join him. He will be very cross with me if I do not deliver you all."

I began to search urgently for excuses that would not excite her suspicions. "That's very kind, but you must forgive us . . .", I stuttered. "We really have to break camp and get on our way. We have delayed far too long . . ."

Douglas had taken my point and chimed in almost too enthusiastically. "My boys will be expecting me down at Edenend," he blurted. "Give my regards to your uncle. Tell him I'll be coming back very soon . . ."

The lady pursed her lips; she allowed her vexation to show. No point in this palaver, I was thinking, I've got to get down to the telegraph at White River – when Schalk interrupted. He gave her his caramel smile. "Hold on, my friends," he said, and, to the lady, "That's very kind of you, Miss Ingeburg. I was sad that I did not meet your uncle yesterday. We can't be in such a hurry that we cannot take coffee with him before we leave."

I was astonished rather than angered at the Boer's presumption. He must have known as well as I that it was vitally urgent to get our news to our masters in Sunnyside. I might have protested, even at the risk of indiscretion, if he had not turned to me as though seeking my agreement and allowed an eyelid to flicker. I paused for thought and in that instant Helga, all sunny again, cried "Let's be off then," and gave her pony its head to prance prettily across the short grass in the direction of the Berg, waving as she did so to the silent figures of her armed companions.

That gave us a moment's private conference.

"Schalk," I hissed, "what sort of idiocy is this? We have to be on our way."

"Gentle, *basie*," muttered the Boer, his eyes on the three ponies. "Do we trust these Germans?"

"No, of course not, that's another reason to be off."

"Yes, but we must try to calm their suspicions. She heard you shouting that we had found something . . ." He was right and I cursed myself. "We think they know too much about our mission. By going to take breakfast with them we convince them that nothing dramatic has happened –"

Douglas interrupted. "I suppose you're right, Schalk. We can still leave before midday."

Schalk had not finished. "And I don't like the way that dirty Portugoose is carrying a rifle, just to deliver an invitation."

He spat in his kaffir fashion, then looked around for the horses, while Helga pirouetted in the sunlight and urged us to hurry.

The Old Man, as I found I had dubbed Helga's alleged uncle in my mind for all time, was waiting for us on the Lodge *stoep*, though whether so grand a balcony over one of the world's finest panoramas could be characterised by the simple local word has to be doubted. He had not met Schalk and the two exchanged courtesies. Schalk, I saw, was intent on playing the humble man and I was not surprised when I overheard him launch into reminiscence of his days amongst the transport-riders, back before the war, when they were the only line of supply between Delagoa Bay and the goldfields of Pilgrims Rest and Lydenburg. The Old Man gave him full attention, occasionally interjecting a question which seemed to betray no mean expertise in the topic, while the rest of us concentrated on the papaya and grapefruit, the varieties of eggs, the bacon, the Teutonic selection of cold meats and cheeses, and the piping jugs of the richest black coffee. The expedition to the waterfall had bred an appetite, and I allowed neither the surly glare of the Portuguese butler nor my frustrated need of a telegraph line to restrain me.

After we had eaten we were invited by our host to inspect his library, an invitation which Schalk accepted more eagerly than I would have expected because I had not thought my colleague a literary man. Douglas was summoned, too, as they argued about the precise chronology of the white man's settlement in these parts. Maps were produced from wide shelves, the Boer quoted the memories of his kinsmen, and I looked on three very different species of African imperialist and found it in me to enjoy their debate. The Old Man, it somehow emerged, was a fellow of London's Royal Geographic Society and claimed to have known Speke.[51] I noticed that Douglas was impressed with this, whereas Schalk showed me another of his flickering eyelids.

That left me to the attention of Fräulein Helga, whose curiosity about my poor self I could no longer in honesty have denied. We strolled through the cool and spacious rooms of the Lodge and then, as if by common consent, out on to the natural lawns of the belvedere. As we gazed out over the plains, down on to the thick haze of the stifling Lowveld at our feet, I remembered, fleetingly, how so few days ago I had saved my life by launching myself out over the precipice and the scree. Here, I saw at once,

51 This seems unlikely, though not impossible, since John Hannay Speke, the famous African explorer, colleague of both Burton and Grant, had died in 1864 in a gun accident (possibly suicide).

I would have plunged to instant death. The cliff was sheer, while to either side the enflanking ravines were the densest ancient bush.

I made some tactless remark on the theme that this lodge was set apart from the outside world. "You have no fear of this isolation?" I asked.

"You mean?"

"Oh, that this wonderful site, this paradise, could so easily be cut off – why, look behind you, you could be blockaded, separated from the Berg and from all escape –"

She affected to shiver dramatically. "Why such thoughts? Who would wish us ill?"

I shrugged and let a fancy seize me, perhaps to distract me from my awareness of her. I had an absurd fear that she would seize my hand, make some advance I did not have the wisdom, let alone the desire, to repulse.

"These are dangerous times, Miss Ingeburg. The war may be over, but consider – there is a local tribe of Natives not far from here whose Chief is called M'Chudi. I may tell you that I had a difficult moment in his *kraal* the other day."

"What on earth do you mean?"

Her blue eyes emboldened me.

"They pursued me over the Berg cliff. That was why you found me painting my face at Edenend – they have a ridiculous grievance against me. What if they were to forget themselves and make demands on this place?"

She had a trick of gazing deep into my eyes, evade her though I tried. "Oh, M'Chudi and my uncle are great friends. We take all our labour from his *kraal*."

At that moment I think I had a moment of instinct and of insight and understood something which had been escaping me.

I remember that I walked rather briskly away from her along the line of cliff, so that I could think it through. M'Chudi, of course, was the element we had left out of our plans and calculations. It was M'Chudi – I realised at that second – the superior, educated, self-confident and rebellious M'Chudi, the chief who had sanctioned my death, who must have led the Native ambush of Kruger's gold. It would have been M'Chudi who had hidden the gold behind the waterfall, it was M'Chudi whose young wife had betrayed him with one of his warriors on the green lawn those few yards from the treasure. M'Chudi would not have lamented for one instant the death of the young man who, more important than cuckolding him, had broken the great secret of the golden hoard. On the contrary, M'Chudi might cheerfully have betrayed the young brave to his torture and death. But M'Chudi would have made his own plan from the beginning. He must have a plan for the gold. He would have the wit to understand that there was no benefit in, no use for, the gold for the time being; he was holding the gold, hiding the gold, in the safest of treasuries until the time was ripe – ripe for whatever, I could not guess, and for however many years that might require. M'Chudi's gold was safe: except that I, and Schalk, had found it. If M'Chudi were to discover that Schalk and I had ventured behind the water-fall, our lives would be doomed. If M'Chudi were to hear that I had emerged from the ravine crying that we had "found" something . . .

Helga interrupted my meditation. "We often visit M'Chudi's *kraal*. My uncle speaks very highly of him. They have long talks together. Don't look like that, they are friends . . ."

"Friends? Your uncle and a mission kaffir?"

"Of course. M'Chudi has told me he will protect us if we are ever in any danger."

"We shall have to leave after lunch," I managed.

"I won't let you. No, I won't!"

Douglas said, "Shouldn't we be leaving?"

"Only when we are sure they know nothing," replied Schalk. His tone was firm, as though he was prepared to argue the case.

I said, "Do we really need to worry about the suspicions of a party of rich Germans?"

We had managed to win a few minutes' privacy in front of the stables; Helga had gone to administer luncheon, the Old Man had pleaded the heat. Schalk said, "I know nothing about diplomacy, but I thought you people were concerned for the German Government and its policies in Africa. I do not believe that these are simple travellers. Do you?"

He asked the question so that it demanded an answer. Douglas glanced at me and we both shook our heads at the same moment.

"Then who are they?" Schalk had seen us and was pushing his advantage.

They waited for me, assuming, I suppose, that I spoke with the authority of the High Commission.

I said, "I'm hanged if I know."

Germany had been actively competing with us in this particular territory for years, as it had elsewhere in Africa, but after the 1898 Treaty the Germans had appeared to accept the spirit of the agreement – the division of the spoils, as the anti-imperialists described it. I tried to explain this.[52]

52 In the mid-1890s Germany had helped President Kruger and encouraged the Portuguese to hold on to Delagoa Bay (later Lourenço Marques, today Maputo). The Kaiser even sent a notorious telegram congratulating Kruger on the defeat of the 1895 Jameson Raid (by the largely English *Uitlanders* against the independent Transvaal Republic), and Kruger always looked to Germany as potentially his most important supporter in the Anglo-Boer war. Indeed, there was fierce anti-British

Douglas, whose biography included South-West Africa and the Hereros, challenged me at once. "The Germans always supported Kruger. Even the Kaiser encouraged him."

"True, but they never endorsed the Boers at an official level. Now that Kruger is in exile in Europe and the war is over, there's no reason to worry that Berlin wants to embarrass our Reconstruction policies." My language sounded too formal out here in the breezes of the Berg.

"Which means," said Douglas, "that we all agree that our hosts are unofficial. Are we all sure of that?" Schalk and I were nodding.

"Then," said Douglas, who had never claimed to like the lady, "we agree that our hosts must be pursuing their own interests. Without official authority or endorsement."

"What interests?"

"Oh, come on!" exclaimed Douglas. "The interests that most of us pursue, if we aren't dried-up civil servants. Our own interests. Money, of course. Riches. Loot. Best of all, treasure!"

"Gold?" asked Schalk softly.

"What better?"

The Boer appeared to be discomfited by this. "I hate the vulture," he muttered. "I have always hated the *aasvogel*. He eats the carrion – he feeds off the corpses after the battle is ended. For us, the war is ended. And now these people descend on us . . ."

"How much do they know?"

sentiment in Continental Europe when the war broke out. But an Anglo-German agreement in 1898, providing for the partition of Angola and Mozambique if Portuguese authority failed (with Delagoa Bay to become British, to Kruger's chagrin) effectively ended competition between the two imperial powers in this particular theatre. Nevertheless, and not surprisingly, British suspicions of German ambitions were to persist, and German nationals travelling in the Eastern Transvaal immediately after the war were likely to attract attention. Throughout the period of this narrative everyone was aware that Portuguese control over Mozambique was precarious.

"We have to assume they know that there's gold hidden some-where in this area."

"They know from the Major that the word is out . . ."

"And that we are looking for it. With official authority."

"But they probably don't know how much gold is involved."

"They know of a single *veldpond*," said Douglas. "They may think we are simply looking for the coin that was struck at Pilgrims Rest in the war."

That seemed optimistic. The Old Man had shown himself an expert on the contemporary history of these parts.

"They also know we are looking for a waterfall."

"And they heard you say you had found – something . . ."

I interrupted. "But do they know that M'Chudi must be the man who ambushed the gold and hid it behind the waterfall? And that if he knows how much we know, M'Chudi will have to kill us. All of us." It occurred to me in that moment that the Old Man could never confide in the Chief that he was interested in the gold or M'Chudi would have to kill him too.

There was a pause. Schalk said, "M'Chudi will kill us whites whenever he thinks he can get away with it. I can live with that. It is these Germans who are the immediate danger. Don't we agree?"

I was thinking: only because you insisted we came to breakfast, Schalk. But I said nothing.

We lunched simply, on pressed ham, omelettes and tropical fruits. Then we sat on the *stoep* and looked out over the panorama as great clouds sailed overhead, dappling the land-scape far below. The Old Man talked on into the afternoon, and I slowly realised that I was waiting for him to broach the reason for our entertainment. Douglas, less skilled in diplomatic prevarication, had twice retreated to the stables to check that our horses were ready.

The Old Man presided from his high armchair and the woman kneeled at his feet – I was obscurely troubled to see how she fed him a grape taken from her own mouth – and at last the moment arrived. He had confessed that he felt the heat, which was why, he explained, he sought the breezes of the mountaintop, but in this mid-afternoon his Pickwick's head was glazed with sweat and, as he mopped his brow with a silk kerchief, I had the first inkling that, if he was the scoundrel I had divined, he might be outfaced and defied. He was horribly intelligent, but he was vulnerable.[53]

"Gentlemen," said he, "I do so appreciate your willingness to attend the table of an elderly traveller . . ." Helga was pouring wine, checking that our glasses were full, playing the attentive hostess.

Heaven knows what he had intended to introduce, but his bland courtesies must have been the last straw for the exasperated Douglas, who was suddenly on his feet in a clatter of coffee cups. He was pale beneath the tan and as agitated as can be imagined of a diffident, a courteous and indeed a conventional young man who has felt obliged to break the rules of society. He was gazing at me, not at his host. Helga, who had been sitting next to me and, I realised, more attentive than she needed to be, looked up from her duties with a start of alarm which she failed to suppress.

"Can we please halt this charade?" the engineer blurted, and waved his arms as though to protest his incoherence. "We sit here as civilised white men, chatting about this and that, and yet we all know what is going on . . ."

There was a fraught silence. Dorando had recently brought

---

53 cf. *The Thirty-nine Steps* (ch. 6).

fresh coffee and I suspected that the Portuguese had not yet withdrawn. The Old Man mopped his brow yet again and directed a placid gaze on my agitated friend.

"Mr Green, you seem distressed."

"That I am," replied Douglas, "and you know why, sir."

"Mr Green," repeated our host, "I trust we are not to betray confidences."

"By God we are!" declared Douglas with vehemence, though he was still addressing his words to me. "Why do we play these games? Don't you realise that our gracious host a few minutes ago offered me one-half of the proceeds of what he described – I don't understand why – as the 'waterfall gold'? On condition, of course, that no one else would ever know of it and on the assumption that I would need to book my passage for next week."

"What did you say?" It was the Old Man who put the question, not me.

"I told you I didn't know what you were talking about."

This time it was Schalk who intervened. He addressed not me but the Old Man.

"Since the cards are on the table," he said, "let us record before my friends that you and I had the same conversation in your study a short time ago. I got to understand that my share of whatever we are talking about might be worth even more than one-half . . . though I'm not entirely sure that I would survive to enjoy it."

"And what did you say, Schalk?"

"I consigned him to hell, as I do again in the presence of all of you." He paused, then began to tap out his pipe before casting a mischievous smile about him. "After that, I reckon we can be on our way at last. The air seems to have cleared."

The Old Man was beaming down at us from his high chair; he showed no sign of discomfiture. He positively chuckled as he said, "Alas, I have offended you all – we businessmen do not always make allowances for finer feelings. How fortunate that I did not venture to approach your friend . . ." And he inclined his rosy skull at me.

"I describe myself as a businessman," he went on, "though I am also, you may have noticed, something of an historian, of the amateur variety, and also, in my modest way, a collector. Of Africana, of curiosities, that sort of thing. The Major in Pilgrims Rest has helped me expand my ethnographic collection and I have even found my friend Chief M'Chudi sympathetic to my interests."

"And you collect gold?"

"Don't we all, to some degree or other?"

Douglas and Schalk, I noticed, had risen from their chairs and were awaiting me. The Old Man twinkled at us all. Helga offered me a lingering smile – of collaboration or apology I could not guess.

The Old Man spread his hands wide, in what I thought to be an appeal with something ancient and Semitic in it. "Before we depart as enemies," he cooed, "are you all certain that we cannot be sensible, adult men?"

That was enough and I hauled myself to my feet, glancing at the angle of the shadows to judge how late it was.

"I insist that the subject must go no farther." I spoke in the accent of Sunnyside and saw the Old Man smile again, inscrutable as ever.

Helga interrupted, suddenly and inexplicably breathless. She said, "There's only one problem –"

"What problem?"

"You won't be able to leave."

"What do you mean?"

"I'm terribly sorry, but M'Chudi and his men have blocked the road."

Schalk swore, a Dutch obscenity, contemptuous and unbelieving. He strode off towards the compound. The Old Man had still not moved, though I saw that Dorando and his Cape foreman were to hand and carried weapons. No one said anything. Helga, I believe, busied herself with cups and so on. Douglas abruptly ran after Schalk. I made a sustained effort to think hard and clean as Lord Milner would have expected of me. There was an unreality to this situation which clouded my rational powers.

Douglas returned first, in a black fury, followed by Schalk, who preferred to offer a seraphic smile.

"So?" I asked.

"Our host is right. The neck of this promontory, between the *skerm* and the cliff, is blocked by a hundred kaffir scoundrels, most of them in paint and spears and apparently hostile. I didn't see M'Chudi, but he must be there somewhere."

"He is," the Old Man proffered.

"And why?"

"Do you mean, why should he be so hostile to you, Mr Minnaar, and to your colleagues? I assure you he is no enemy of mine."

"You are playing with fire, my friend," observed Schalk. "My people have learned not to play games with the kaffir. So – what have you told them?"

It was Helga who answered. She said, and was speaking urgently to me, "I'm afraid they have realised that you are the white man who escaped from them the other day – as you were telling me, do you remember? – the man who went over the Berg so bravely. And they are beginning to think that Mr Minnaar was involved in your escape. But they are not angry with you, Mr Green."

I suffered an instant memory of my admission to Helga this morning – perhaps I had been boasting – that I had escaped from M'Chudi's *impis* over the cliff. I had no wish to meet again that unkempt gang of kaffir youths, and I would have dearly welcomed the arrival this very minute of a company of Wheatcroft's horse.

"You look alarmed," the Old Man had the impertinence, and the accuracy, to observe from his chair. "Believe me, you remain under my protection. They will not enter my perimeters."

Helga said, "I promise you are safe with us. You must stay as long as you wish."

And the Old Man added, purring like a very comfortable and privileged cat, "Do please think again about my proposals – all of you . . ."

The sun was lower in the sky. Soon it would fall beneath the rocky wall behind the Lodge and abandon us to the dark African night. No doubt our host would invite us to "sundowners", and no doubt he would find a way of repeating his invitation. The very thought was an outrage. I said, "Right, you fellows – when do we leave?"

We had been permitted to stroll and smoke on the terrace though we were aware that Dorando and his crew kept watch with their Mausers at a discreet distance. Schalk had repeated his reconnaissance of the perimeters and reported that the blockade was complete and the sentries hostile. Douglas, when we offered him the chance that he take up the Old Man's promise that he alone was acceptable to M'Chudi, firmly declined to desert us.

"Then we have to make a break for it," I had said, though with more confidence than I felt. It was a pity, I thought again, that Schalk had insisted on accepting the breakfast invitation.

He may have been thinking the same. "The sooner the better," was all he said. Perhaps he was wondering whether he might carry off another disguise.

"It's vital that we get word to Wheatcroft – he was moving up to Sabie," I said, and a glimmer of an idea began to take shape in my mind. No, I did not relish the thought of going over the Berg again with M'Chudi's lads in pursuit – the recollection gave me a chill even as I remembered that the cliff beyond the Lodge was so sheer that the effort would be madness, it was a precipice, not the steep scree behind the *kraal*. Somehow or other we would have to penetrate M'Chudi's cordon. But how? Not even Schalk would find a disguise that would make him invisible to that lot, and there were three of us . . .

It made better sense to split up. That way there was a double chance of getting through to Wheatcroft. I said, "Look, you chaps, I'll stay behind. You two make the first crack at it and – well, if it doesn't work, I'll think of something else . . ."

It sounded pretty cowardly stuff to me, though the others seemed to think that I had volunteered for a hero's fate. "By God, you'll do nothing of the sort," protested Douglas. "I'll stay with you and Schalk can do one of his vanishing tricks." I shook my head. My motives were, I now see, as mixed as ever. As I say, I didn't have the nerve for a chase. I knew it was right that Schalk and I separate, but I had an instinct that Douglas should stay with the Boer – if for no other reason than that he might be able to persuade M'Chudi to spare Schalk if they were caught. Anyhow, I was the prime target of M'Chudi's warriors: they might not even associate the trim Boer hunter with a verminous old kaffir who had briefly visited their *kraal*.

"I'll find some way to distract Helga and her uncle when you make a dash for it."

The reference to our hostess appeared to impress Douglas.

"Rather you than me," said he. "I'd rather take on an *impi* of Zulus fresh from Isandhlwana[54] than be entertained by that woman."

Schalk, I could tell, was also going to agree. I could see that he had been studying the terrain – measuring the distance to the crags above us, the depth of the bush, the calibre of the rough log gates – though not in a manner which Dorando could have noticed. Douglas was still worrying about me. He kept repeating that I would be helpless: there seemed no outrage on me which he did not suspect of the Germans. Schalk laid a hand on his arm and chuckled: "That's where I like the *baas*'s plan," he murmured. "Once I have gone away, his health will be very precious to his jailers. Think on it, Douglas – only *he* will then know where the gold is hidden. So they will have to protect him from the kaffirs. As the lady said, he will be safe with them."

"Then that's agreed," I said brusquely, not feeling quite so confident that Schalk was right. "Then let's make a plan. Schalk! *Ons sal 'n plan maak . . .*"

54 Isandhlwana was the site of a famous battle in 1879 when the Zulu *impis* (regiments) slaughtered 1600 British troops. (The young Kruger had warned the British generals not to underestimate the Zulus.)

Chapter Nine

*[These next chapters are Douglas Green's story.
He wrote it down for me afterwards and I reproduce his
account, in his own words, with only slight editing
of duplicated material.*

                                                        JB] [55]

I T WAS, as we all knew, a damnably risky plan, but for the life of us we could come up with nothing better and at least it had the virtue of simplicity. In the minutes before dark I had strolled down to the fence to see whether M'Chudi's fellows had got bored and taken themselves away. No such luck, they howled insults and brandished their ironware and shouted me down when I tried to strike up a chat with a couple of youths I thought I recognised from my last picking season.

That took us to dinner, where we had agreed we would be polite but cool so as to raise no suspicion. It ought to have been

[55] It becomes clear from what follows that Douglas Green did not have the affecting and fluent literary style which JB was later to give Sir Richard Hannay. Perhaps that was too much to hope.

This may be an appropriate point at which to ask again whether the literary *style* of these pages is true enough to the Buchan we all know. But what was Buchan's prose style at this time? We can assume that he wrote this text some time between 1903 and 1905 when he had not yet achieved the effortless rhythms of his post-war maturity. In these early years he had not found one style, he had a choice of them. There was his official voice (as in *The African Colony*) – a combination a sticky evening, but to my surprise the old boy set himself to play the gentleman. I calculated that it would have been churlish to refuse the first-rate champagne he brought out for us, followed by a very decent port, and then the lady, who has always terrified me, Lord knows why, sat down at the piano and sang for us. I am not a musical type, but I have a weakness for a woman's voice, while my companions, I saw, were all equally entranced, so that the evening passed in a civilised fashion.[56] Buchan felt obliged, before we went to our quarters, to deliver a rather formal statement of protest – outrageous discourtesy to the High Commissioner's emissary, willingness to forget it if no more problems in the morning, that sort of thing – but Madame was by this time flirting with him quite brazenly (which, I observed, made him pink and flustered) and she and her uncle absolutely declined to entertain an argument. In the circumstances, of course, we had no wish to excite their suspicions and so we withdrew without further discord.

Usually I am awake an hour before dawn, but the evening's entertainment must have taken its toll and I may have overslept, so after the first moment of bewilderment in the darkness I was

of the self-conscious, elegant and pompous, even the Augustan, with a touch of what-I-did-in-my-holidays. Before that there had been the bright undergraduate's florid artifice. A little later there was *Prester John*, the so-called boys' adventure story, the prose simple, clean, fast – surely the first *good writing*. Then came the famous mid-career novels, very often told in the first person and so the language is subtly different depending on whether the narrator is, say, Richard Hannay (bluff, idiomatic) or Edward Leithen (cooler, lawyerish). And there is a lot of Scottish embellishment, notably the series in which the main protagonist (but not the narrator) is Dickson McCunn, the retired Glasgow grocer. There is therefore no "real" Buchan style.

56 Buchan's heroes frequently fall for a girl's voice: see for example *Salute to Adventurers* (ch. 1) and *Huntingtower* (ch. 3). In *Mr Standfast* Hannay first meets his wife-to-be, Mary, when he hears her singing "Cherry Ripe" (ch. 1). (She whistles it again, to even greater effect, in chapter 13).

relieved to be woken with the old hunter's trick – a finger pressure on the earlobe – and to find that Schalk had had to arouse me.[57] It was essential to be up and about ahead of the staff because Schalk and I must take up our positions before daylight. Everything then depended on the hour at which Dorando would drive off for provisions – for that much we had overheard in an exchange between our host and the butler: this was the day on which the Portuguese drove the Cape-cart to Pilgrims Rest.

The plan, in short, was to get out by hiding ourselves in the cart – or rather, by hiding ourselves until we had the opportunity to convince Dorando that we would blow his brains out if he did not take us through M'Chudi's cordon. I did not seriously doubt that Dorando would turn out to be a yellow-livered cur like most of his compatriots (I had spent a part of the recent war in Delagoa Bay on confidential business where I had formed an opinion on such matters) but first we had to get ourselves to the vehicle, and then hide ourselves, at least until Dorando appeared. The problem was that we did not know the hour he intended to leave, so we had to find the cart in darkness and install ourselves in it with the awkward prospect of a long wait. It will be evident at once that there was the constant danger that our absence from the Lodge would be noticed. The best we could manage to come up with to cope with this prospect was to agree that J. would if necessary create a diversion, probably by pretending to mount an "escape" over the cliff; his recovery would distract attention from our absent selves and the Cape-cart. With hindsight, the plan was woefully thin, but it worked in practice better than we deserved.

This was because Dorando turned out to be an early riser. Perhaps he relished his weekly trek to Pilgrims Rest, where I have

57 This trick is mentioned in *Greenmantle* (ch. 18).

no doubt he got up to the mischief of his race. Schalk and I had snaked our way to the stable area just as first light was showing in the east. There was no difficulty in it, though Schalk was twice as quick as I, and when we arrived at a sort of godown he had to move very fast to slit the throat of a dog who was about to wake the whole party.

A Cape-cart, as you know, has a loose canvas covering which wouldn't give much shelter to two grown men, but what saved us was, item, that Dorando kept it in a scandalous state of rubbish and disarray – presumably Madame never had occasion to travel in it – and, item, he had had it loaded for his journey the previous night so it was piled with empty crates and barrels in all manner of disorder. Come daylight, we had arranged ourselves inconspicuously beneath this shambles, Schalk had selected a slim iron curtain-pole which would, with firm pressure from the rear, give a satisfactory impression of a Männlicher, and I was rehearsing my Portuguese oaths from my not-so-distant days in Delagoa Bay.[58]

That's really all that needs saying. Blessedly early we heard the stumbling arrival of a heavy body, heard him call for the mules, braced ourselves as he thumped on to the board seat, breathed the stench of the man, and waited as we were hauled halfway down the bumpy stone track towards the Berg. The cart made a deuce of a row, which must have helped our cause. Schalk squinted at me through a gap in the furnishings and raised a thumb. Simultaneously Dorando felt cold steel jabbed into his lower spine and heard my most villainous Portuguese accent. There was a moment, I think, when he seriously considered raising the alarm. It was Schalk's voice that must have convinced him. It was

58 In *The Thirty-nine Steps* Hannay refers to his wartime role as an intelligence officer in Delagoa Bay. But in *The Green Wildebeest* he also says that in the war he did "two years campaigning with the Imperial Light Horse". Is there a contradiction here?

quiet and conversational, not a tone that would carry far or alarm the horses, it was in Dutch, and from my own limited knowledge of the *taal* I can certify that it conveyed in terms of extreme vulgarity what my friend's weapon would do to the wretched man if he did not obey our every wish.

That was enough to take us to the gates, where we could hear sounds of movement and agitation, presumably because M'Chudi's sentries were summoning their sleeping friends. Schalk murmured, in English this time, "You half-caste bastard, you are dead in three seconds if we don't get through."[59] I believed him, and so did Dorando. We half-halted, the Portuguese gabbled something in a falsetto – of course, they knew him – and there was a crack of the whip, a rustle of reins, and we were lurching and bumping down the rough track.

Schalk said, so that the three of us could share the conversation, "Shall I put a bullet in him?" There was a yelp of protest from our driver. I took the point. "Let's see if he behaves himself," I replied, loud enough, and added a few words of advice in my rusty Portuguese.

We tipped him off the cart after about eight miles and one of the reasons was that we were weary of the stink of the terrified creature. His gun we had removed much earlier – I don't know whether he ever realised we had been unarmed – and he did not even have the gumption to curse us when I looked back at the dishevelled lump of lard sprawling in the dust. Schalk had taken the reins.

"You know the way?" I asked, foolishly.

"*Meneer*," he said, polite as though we had just taken tea in the Carlton Hotel,[59] "I used to be a transport-rider in these parts.

59 Here and elsewhere JB's awareness that this manuscript could never be published allows him to employ realistic language of a sort which he would never have considered including in his public volumes.

Now I shall show you some tracks that even M'Chudi has never dreamed of . . .''

But it was not going to be easy. The mules were willing but unable to keep up a decent pace, Dorando would be back at the Lodge in a couple of hours and M'Chudi's boys would be on our trail with a vengeance. We had one gun between us, no food, and too many miles to cover before we could look for Wheatcroft's protection in Sabie.

I had come too recently to this territory to know the transport-riders, that wild breed of men who used to ferry our provisions across the desperate terrain that separates the ocean from the Berg. They were heroes, I had heard, and rogues at the same time, and Schalk now gave me a demonstration of their skills. He took the cart down that mountain at a pace which sometimes put me into a blue funk. How the wretched mules survived the race I have no idea, nor can I now believe that a simple wooden cart can take such punishment, for nowhere did we rely on the main tracks. Schalk was constantly twisting into thick timber, doubling back under great granite outcrops, forcing the beasts through deep tunnels of greenery. I soon lost any precise sense of our direction: we were going east, yes indeed, but we seemed to be cutting far to the north while White River lay to the south-east. Not that I thought to mention it, I was in the hands of a professional and I held my peace in the consciousness that I would not have been amused if Schalk had queried my assessment of an out-crop of oxides. One thing that I did work out and understood for myself was that he was wherever possible keeping to the untrodden greenery of the bush, so as to avoid the thick white dust of the established tracks, which set up high plumes of yellow smoke which lingered for long minutes in the sun-baked landscape. M'Chudi's men would be able to track us, but that would take time, whereas any dust trail from us could be seen from miles away and would warn them to cut across country to intercept us. It occurred to me that a brief sharp storm might settle the dust and speed us on our way: I had the impression that the bank of storm cloud was beginning to move in our direction, but slowly.

Our immediate problem was that we had no food and, speaking for myself, were getting to feel famished since we had hardly been in a position to take breakfast before our departure from the Lodge. In early afternoon, with the sun high overhead, we stopped in a discreet glen to find water. Schalk seemed to content himself with his pipe, but I lay on some sacking in the cart, squinting through the canvas at the diamond-sharp contours of the Berg and suffering the first tortures of starvation. We would have to shoot a buck – but no, that would raise the alarm, and we certainly could not risk a fire. I was driven to the indignity of searching the cart for a fragment of biscuit, but we had thrown out most of Dorando's rubbish and all that remained was a few empty cans of paraffin and cooking oil.

The mules, I knew, were flagging and I had very little idea of where we were. The Berg wall did not seem to have retreated perceptibly and we would soon be off on yet another corkscrew digression. I said, "Schalk, I haven't a notion where we are heading and I still haven't seen a smidgin of the enemy, but I'm getting hungry. Shouldn't we be aiming for Sabie?"

Minnaar puffed away at his filthy pipe and glanced across at the wretched beasts which were cropping at the verge. "I was beginning to think," he said, "that M'Chudi's boys may not be so keen on the chase."

"What do you mean?"

"Why should they worry so much if two of us have got away? It's the German pair who will be sorrowing, not M'Chudi. And they have still got one of us – in the *tronk*." He busied himself with his pipe; I used to notice how pipe-smokers spend more time playing with the thing than smoking it and Schalk was no exception. "Douglas, I was wondering whether we have done right to leave him up there . . ."

I had been thinking the very same thing. Yes, we had to get word to Wheatcroft. But did that mean we abandoned a hostage in the German camp?

He said, "Come, we must keep moving. But we must shoot for the pot because we shall have to make camp tonight. How much ammunition was the Portugoose carrying?"

"Do we risk a shot?"

"We need to eat. Yes, both of us!" and he chuckled.

We left the cart and struck off on foot down a long valley, making for a stretch of *vlei* which was hedged by thick bush and tucked under a line of steep *kopjes*. Schalk, being the famed hunter, had the gun and began scouting around for a spoor. I need hardly have bothered to accompany him. It was very hot indeed, with the intensity that builds up before the summer storms of Eastern Transvaal, and the blood was beating in my temples as we crested one of the crags. Schalk had seen something – I did not shame myself by asking what – and gestured that we must hurry on to the next cliff. To my right I noticed the smoke of a grass fire. The game would be asleep in deep shade at this time of the afternoon.

For the first time all day I felt a wind on my cheek, and welcomed it, half-thinking of the clouds above the Lowveld. Schalk had found his spoor and paused to show me; in the infuriating manner of these people he pretended to know the life history of the poor buck from the scrawl of a hoofmark on a patch of sand. We followed it west, towards the *kopjes* at the foot of the Berg. He offered me the gun and I hastily declined. There was no sign of M'Chudi and I began to forget him. I had a headache.

Five minutes later we pushed through a thicket of thornbush and, as we came out on the other side, we felt the wind again. And this time we heard the noise. It sounded like a rhythmic and distant rumbling, but it wasn't the wind in the trees, it was different, and something dangerous. It was the grassfire I had already spotted, but the grassfire had become a bushfire, which is not at all the same thing, and we both realised at the same time that it was moving in our direction.

"Let's forget the buck," I said, in a tone as casual as I could manage, though I knew that we were both old Africa hands and would both understand that we must move fast. Which direction? "Towards that *kopje*!" said Schalk, and we set off at a brisk march across the tinder-dry veld towards the nearest line of boulder-strewn cliff.

Now the smoke overtook us, which was unpleasant, not just because it made our eyes smart but because it was thick with a million flying beasties. Around us there was a rippling panic of wildlife – the *klipspringer* that leapt across our path was probably the same one we had selected for our supper – but it was the noise that always scared me in a bushfire, the deep ripping and crackling of it, so far and yet so near. The flames could not yet be seen, but the smoke was thickening rapidly and, I noticed with a pang, had spread to both left and right. Fortunately the cliff was only a quarter-mile away and it was high enough to defy the flames to jump its granite face.

There was our error. We pounded towards our exit, and at this last we abandoned dignity and allowed ourselves to run. In mere minutes we had escaped the bush and reached the clean rock.

We found disaster. Rather than the steep and slippery scramble of the usual *kopje* we found an overhang; the cliff face was indented with caves but there was never a sign of a defile. I used to enjoy scrambling on the Matopos and at Inyanga, but this was beyond the skills of even an Alpine expert. Perhaps somewhere there was a corridor, but we certainly did not have the time to look for it. We might hide in those caves and be smoked to our death. Or we might attempt the ascent and assuredly be flung back into the flames. That was our choice.

Schalk had sworn savagely under his breath when he saw the overhang but he instantly drew the only conclusion. He had halted, taken out his matches from his pipe pocket, and was furiously harvesting bundles of dry grass. "Too late to get round it," he shouted through the furnace-wind. "We need a firebreak. Take these brands – we must clear a line . . ."

He was right, I acknowledged, and we hurled ourselves into the attempt. Within minutes we had made our own modest fire, fifty yards of blazing grass, scorching our eyelids in the process, scalding the sweat even as it burst from our flesh as we raced to and fro with our flaming torches. The trick was rather like immunisation against smallpox: to create our own and frailer version of the fire that must otherwise destroy us. The veld grass was like straw and burned merrily at our bidding along the cordon that Schalk had defined. Then we broke new green branches from a *mopani* tree, drew a deep scorching breath, and charged out to destroy our own creation, furiously beating out our own flames, trampling on the embers until our *velskoen* sizzled. It was a matter of minutes before we had withdrawn, panting like old men, from a frail strip of black ash that was all that stood between our lives and the belching flames that were racing down on us, turning the afternoon sky into night, bombarding us with sparks and brands and splinters of flickering fire.

We paused, gasping for a breath of cooler air, our backs to the fatal cliff. I confess that my main emotion was neither panic nor resignation but indignation. It seemed such a ridiculous way to end, so unnecessary, such appalling bad luck, after Africa had given me such splendid years and had seemed to promise so many more. I had had, I thought, a good innings and I did not for a moment regret the circumstances of my come-uppance. I knew that I had not needed to involve myself in this business, but I had always had a sense of duty, even in my wilder years, and I was happy to have been able to do something for the old country – but how I wished that the mission had been accomplished. I looked across at Schalk, wondering whether one of us might yet sacrifice himself to enable the other to scale the cliff, but he must have guessed my thoughts, he shook his head and I saw him attempt a smut-blackened smile.

The bellow of the fire was louder than ever and he had to lean across to grip my arm and speak into my ear.

"I'm not so sure that our firebreak is wide enough to work," he said, his voice wonderfully calm. "Douglas, my friend, I think it is time to look to our Maker. Will you join me?"

He removed his hat, joined his hands in the universal gesture of private prayer, and raised his eyes to the smoke-tattered heavens. Then he spoke aloud – quietly yet clearly, in the *taal* – to his Creator.

I understood him to be accepting divine judgment, admitting a lifetime of error and inadequacy, refusing to protest against this destiny, commending us both to infinite mercy. I am not a man who has kept a close acquaintance with the Kirk and I stood next to him rather shy and diffident, not quite sure how to hold myself, and distressingly conscious of the din of the approaching flames.

Schalk said, in English and in the same conversational tone, "And now a moment of silent prayer . . .", and I think we both sank to our knees. We stayed like that for a long minute.

The wind, I realised slowly, had shifted. There was a new fury to the roar of the flames, a deeper, harsher, more percussive element. I felt a gust of even fiercer smoke but it was followed by a different blast – cold, dank, blessedly different. The ashes were still whirling against my head, but there was something else, a sensation of violent blows, yet blows which soothed rather than injured. The smoke was even thicker now, we coughed and choked and I realised it was very dark as though the sun was in eclipse. The smell of the place had changed. The air was pungent with all the riches of Africa. It is a smell that no one who knows Africa ever forgets and I suddenly recognised it – it was that wonderful fragrance that is disgorged by the soil at the first rains of spring.

I put my hand on my face and, unbelieving, found it was wet. I felt those blows on my bare head and realised they were heavy raindrops. Then the thunder smote at us with a colossal explosion, and lightning forked into the headland not half a mile away, and the rain became a downpour, a deluge of solid water, fresh and cold and life-affirming – and the flames went out, as we knelt trembling in the bush, side by side, drenched, sodden, laughing like idiots.

Curiously enough, we never talked about it again.

We found the Cape-cart and the mules unharmed at a safe distance from the fire after we had tiptoed across the damp but smouldering veld. There would be no food but that no longer mattered. "Do we keep watch?" I asked Schalk, deferring to his age and experience, and he shrugged. "They will not try to take us in the night. They have no stomach for this quarrel of white men. And they respect us both, in their fashion." I reckoned he was right. We tried to wrap ourselves in scraps of sackcloth and cardboard, but our clothes had scarcely dried in the brief evening sunshine that followed the storm; we might have used branches and undergrowth, but that, too, was still wet. It was going to be a miserable night.

When I woke I was cold and stiff and suddenly panicking about our friend on the mountain. We had blundered, I knew it. We had calculated that his health would be precious to them, but that need not necessarily be true. Once they had extracted the secret from him they might as well toss him over the cliff or bury his body under a scree: we were fools, all three of us, and I may have groaned aloud in misery because I heard Schalk stir next to me and knew he was awake. It was, I guessed, the hour before dawn.

I said, without need for explanation, "It's that woman who frightens me. I hate to think what she could be doing to him."

The Dutchman seemed to consider my point with due solemnity. He said, "I'm worrying more about the other one. The uncle. I don't like his eyes. They are like the eyes of a snake. He's a bad bugger, I reckon."

We lay there for a while, with no thought of action or prospect of sleep.

Later, I said, "Schalk, I'm going back. We must split up. You go to Sabie and alert Wheatcroft. I could never forgive myself if I didn't go back." There was another long silence, in the dark.

"Are you sure?"

"Sure . . ."

* * *

Sun up and decision taken, we both felt better. We would aim for the first homestead, where I would beg, borrow or steal a horse and Schalk would make his way, as fast as the mules could sustain, to Sabie. I still didn't understand exactly where we were, and whistled when Schalk told me: we were closer to Pilgrims Rest than to White River – but no, we would not trust our discovery to the Prussian Major, even for the sake of a telegraph line to Wheatcroft. The Major was the last person to deserve our confidence.

This, I remember, must have been the Thursday, and by the luck of the devil Schalk within the hour found us a farmstead where I was recognised, thanks to some common business at the Nelspruit market, and where, more to the point, the breakfast table had not yet been cleared. We gorged ourselves on ham and eggs and porridge and pints of coffee, to the astonishment of the farmer's lady, to whom we had made a tale of a misadventure on the mountain to explain our ragged and blackened appearance, and our good fortune was complete when our host, after private discussion with Schalk, offered the loan of a horse since I had indicated that I needed to get back to Edenend. My farewells with Schalk were therefore not private. "Remember –" I managed to say – "Wheatcroft must get up there as if the nation depended on it. It's not the waterfall I'm worried about . . ."

He smiled that wry, unforgettable smile and leaned forward to touch me gently on the sleeve as though in reassurance.

"*Tot siens*," he said, and shouted to the boys to bring his mules clattering across the yard.

That was the happy beginning of a desperate day. My only concern was to get back to my young friend on the Berg; to Schalk's well-being I did not from that moment give another

135

thought, he only had to trek down to the cantonment in Sabie where, I was sure, Wheatcroft would be speedily found to take responsibility for the final act in our drama.

My farmer-host produced the promised horse, we made our farewells and then – confound it – the creature went lame soon after I had left his orchards. It was fortunate, I told myself, that I had not gone farther because I could walk back with the wretched beast and resume those endless sequences of coffee and Boer cakes – *koeksisters* – which are necessary in these parts, and with many an unnecessary apology from my new friends before I emerged an hour later with another pony. Where, I had asked, was Schalk, and was impressed to hear that he had been on his way only minutes after my own departure. Evidently, said the wife, he was engaged on the most urgent business; I wondered whether the old charmer had for once been hasty in his courtesies.

I am no particular horseman, but we made five brisk miles before my nag threw a shoe and I had to return yet again to the homestead, this time feeling a thorough idiot! There is something in the Scriptures about the treachery of horses.[60] They forced me to drink more coffee and somehow found me another broken-down brute, and when, in a fever of urgency, I implored them whether there was a shorter route, they urged me down a sandy track which after ten miles deteriorated into a quagmire without path or exit. That was the moment when I called myself to order. Too many hours had been lost; I realigned myself to the line of the Berg to the west and set myself to a long and, if need be, a slow recovery. That took another two hours of infuriating

60 cf. "My head was full of a text from the Psalms about not putting one's trust in horses . . ." *Prester John*, ch. 18.

perambulation as the sun began to fail and my hunger began to grow again – when all of a sudden I spotted an unlikely landmark and realised with a start that I was not so many miles from my own Edenend. I dismounted, drank from a sour pool, and allowed myself the time to take a miserable but considered decision. There would be no chance of regaining the Berg that night. I would be wiser to change out of my fire-scorched kit, sleep in my own bed, rest, re-supply, and resume at dawn. And that was what I did . . .

Chapter Ten

I INTENDED TO LEAVE Edenend, as you will guess, very early. I had made my plan and first I had an errand in Pilgrims Rest; then I would break all records up to the Berg. I would saddle my favourite horse and load my best rifle, but what I needed was the luck of the Gods, and even with that I had a sick feeling that I might be too late. When I woke to see the dawn streaking the hilltops, I was, for once, not soothed and gladdened. I was in a thoroughly rotten frame of mind.

All things seemed to conspire against me. My breakfast arrived late, and when I cursed the boys they protested some overnight commotion in the compound. I could hardly leave them in a pother so I walked across to the native huts and discovered the cause of the crisis – something to do with the headman's daughter. Then I was called over to the drying sheds, where my foreman insisted that the flues, not he, were at fault. This was, after all, my living, so I was compelled to spend an impatient thirty minutes with him. Meanwhile, the sun was rising too rapidly in the sky.

I arrived back on my *stoep* in a short temper. To my astonishment it was occupied – and by a stranger, a young fellow whose kit was dusty and who sprang to his feet and gave me the cheeriest greeting. Most surprising of all, my dogs were fawning at his feet (I had not heard them bark as they normally would on the arrival of a visitor), and my boys had furnished him with what I could see were the remnants of my own breakfast. Hence, I reckoned, my stranger's good spirits.

He pumped my arm and made the usual greetings with an adequate element of apology for the surprise, the discourtesy, the early hour, and so on. He may have been young but he carried himself with confidence; I guessed that he had good reason for it, for this was no rough colonial like me but an English gentleman and, I suspected, a soldier as well. I am no dwarf, but he towered over me by half a foot, and I could see that he had the build to go with it. His eyes were friendly, his manner was full of charm, and he wore a small ginger moustache which I am sure was much appreciated in Johannesburg.

I said, "You find me as I am on the point of leaving . . ." and added my name.

"That I know," he replied, with the same geniality. "And that is why I am here. Again, I apologise. My name is Ironside. Captain Edmund Ironside. I am based at Sunnyside."

I must have betrayed my bewilderment.

"I am attached to Lord Milner's staff. I understand you are a familiar of one of my colleagues."

"Up to a point," I said. "We went up on the Berg together last week – I mean, this week."

"Then I have found the right man. May I beg some more of your excellent coffee?"

Ironside then told me his tale. I suppose I believed him because, with his fresh face and hearty laugh, it was scarcely possible to imagine that the fellow was an impostor. He told me that he worked, like my new friend, in Milner's private office – "But, unlike Buchan, I am attached to what we now call the

'Intelligence' department," he explained. "To give you an idea of what I do, I have recently returned from Damaraland . . ."

"Great heavens," I interrupted. "I know the South-West well – I worked there for a time."

"Then we'll have to exchange notes. Wonderful part of the world – pity about the Hun! But first, there is work to be done nearer home, and His Excellency was hoping that you might be persuaded to help us . . ."

This was a bit steep. I said, "I'm just an amateur farmer. A mining engineer before that – I came down from Rhodesia only last year. How could I possibly help?"

"Because, Mr Green, I think that you are already helping us."

We seemed to agree to lay our cards on the table. He told me that he understood that I had met Buchan and a Boer friend, and he guessed that we had had our adventures together, to which I agreed. I had to ask him how he knew, since I doubted that Buchan had been in a position to communicate with his colleagues in Johannesburg. (That thought reminded me that the poor fellow was at this moment imprisoned in the Lodge on the Berg, and in my agitation I strode the length of the *stoep*, wondering whether and how I could – should – get rid of my guest.)

"We do not know where Buchan is," volunteered Ironside. "Indeed, I have no idea where he has got to, because we have had no word from him – directly. Nor can we contact Colonel Wheatcroft, who is out on patrol. But we have received another message, which is why I have travelled down here post haste and why I am so relieved to have found you."

I threw myself back on the couch, abandoned my plan for a speedy departure, and shouted for more coffee. I said, "I think you had better explain."

* * *

The essence of Ironside's story was that, less than twenty-four hours earlier, the High Commissioner had received an urgent telegram using the military cypher and which was signed "Springbok". "That is the *nom de plume* of Minnaar, when he condescends to work with us. I have the text of that flimsy clear in my head," said Ironside, who was skilled, I supposed, in committing such things to memory. "It read as follows: 'We make progress on the Berg but understand further consignment sighted at Rooi Rand in Number Four Shaft. Since we are fully engaged here, urge you investigate by making contact with our new and trusted associate' – that's you, Mr Green, he gave us the name of this farm – 'who would be best guide as he is mining expert and is fully in the picture . . .'

"So!" continued Ironside, whose self-confidence seemed remarkable in a man who must be younger even than Buchan, "His Excellency ordered me to proceed with utmost speed since it is essential that this business be restricted to the smallest circle – which, sir, evidently now includes you. They gave me a special train down to Nelspruit, which got me to the Lowveld in no time. Then I rode up here like the devil, through the moonlight. I had a bit of a turn when your boys said you had just left, but then they realised that your horse was still waiting at the stable, and here you are!"

I said, "I'm very anxious to get back to the Berg. My friends have a few problems up there, and we'll need to find Wheatcroft . . ."

"But I suppose that you managed to find part of the treasure. Well done! You'll all get a medal, mark my words."

"I think we assumed we'd found all the treasure. It's under a waterfall – at least I think it is, I didn't see it myself."

"But now we are told there's more of the gold, across in the other direction at Rooi Rand.[61] So we'd better dash off and get it."

"We?"

"But that's why I'm here. You're the mining engineer and I'll need your help in getting into the Rooi Rand shafts – I've never been underground in my life, and this is all so desperately confidential that we have to use a mining man we can trust. That must be what Minnaar was getting at . . ."

Now hold on, I thought, why should they assume they can call on me like this? Schalk went off to find Wheatcroft, that was our agreement, and he must have sent off this message about Rooi Rand pretty soon after we separated, though goodness knows how he discovered there was another hiding place. My responsibility is to get back to the Lodge to relieve young Buchan.

I tried to explain this to the Captain, but he had little time for my protests about the perils on the Berg. Nonsense, he said, you are surely exaggerating. "I promise you, Douglas" – I noticed that we were by now on intimate terms – "I have more faith in my colleague's stamina than you – and I have known the fellow much longer! He can surely cope with one old man, one pretty lady, and a crowd of kaffirs at the gate. He can't be in real danger because, as you have explained to me, they need him since he alone can tell them where the gold is. And you and I both know that he would never, ever divulge that secret. Do we not?"

It occurred to me to wonder whether Ironside was truly a friend of Buchan, but I have never been fast-witted in debate and I had to concede his point, which was that we could risk

---

61 JB appears to be concealing the true name of this mine. There is no "Rooi Rand", though the name appears on a map in *Prester John*. There were many small gold mines at this time, along the length of the Berg.

leaving Buchan another twenty-four hours on the Berg while we – Ironside and I – made a rapid diversion, at Lord Milner's express instruction, to Rooi Rand to investigate Schalk Minnaar's report. I had to grant that it was not possible to confide this mission to any of the other mining men in the district.

I made my last protest, even as I rose to my feet and summoned my boys. "Edmund," said I, "I promise you that I don't like this. Not just because I think we should both be riding for the Berg. Not because I hesitate to do my duty – I'll do whatever the High Commissioner requires . . .". I stopped. I did not want to add that, deep in that instinct which has saved my skin over the years, I did not believe in Rooi Rand.

He gave me a charming, daredevil grin. "Let's drop this 'Edmund'," he said. "All my friends call me 'Tiny'. Heaven knows why!"

I had a couple of decent horses, so we left Ironside's exhausted creature at Edenend and we made pretty good time. Ironside claimed to be an Artillery man but, as I said to him after a few miles, he would have qualified for any Cavalry regiment of my acquaintance. We did the sensible thing and dismounted every hour, and in these intervals we began to know each other. He had fought in the recent war, he told me, and had then been seconded to Intelligence, which took him to South-West;[62] he had, he modestly confessed, a talent for languages and had soon picked up the *taal* so that he soon spoke it as easily as he did German, which meant he could move around Damaraland like a fish in water. I admitted to him that I shared some of these qualifications,

62 Ironside would return to South-West Africa in 1904 when he used his languages to pass as a Boer transport contractor working for the Germans (and reporting to his British superiors). He was awarded a German medal.

which soon led us to talk of our respective adventures in the territory, of our friendship with the Herero tribe, of treks into Etosha and Owambo, and, inevitably, of our experience of our European brothers, the colonial masters of that vast and tragic land. In this context I mentioned Major S. Ironside hastily prayed me to say no more of the man, which I took to mean that it would embarrass him to be required to explain why we employed such characters. So we chatted, and we rode again, and I was still in a funk. It was all very well for Ironside to assure me that I was doing my duty, but in my heart I knew that I was betraying a truer loyalty.

It was on these dusty tracks, I now realise, that Ironside unburdened me, so cleverly, of the story of the past week. I scarcely noticed at the time that he can have known nothing of Schalk's arrival at M'Chudi's *kraal*, of our encounter with the German party, of Buchan's understanding of the meaning of the waterfall, of his and Schalk's discovery of the gold, and of our subsequent confinement and escape. I told him everything and Ironside listened as casually as though he was merely humouring me in the re-telling of an old story, yet he must have been memorising my every word. Only afterwards did I see that here was another reason why Lord Milner had sent his captain to Edenend – to discover for himself what had been happening to his silent envoys. Whatever ensued, Ironside would survive and would report back. That was his role. I reckoned that Tiny would rise very high in his profession, if he didn't stop a bullet on the way.

The face of the Berg, as it travels for hundreds of miles from north to south, is honeycombed with mineral deposits which promise gold and a variety of other metals. Sometimes the gold has been found, either by panning the streams, as in Pilgrims Rest, or by following the outcrop deeper into the rock, as in

Fairview. Even before the discovery of the great gold reserves on the Johannesburg Rand, there was mining fever in the Eastern Transvaal, centred around Barberton, which briefly boasted its own stock exchange, and the small gold mines of the district had helped fund the Boers throughout the war. But most of the mines were small in scale and low in output. Your local miner, generally a rough type, would arrive in hope, direct his labourers to dig a hole in a mountain, and then, more likely than not, depart in search of greener pastures. I am a copper man by background but gold is an associated trade, and when Ironside told me of Rooi Rand my heart sank, because I guessed what we would find.

True, from the point of view of a band of thieves seeking to hide a consignment of gold bars, the location might make sense, since Rooi Rand was a warren of caves and cavities, shallow shafts which had been opened, and soon deserted, by greedy and under-funded miners; to my knowledge no significant quantity of gold had ever been extracted from that particular mountain.[63] However, I realised that if you could hide a treasure in a waterfall, an abandoned mineshaft might do as well.

We made record progress and arrived in early afternoon. The track petered out in front of a decrepit and deserted corrugated-iron shack which, according to a faded board, had once been the head office of "The Rooi Rand Gold and Minerals Exploration Company, Ltd." We tethered our horses there. I said, "Now we'll have to climb. But which is Number Four shaft in this godforsaken place?"

The view beneath us belonged to a minor paradise, a deep and steep vale of grassland and bracken, with a small stream sparkling

63 Nearly a century later, Gencor was still extracting significant gold from its mines at Fairview, near Barberton, where it had introduced a modern technology in which "bugs" processed the gold-bearing ores.

far below and new hills rising beyond. There was no sign of human presence. I could summon no image of the miners who must have slaved here not so long ago, dumping their tons of yellow spoil and slimes on the green hillside and staining the bush with their acids. I used to be a miner, but when I looked out on this landscape I was happy that my colleagues had departed and left the place to wilderness.

Ironside said, "How do you mean, a 'shaft'?"

"It will be what we call an 'incline'. A vertical shaft is far too expensive, and anyhow it wouldn't be needed in a prospect like this, where the reef outcrops through a steep mountainside. The trick is to find the ore and then keep track of it – it's difficult mining, even when the gold exists."

"Will we have to go underground?"

I said, "I imagine so, once we find Number Four. I brought lamps and I don't expect we'll need go very deep."

Ironside said – and his voice was less commanding than usual – "Fine. I mention it because I haven't been underground before."

"Not even in a cave?"

"I hated caves when I was a boy."

That came out reluctantly, and when I glanced across at him he evaded my eyes. I had seen this before, it can afflict the bravest of men. I said, "Think nothing of it."

"So lead the way, Douglas!"

We toiled up the mountain for no more than a couple of hundred yards when I spotted a ruined ore trolley – a *kokopan* – and a whitewashed arrow pointing down a narrow track to "No. 4". I had no intention of going deep into any shaft. If anything were hidden here – and the bullion would be heavy, very heavy – it would have been taken only far enough to escape casual visitors.

More important, I had survived my time as a mining engineer and I had no intention of getting myself into a dangerous situation inside a network of deserted and interconnected tunnels in unstable rock. Ironside had no need to worry: I was the last man in the world to take risks inside a worked-out gold mine.

But the man was evidently unhappy. I said, "Look, let me do this," which he must have taken as an insult to his military pride, because he said, very quickly, "Not at all, I'm right behind you . . ."

"As you wish," I replied, and lit two lanterns – I would have preferred to have helmets and reinforced boots, but I thought it wise not to alarm my companion any further by mention of it. "Now follow me, and keep your head down."

That would be the smaller part of Ironside's problem. The shaft narrowed quickly to about four feet in height, which was bad enough for me – and I had spent years forcing my spine into a semi-crouch – but for this giant soldier it was bound to be an ordeal in itself. The incline was steeper than usual, so we had to steady ourselves by grasping at the rock face as we seemed to dive downwards into the dark heart of the mountain. Suddenly it was cold, and our sweat-soaked shirts were chill and clammy. Our lamps threw only a narrow beam, flickering, swaying, as we stumbled over the rough scree of the passage. Sometimes we tripped on the remnants of rusted tram lines; most of the track had been ripped out and removed. There was too much water for my comfort; we had to splash through stagnant pools, and the constant dripping from the roof became a loud cascade and we were soaked again and again. Nor did I like the piles of loose rock which obstructed our progress: this was not, I reckoned, a safe mine. I had made my career in these places, and I had made my pile out of them, but I cannot deny that I always hated the stink, the danger, the stale and dank air, of the underground. Yet I have never been afraid of it. Ironside, I knew, was afraid.

I said again, "Go back, man. This is my world, not yours."

"To hell with you," he replied, though his voice quavered.

"Tiny," said I – it is odd how one speaks so quietly in these tunnels, as though fearing that the mere vibration of a human voice will bring down the whole caboodle – "we needn't go much farther. Look!" – and I directed my lamp at our feet – "There's no sign of a spoor, no track, no footprints. No one has been here for a year."

I have rarely been so conscious of another man's terror. He was breathing too fast, I could hear him, and he was shaking – the beam of his lantern lurched uncontrollably – and I had the sense that he was on the brink of panic. No shame in that, I repeat: many a brave man has this private weakness, though it takes a braver man to confess to it.

"Another hundred yards," he managed to say.

That was a mistake. We had come to a junction, and I was going to be very careful in making my choice: this was no time to get lost in the labyrinth which lay ahead of us. I chose the left passage – there was less water underfoot – and took care to place a boulder to point our return. I stepped over another piece of rail, plunged one foot into an unsuspected puddle – and measured my length. My lantern went out. I heard a stifled cry of alarm from Ironside and, rolling on my back, saw his silhouette rear upwards in alarm. I heard the thud of his unprotected head as it hit the low roof of the shaft – and he, too, dropped his lamp, which also went out.

We were in the blackest species of darkness.

I must insist that there was no crisis in this. Ironside might well be stunned, and I had twisted an ankle, but I had dry matches and there need be no problem in finding and re-lighting our lanterns.

I don't enjoy lying in a filthy puddle in pitch dark in the depths of a mountain any more than the next man, but there's no need to *panic*. Which is what Ironside did. I won't dwell on the detail. I repeat, we all have our frailties. But the gilded captain broke down and howled, which began to give even me the heebie-jeebies, because here we were, deep in one of the remoter mountains in the colony, and His Excellency's envoy was indulging in a fit of hysterics.

I suppose I must have said something like, "Ironside, get a grip on yourself!" – words to that effect, though not, I now see, very helpful.

He did not seem to hear me. I said, "Great Scott, man, pull yourself together . . ." (All this was in total, stygian blackness, I did not not even know where the poor man was lying, though he must have been within feet of me.) He answered with an explosion of sobs – the memory of it still embarrasses me.

My only recourse was to find my matches, grope for my lamp, and – after several failures – to re-light the wick. To me, there was no great drama in our situation: we were huddled in a low shaft which led either down into an underground mystery or back to what I knew to be the certainty of the sunlight of a Transvaal afternoon. My point is that we were in no real danger. One more thing I knew, which was that there was no sign of Kruger's Gold. We had been following a false trail.

But for Ironside, the wound to his head, the sudden dazzle of the lamp, the looming shadows as I raised it to take my bearings, seemed to conspire to bring his nightmare to a climax. He gazed around him, near-screamed, leapt to his feet – and thereby dashed his bare head once more against the roof of the shaft – and raced off down the passage, in the wrong direction, *into* the mountain and into the darkness. I began to fear for him.

I bellowed, "Come back, Captain! Over here! We can leave now – our job is done!"

I fear that he could not understand me. "Douglas!" he screamed, and his voice echoed, falsetto, the length of the tunnel. "Follow me! The gold is down here. . .", and he vanished into the emptiness, where I could hear him stumbling, falling, sobbing.

I shall not dwell on the episode. I have learned in the past how to deal with panic, and I know how dangerous it is when it occurs underground. Some things have to be stopped at once. Suffice it to say that I followed the Captain, with the aid of my faltering lantern, that I persuaded him to allow me to overtake him, and that I then, with a very unsporting blow with a lump of ore, rendered him insensible. (I afterwards told him that I had had no alternative. He neither agreed nor disagreed with me, because Captain Ironside preferred to forget the episode.)

That left me with the problem of removing the body, so to speak. I could not possibly have carried him on my shoulders because, although I am no weakling, the Captain was a weight beyond my powers, leave aside the fact that in a four-foot tunnel it would have been impossible. So I stripped his trousers and made them into a halter to tie under his arms, and in that fashion I dragged him, like a dead buffalo, the length of the shaft and out into the sweet sunlight of the valley. I record it briefly, but the gradient was steep and the effort was almost too much for me. When we emerged and I had dumped him, without ceremony, on the ledge outside the shaft, I may have passed out for a moment. . .[64]

When I woke, Ironside was standing above me, swaying a little. He was blackened, soaked, bleeding from above one ear,

64 Note that this passage has no parallels with the heroics in *Prester John*, when Davie Crawfurd escapes from the cave.

and was offering me a canteen of water. I gave him my thanks, and drank deeply. He made a bit of a speech, until I told him to stow it. Then he asked me for his trousers, and complained that I had ripped his boots to shreds when I dragged him out. He was trying very hard to recover his old, debonair self, and I knew that he would never be at ease with me again. There was no need to discuss it.

I said, "No gold in that shaft. Never was and never will be . . ."

"False alarm?"

"Red herring."

Tiny, who must have had the constitution of an ox, was recovering faster than I was. "Sorry about that business," he offered. "Must have hit my head on the roof – that's a problem if you're built like me."

I said, "Forget it. Now I need to get back to the Berg. Our friend is in danger. Will you come back to Edenend with me? You can rest up . . ."

He hastily demurred; Rooi Rand had made us shy of each other. We agreed, rapidly, that we would separate at once: he would pursue Colonel Wheatcroft, through White River and up on to the Berg, and I would attack the Lodge by the direct route through Pilgrims Rest. That must take me back past Edenend for another night. Precious time had been lost which, I knew in my heart, must have cost Buchan dearly. I dreaded the discoveries that lay ahead.

Chapter Eleven

AT EDENEND, as I descended into a necessary sleep, I cursed myself for the wasted day. It was a night full of crowded, uneasy dreams, and when my boys woke me at dawn I was still worrying about the Rooi Rand business: what on earth had given Schalk the idea that there was treasure in that hillside?

But I had learned in the Matabele affair that it's a mistake to dwell on the downside immediately before an engagement – it seems to slow the reflexes – so I spurred my beast down the rutted tracks and was rattling down the main thoroughfare of Pilgrims Rest soon after the sun had climbed over the steep mountain rim that dominates the village. I looked to my errand at the local mine, but decided first to water my horse at the hotel and leave my kit in the stable lad's safe keeping while I washed the dust from my throat. At that time of morning the saloon was near-empty and I had completed my business when, through the mottled shadows, I saw a group of scallywags huddled around a table. But where I would have expected raucous laughter and the jingle of glasses from the sort of white flotsam that has nothing better to do in the middle of the morning – down-at-heel miners, long-dismissed transport-riders, the odd trooper on furlough, that sort of creature – there was only an intense murmur, a muttering of serious voices speaking Dutch, I fancied, for all the world as though a Commando of Boers was democratically planning its sortie for the next day. I snorted at my own imagination – the war was over! – and strode to the door, but when I glanced back the sunlight darted into the room and I saw that at the head of the group was a familiar figure. He was perfectly clear, I could not be mistaken, it was Schalk Minnaar. He looked up and saw me.

He smiled, like an uncle who has seen his favourite nephew, and when I paused in the doorway – because I was nonplussed, I didn't quite know why – he said a word to his friends, slipped through the thicket of benches and tables, and laid his arm on my shoulder, guiding me out into the street.

"Douglas, my friend, I thought I had missed you."

"What the hell are you doing here?"

It may have come out a little stronger than I intended, but I had been startled, and almost, for some instinctive reason, alarmed: this had not been a part of my plan.

"How do you mean?" His eyes gazed into mine, half-surprised, half-mocking.

"Schalk, you're supposed to have gone to Sabie."

"So I did."

"And brief Wheatcroft."

"As I did."

"Then – why didn't you stay with him and lead him back to the Lodge?"

"Because, my friend, he decided to take the route through Lydenburg and approach M'Chudi from the west. I preferred to get there quicker, so I came round this way . . ."

"And then you telegraphed some nonsense about Rooi Rand."

"Was it not true?"

"Nothing in it. They sent down Ironside and I wasted a day."

"I am sorry for that. It seems I was deceived."

He paused and then looked at me thoughtfully. "But why did Ironside's visit concern you? I assumed you would have left by then. I told the Colonel you were in a hurry."

I must have looked abashed. "I had a bad day after I left you and had to spend the night at Edenend." Schalk was giving me a very candid gaze. He said quietly, though it only compounded my guilt, "I hope the little *baas* up on the Berg is holding on."

"Good God, what do you think they are doing to him?"

Schalk said, "I have never loved a German since I saw them at work in South-West. Remember, there are three of them to keep in our sights, not two – the third is the worst of the bunch and he's down here in this very *dorp*. He frightened me in Swakopmund many years ago and he frightens me still. And he had a visit this morning from the Portugoose."

"Dorando?"

"The same. He was travelling like the devil. He spent ten minutes across the road there, where the Major does his dirty work, then he galloped off again just before you arrived."

"So he must have been bringing news from the Lodge."

We looked at each other and kept silence. Why would Dorando have brought a message to the Major if his master and mistress were not in some alliance with the Prussian? And what would that message tell if not to confirm that the gold was found and they were ready to bring it out, presumably under the Major's protection – and yes, the Old Man would need transport, because we had borrowed his Cape-cart and the gold would need a wagon, you don't carry bullion and coin on pack-horses? But would the Major get to the Lodge before Colonel Wheatcroft? And what of M'Chudi and his warriors, and Buchan so vulnerable in that house? . . . All this I stumbled to explain to Schalk, who winced and frowned and then said, "Not so fast, *Meneer*.

The tracker does not overrun the buck – you are reading too much from a thin spoor."

I have never laid claim to great schooling, and my wits may not always be of the fastest, but I saw no need to defer to this old Boer as meekly as Buchan invariably did.

"Then why else should Dorando ride down here in a muck sweat?"

"All we can be sure of is that they need something of the Major."

"Then we'll have to take a shufti at the police station to see what's going on . . ."

That was a mistake, and Schalk ought to have forbidden it, but there was a tension between us and we did not talk it through. He looked as unhappy as sin, but I would have none of it: "Here's a chance for you to test your Theory of Disguise," I mocked him, which made him angry, so he said, "What are you telling me I must do?"

"It won't take a minute. We need to know if he's getting ready to move. I'll walk in at the front gate and distract the sergeant, while you scout out the yard at the back."

"What about the kaffir guards?"

"Come on, Schalk, they'll never dare challenge a white man, you know that."

The sergeant was a pleasant lad who turned out to come from Norfolk, and he showed a proper concern for my tale of stock theft at Edenend. We were starting the paperwork when we both heard a noise like a fox in a chicken roost coming from the direction of the stable yard in the rear of the station. Off rushed the sergeant, followed by me.

There, in front of a couple of long-axle transport wagons and a trio of astonished Native constables, a great giant of a European, in army uniform but hatless, was holding the wretched Schalk high in the air. He had him from behind, gripped by the shoulders and the armpits in an enormous, ape-like grasp, and he was shaking him as a bad-tempered child shakes a rag doll, bellowing the while in a stentorian rage. For the first and only time I saw an expression of terror on Schalk's face, as though he knew that this animal was perfectly capable of undoing every bone in his body. He kicked and struggled and roared his own defiance, but it was an uneven match and the reproachful expression he cast me showed that he knew it.

Schalk had no gun and I had left mine at the hotel, and anyhow it would not have done to open fire on a Major in the British Army even if he were only a hired hand, at least not while there were witnesses, but Schalk, although he must have feared that his life was being squeezed out of him, kept up a torrent of the foulest Dutch leavened with German words which I had never heard even in Windhoek, until I decided that, irrespective of Schalk being my friend, this bullying must stop – I have all my life detested a bully – so, as the blood roared into my ears and my eyesight misted over, I stepped up to Major S. (for I had realised this giant oaf must be he) and punched him with all my strength on the nose. Then I became unconscious.

When I came to, I found that I was in a well. At least, it seemed to be a well because there was blackness to all sides, and I was lying in water, and far, far above there was a circle of blue sky. A steam hammer was pounding at my head. I sank back into oblivion.

I woke again and may have groaned out loud and a familar accent said, "Douglas, are you with me? That *Engelse* sergeant gave you one hell of a thump."

The proportions of the well had shifted. I was in a pit, a circle of darkness, but the sky was closer and I could see that it was the pale blue of early afternoon. My clothes were wet and something was stinking and foul. I said, "Where are we?"

"In the Major's private *tronk*. It's an old blockhouse, down by the *spruit*. He doesn't want us in the town gaol, he's giving us first-class treatment."

My sight was coming back fast. I could see now that we were on the bare earth of a stone tower: to judge from the black patches on the rounded cement wall it had probably been burned out at some point in the fighting. There was no roof left and when I turned my head – cautiously, carefully, painfully – I saw a massive oak door against which Schalk Minnaar was leaning, as relaxed as a Free State farmer watching his mealies grow. There was nothing else: not an item of furniture, not a jug, not a bucket. The ground was a foul midden; the place must have been recently occupied, and were it not for the open roof the stench would have been overwhelming.

I said, "The man must be mad – to assault and lock up the High Commissioner's men like this . . ."

"Not so fast," said Schalk, for the second time that day. "He can claim he didn't have any reason to connect us with the young *baas* from Sunnyside. He recognised me as an old *skelm* from his past, and he'd never seen you from Adam until you bloodied his nose."

I snorted, not without satisfaction. "How is he?"

"He'll still be bleeding. Like the pig he is."

"And you?"

"He let go of me pretty damn quick. *Dankie*! He's too big for me, that one."

The clouds were lifting, but only slowly, from my brain.

"So what do we do?"

"We can't stay here. We're at his mercy."

"But he can't *do* anything to us. We can insist he check with Jo'burg and with Wheatcroft."

Schalk shook his head. "I think he's going to kill us," he said, with a nonchalance that froze my blood.

"Why? How could he get away with it?"

"Because he must know he is very close to the gold. Then he can pop over into Portuguese East in a few hours and he'll be safe. You and I know too much. And he's mad, as you just said."

"So we have to get out – somehow – at once. Then get word to Wheatcroft up on the Berg."

"*Ja,*" said Schalk Minnaar. "Pretty damn quick . . ."

Best to clear my head and check the damage, he told me, so he gave me an arm and hauled me out of the filth, then probed my scalp with sly and gentle fingers, tut-tutting as he found a lump that felt to me to be the size of an ostrich egg. It was fortunate that I had a skull as thick as Lobengula's. "Walk," he commanded, and I set off on a circuit of the pit. The slabs had been mortared flush together, smooth as a billiard ball, and on the smoke-blackened patches there were scratches and scrawls, unreadable, indecipherable, the frantic messages of desperate men. The door was made of railway sleepers, hardwood pitted by termites but massive, hopeless.

"There'll be sentries."

"I think not. I heard him ordering them back to the station. He won't want any witnesses, and he knows we'll be safe here, like cattle in a pen. I reckon he'll deal with us as soon as he's ready to break camp, because he won't be coming back. But he can't tell his men that."

"Doesn't he know that Wheatcroft will be up on the Berg before him?"

"Let's hope not," said Schalk.

That, I realised, was no great consolation for us. I said again, "We have to get out. Let's make a plan . . ."

It was absurdly simple, there was only one way out, it was perfectly obvious – we had to go through the open roof. We circled the wall very slowly, separately, again and again, searching for a toehold, some sort of ladder to the heavens. There was nothing, it was as if the cement had been sanded to a fine art, the thinnest fissures plugged with mortar. I reflected that we were not the first of the Major's victims to perform this exercise. The wall was sheer and unclimbable: only a gecko could have escaped. Could we gouge out the mortar and make ourselves a stairway? Impossible, we had nothing, our knives had been removed.

Schalk said suddenly, "How tall are you?"

"Well over six."

"And I've always been the runt of the litter, but I'm not so short . . ."

He was also, I suspected, stronger than I, but let that be . . .

"How high is this damn wall?"

"I guess fifteen feet – give or take a bit."

"Then we'll have to measure it."

His idea had the simplicity of desperation. He would climb on to my shoulders. Then, while he maintained his balance by leaning against the tower wall, I would put my hands under his feet and try to lift him, vertically, in the hope that he would be able to reach the ledge. From there, without any help from me, he would have to haul himself up by his fingertips. Once over – if undetected – he would send over a rope for me.

I said, "It's impossible."

"It mustn't be."

"If you fall backwards, you'll break your back."

"So I'm in your hands, Douglas."

"Why don't I try first?"

"Because you'll have a longer distance to pull yourself up – and a lot more weight to lift."

"Then it's worth a try."

The first bit was easy. I braced myself against the wall with my hands and he hopped, light as a *duiker*, on to my back, then scrambled on to my shoulders. Very cautiously, muttering to himself in his lingo and hanging on to my scalp, he settled his *velskoen* on my shoulders and levered himself, inch by inch – I couldn't risk looking up – until he was standing, full-length. I sensed that he was groping higher, and realised that if we had been acrobats all this would be child's play. "Now lift me, *basie*," he hissed. I took my hands away from the wall: we swayed slightly and I felt him correct the balance. I wiggled each hand in turn under his feet, steadied myself, took a deep breath and lifted. He went up much faster than I had intended: he was lighter than I expected. There was a gasp, a curse, a moment of confusion and panic, and he crashed down upon me in a flurry of limbs.

"Are you in one piece?"

He was cursing me and all creation, panting, white-faced, and there was a long scratch on his face where he must have scraped the wall. But he grinned at me, fierce-eyed.

"*Onse God*, Douglas, I touched the top. Let's do it again – but this time don't try to throw me over."

Again, the hands under the heels. Very slowly – and this was much harder for me, I felt my shoulder muscles cracking and bunching – I hoisted him higher, until I sensed his weight lift away from me. He was panting and whimpering with the effort. My arms were at full stretch, and I let go his heels and stepped back to see him clinging like a bat to the upper wall, his toes scrabbling in vain at the bricks. Suddenly he snapped, "Catch me!" and before I could move he landed full weight on my head and sent us sprawling back into the slime.

After a stunned minute of silence he said, "*Godsverdomp,*" very softly, and I said, "It's no good, Schalk, it's too high for you."

"No, no, no," he snapped, and this time the lazy charm had vanished, there was a naked ferocity of determination in his voice such as I had never heard before. "That time, just before I fell, I felt a handhold. It's a foot to the right of where you've been standing . . ."

So we tried a third time. The blood was caking on his cheek and he punched me on the shoulder, positioned me, and leapt, easy as a monkey, on to my shoulder. Again, the bracing, shuddering elevation until my arms were stretching out of their sockets. Again, the sudden awareness that he, not I, was taking the strain. Again, the scrabbling feet, the curses, the groans, then a stifled yelp of triumph, a pause, as though to muster a last, death-defying effort, a violence of scuffling and gasping and – silence.

I looked up and, sure enough, he was straddling the wall. In the next instant – we must both have had the same thought about sentries – he hastily leaned forward, pressed himself against the skyline.

"Can you get down the other side?"

"There's a *wacht-en-beetjie* bush. I'll bounce like a kiddy and never mind the thorns."[65]

"So don't be long. Make sure it's a long rope, and strong enough."

65 "Wait-a-bit" – the charming name of a species of thorn bush (e.g., see *The Island of Sheep*, ch. 4).

161

He was silhouetted against the afternoon glare, but I could just see that he was smiling down at me – that sweet smile which used to charm young Buchan.

"Douglas," he said, "thank you for your help. I'm sorry. There's something I have to do. I hope you understand."

"What on earth . . . ?"

"*Go well* . . ." he called, and dropped out of view.

I never saw him again.

Chapter Twelve

For the next five minutes I didn't believe it. I must have misheard him. He was going to get a rope. In a moment I would hear his whistle and see it floating over the parapet. So I gave him another five minutes, then another ten for good measure. I worried for him: had he walked into the arms of the sentries? Surely not. So what had happened? Another ten minutes. After that I began to think some bitter thoughts. This was more than *slim*, this was sheer bloody treachery. Why hadn't I trusted my hunter's instinct? Why had I allowed Buchan's boyish sentimentality for the Boer to distract me? Why had I decided we should split up, when Buchan had clearly meant us to work together? Why hadn't I asked what he was up to with his cronies in the saloon when he was supposed to be in Sabie? – Good God (the thought sprang unbidden into my head), could I even be sure that the message had been given to Colonel Wheatcroft? If Schalk had betrayed us in this, too, my friend was still a prisoner in the Lodge, with no rescue under way . . .

No, I was letting my imagination run away with itself. Schalk would have his own reasons for disappearing. Perhaps he was waiting to return at a safer time. Perhaps he had run into the Major – I hadn't thought of the Major for ages. Schalk had said the Major was going to kill us and he had sounded quite certain of it. I had agreed with him then and I agreed with him still.

The Major struck me as a man who was working out the last hours of his King's Commission. With Schalk on the run, he'd be even less inclined to waste his time on me, and this was a country where a body could disappear very easily. I was a Rhodesian newcomer, a stranger, a single man who kept to himself; my neighbours would scarcely notice that I had vanished. Only Buchan would worry himself about me, and like as not he was already a meal for the jackals.

This wouldn't do. I had been in some nasty scrapes before and come out in one piece. The trick was to keep one's nerve and, above all, to stifle the imagination. Fair enough, I was helpless in this trap until my gaoler came. There was no chance he would leave Pilgrims Rest until he had dealt with me. So all I had to do was wait, in the certain knowledge that my fate would not be long delayed. I sat in the dirt and watched the sky turn pale.

Major S. came for me in the gloaming. He came alone, as he must do, and he carried a pistol very carefully directed at my belly. He waved me back against the far wall – I considered a charge for the door, but what was the glory in suicide? – so I obeyed. He locked the door deliberately, without taking his eyes off me. He was smiling, I remember; he was the very image of the jovial, convivial Hun, a man of large appetites looking forward to his pleasures – until he realised that only I was there. It was ridiculous, I noted, but his brain had not conceived the possibility that there would not be two of us, and it took whole seconds for him to adjust to the shock.

I reckoned that this was going to be the only moment of the evening when I would have the advantage: sadly for me, there was little way of exploiting it. So much for my theory that Schalk had not abandoned me but had been picked up by the police.

I attempted a triumphant smile of apology: "My friend regrets that he had to leave, Major." Something like that. He took it very well. His great pear-shaped face (the nose was wonderfully swollen) flushed dark, but he managed a grimace and his voice was under control. "How?"

I shrugged like a stage Frenchman, then pointed upwards to the sky. While he was working it out, I delivered my protest, with as much dignity as I could muster. This was an outrage, etc., I was assisting my friend from Sunnyside on an official mission of which he, the Major, was well aware, my Boer colleague who had been abducted with me was on the same mission and was even now on his way to Colonel Wheatcroft to report this scandal, I demand that he telegraph the High Commissioner . . . and so on and so forth.

It was well done in the circumstances, though I say it myself, but the trouble was that it gave him time to recover himself. He let me rabbit on until I ran out of words. He was still pointing the gun, unwavering, at my stomach and the light was still bright enough for him to run no risk of missing. Would he dare shoot me on this spot? Would the tower muffle the sound? How far were we from the street? Would anyone have the nerve to inter-fere? Would anyone care? He was staring at me as though I was some sort of vermin and he was trying to identify my species. He allowed a silence, as though to show me that nothing remained for me to cling to. Then he laughed, a deep, bass chortle, a gurgling delight in this situation, and in what we both knew was to be the certain end of this encounter.

"I spit upon your Wheatcroft and your noble Lord Milner and your Sunnyside!" he declared, affably enough. "I am soon to leave this goddamn *dorp* and this miserable country. I am sick of you high and mighty English and these idiot Dutch peasants.

Tomorrow I go to collect my earnings. Then we shall be finished with you."

"So you have the gold?"

"Of course we have the gold. What are we talking about? It is you and your friends who have found it for us. I say *Danke schön* to you, sir!" and he bobbed his great head in absurd courtesy. It occurred to me that he was not entirely sober.

I said, very earnestly, "No, you don't have the gold."

"You lie. My friends have sent word and I go to collect it. But do not concern yourself, you will not be here when Lord Milner learns of it."

I said, with all the conviction I could muster, "By heaven, I assure you that your friends do not have it." Perhaps M'Chudi's warriors on the belvedere were in the back of my mind, though goodness knows that was days ago and Dorando would have told him of them.

The Major showed no inclination to end the dialogue: I was sure he had been drinking. He shook his head, as though he knew he was humouring a condemned man. "By now your young friend will have spilled the oats, as you say. Either to the oh so delighful Fräulein Ingeburg – or, if that fails, to other persuasions. There is no way he can resist, believe me! I know about these things."

"That is a very damnable lie!" I protested, and my honest indignation must have been plain in my voice. "Buchan would give his life rather than tell them where the gold is. The secret is still safe, I promise you. All you'll do is ride into the arms of your Colonel . . ."

For a moment I thought it was the end. The giant was standing poised, the gun levelled now at my head, his stubby finger taut on the trigger. But even as I readied myself I sensed that he was thinking furiously, struggling to force his addled, clumsy brain

166

to assess what I had said. Then his frown cleared and he glared at me, with a curious and surprising mischief in his eye.

"That is interesting. You make sense, Mr – I do not know your name, do I? You may have a point. There is no harm in making doubly sure, the Professor will agree. So – before I leave – *you* must tell me where the gold is hidden. Just in case you are right."

"I'll see you in hell first."

"Come, come! I told you, I am expert in discovering the truth. Do not make me angry with you – you will regret it by the time I have finished with you –"

"And then you'll shoot me. You might as well do it here and now. Because, you see, *I do not know* where the gold is. It was the other two who found it . . ." And as I said it I thought: My God, that's torn it, because he'll never believe it, although it really is the truth. Schalk and Buchan had gone to the waterfall without me.

He shook his head at me in admonition, and at that moment I thought, I have nothing left to lose, I'll have to rush him, which I did, and which he was waiting for, but he did not fire because I had persuaded him that he needed me alive, so he held me off with one gorilla arm and I even heard him bellow with glee as the gun descended above my ear, and I pitched forward, for a second time, into a dark pit.

When I swam up out of the darkness, through swift currents of nausea and pain, I was in a different place. There was no circle of sky above but a lamp was burning, low and soft, somewhere behind me. There was a strange, fusty aroma which I couldn't identify though it reminded me of something. Above, as my eyes slowly focused, was a rough plywood ceiling; the wall to my right seemed to be covered with a jumble of papers and maps. And I was bound to some sort of long wooden surface: there were cords – belts? – around my chest and hips and my legs were lashed – I couldn't tell how – and my arms were twisted, awkwardly, behind my back, manacled to two hooks. I tried to shift, and couldn't.

"Welcome to my quarters," said a familiar gruff voice. "I am over here if you can still move your stupid head."

I could, and I turned it to see the Major sitting at his ease in a swivel desk chair. He looked as though he had all the time in the world, he was almost benevolent, and there was a glass in his hand and a bottle on a table.

"Where are we?"

He must have carried me from the blockhouse.

"In my quarters, as I told you. Do not bother to make a scene. It is late and I have dismissed my men. We shall not be disturbed."

"You are mad, Major," I said. "You are out of your head. You disgrace our Crown."

"Say what you wish," replied the Hun happily. "You will soon be singing a different tune."

I said, "I repeat, I do not know where the gold is. I was not with the others when they found it." It was too late to worry that I might be betraying Buchan, not to speak of Minnaar.

"I wish I could believe you, but I cannot take risks, and you persuaded me of that. My friends are waiting for me on the Berg." He poured another glass, appeared to consider offering it to me, changed his mind, drank deeply: he seemed disposed to talk.

"Your 'friends'? You and they – *friends*?"

"But naturally. We have been friends – colleagues, partners – since they arrived here last year. The Professor is a great and wise man, a true scholar. He has advised me on my ethnography, my collection . . ."

I remembered Buchan's tale of the Native jumble in the

German's office, and now I put a name to this strange, dusty smell in what must be his inner sanctum – it was the African stink of woodsmoke and dry grass, fungus and dust, half-cured leather and old sweat. I strained to look about me in the shadows and saw with astonishment that the place was stacked high like an Indian bazaar in Mombasa. There were textiles and mats and *karosses* and beadwork, bows, arrows, quivers, knives, axes, spears long and short, dozens of clay pots in every size and style and scores of decorated gourds, cowbells, marimbas and nose-flutes, baskets of every shape and ornament, mysterious little bags, bundles of herbs, a bowl of bones – all the dusty paraphernalia that some white men think is the best part of Africa. I call it rubbish myself, but I did not want to irritate the man.

He was saying, "We are the best of friends, the Professor and I. Fräulein Ingeburg does not care for these things, but no matter –"

"And was it the Professor who knew of Kruger's Gold?"

He nodded, still perfectly amiable. There was no need for him to be discreet. "Yes, the Professor was convinced that the gold was still here in Pilgrims Rest, and honoured me by inviting me to join them. He said I would be best placed to track it down. And see – he was right!"

"But you are a soldier, Major. It is your profession, your *métier*." (I had to keep him talking, and drinking. I was straining secretly at my bonds, trying to find a point of weakness.)

"Enough! I have enough. For Germany, there is no future here. You damn English have blocked us. South-West is ours, yes, but I have enough of the desert, and there has been too much blood there – even I say it, and I am accustomed to these things. Perhaps we will defeat you yet in East Africa . . . But that is too late for me, I want to go home. I shall take my gold and retire into private life and make my family respected again. And I shall have my collection to remind me of Africa . . ."

"The Professor goes home too?"

"Ah no," said the Major, mysteriously. "It is sadly not possible for the Professor to go home."

"Miss Helga?"

The Major shrugged, and I could have sworn his expression on more sculpted features would have amounted to a hint of distaste.

I am no fool, though sometimes I may appear one, and I realised that in this deathbed confession the deathbed belonged to me. He was enjoying the secure satisfaction of gloating over his triumph. It was gratifying for me to observe his ruined nose, but that pleasure was too modest by far. I tried to shift my weight on the wooden board. It seemed to be a great battered desk, and when I squinted sideways I could see scuffed and scarred leather. I looked again and part of it was stained near-black as though an ink pot had overturned; I guessed that I was not the first to lie here, and I resolved to show this Stone Age heathen that I could play the man. But could I trust myself? Had Buchan passed through these gates before me? I strained again at my cords. There were at least two broad belts around my midriff, and the buckles held so tight that I could breathe only with caution. My arms, too, were lashed firm with ropes that cut into the flesh of my wrists. My feet protruded over the edge of the desktop. I flexed my knee, strained as though I had a savage cramp, and felt the knots ease just a fraction. I flexed again, and again . . .

The Major had been talking of his beloved collection. "Who would believe it of these animals?" he was saying. "Such simplicity – and yet such sophistication. Such variety. Every pattern, every decoration is different. And all so *primitive*, you observe, so basic, so effective. You see, they understand, and they accept, the brutish reality of their lives, as the Professor explained to me . . ."

He hauled himself to his feet, drained the glass again. "Time passes," he murmured, almost to himself. "Now will you remind me – just in case you are right about your friend – where the gold is hidden?"

I answered him with an oath.

"What was I saying? Ah yes. The Professor asked me if this means the kaffir also accepts primitive *pain* as part of life – and how long he will tolerate it. I was able to answer him, I think, in good detail. So then he wanted to know whether the white man, whose life is not so basic – you understand me? – could tolerate that pain better, or worse. You see his point?"

There was definitely more play on the rope. I wished him to keep on talking, crazed gibberish though it might be.

"I said I did not have so much experience of Europeans. I guess, I told him, that the white man is braver than the kaffir because he can understand a bigger loyalty – a wider society. The Professor said he did not agree. He said the white man can be brave under the white man's persuasions, but – and this, my friend, is what I found very interesting in the Professor's theory! – he suggested the white man will not be so brave when he is submitted to the kaffir's tricks . . ."

I said, "You're mad, both of you. Stark staring mad."

He ignored me. He was beyond my view, shuffling around in the shadows, rummaging for something or other. He loomed into view again, and this time he stood next to the desk, gazing down on me. He was flushed and sweating and I did not like his eyes.

"Consider," he murmured, "the simple requirements of the best of their witch doctors. You will have seen the bodies that are left on their miserable battlefields – you will have seen what they do to their enemies?"

I had indeed and I shuddered at the memory. After Mashonaland it was one of my few regular nightmares.

"You will know what they call *muti* – the things their witch doctor needs for his filthy brews. So they remove various – 'items', is that the word? – from their enemy's body. In particular, the intimate items . . ." He specified a number of particular favourites, still gazing down on me.

"The Professor tells me that for the best *muti* these ingredients should be taken from a living body. Had you heard that?"

Staring mad, I thought, but there was a hammer beating in my temple, I was sweating like a horse, and the Major, I could see, was sweating too, and his breathing had quickened.

"In my collection, I have some of the witch doctors' instruments. Have you seen any before?" – and he abruptly pushed in front of my face a handful of rusty ironmongery: there were a couple of short knives, a long carpenter's pincers, and an object my herdsman uses to geld the lambs.

"Interesting, no?" asked the Major, and I felt that his gaze lingered on me in a way that suggested he had forgotten he was in a hurry. "So you are certain that you cannot help me?"

"I am, you swine."

"A pity. That was what the kaffir boy said. And he was lying."

I said, "Colonel Wheatcroft will have you shot."

"Nonsense! When they find your body, it will be near the *kraals* and – if the hyenas and vultures have not got to you – they will see that you have been killed by the kaffirs and used in their traditional ways. They will be shocked because, I promise you – and I do not say these things to make a joke – you will not be a pretty sight. So sad for a handsome young man . . ."

He was very close to me; his other hand lingered, almost touching my shoulder, and another thought rushed into my mind, it was almost more unspeakable than his earlier menaces. I had heard of these foul things – there had been gossip in South-West about this side of the Prussian military – and I had always been revolted by the very idea. I caught his gaze and turned my head away, my suspicions near-confirmed. I strained frantically with both knees, levering with all my strength against the broad belts at my chest. I heard him toying with the *muti* tools; I could smell his whisky breath.

"A last time," he cooed, almost imploring, and I fancied I heard in his accent an echo of the seductive tones of Helga Ingeburg. "You can save yourself such – sadness!"

"Yes, tell you what I do not know, and then be killed for it."

He paused – he was rolling up his shirt sleeves – as though to give it serious thought, then he shook his head sadly: "You are right. I cannot let you run back to your chiefs. But on my oath, it will be an easier death for you if you are sensible . . ."

I cursed him in the foulest German I could remember from my days in Swakopmund.

"God in Heaven, it is hot in here," said the man, and proceeded to remove his shirt, tossing it behind him on to the swivel chair. His body was white and hairless and the fat hung in loose folds like an overlarge Shetland jersey.

He turned back to me and again there was the fevered, perverted gleam in his pig eyes as he stood above me. The sweat was pouring off his forehead, salt drops splashed on to my face. I blinked, twisting my head, trying to see where the blade might be – and then, it's a moment I shall never forget, I felt his paws groping at the buttons on my shirt. They lingered, as though this could only be the beginning of some filthy caress, he was

173

panting over me – and in an explosion of horror my feet lashed out in a superhuman spasm and I hurled myself away from him.

That would have saved me nothing except for the fact that I had been lying on what I believe is called a pedestal desk: that is to say, the horizontal writing surface slots into, but is not locked to, the two separate side supports which each contain a stack of drawers. What I had done was to snap the halter on my feet and to wrench the topboard from the stacks so that, after a colossal upheaval, I half-stood, swaying, staggering, in the middle of the room, but I was still strapped by my waist, chest and arms to a massive six-foot mahogany board, my heart and belly helpless to his knife.

He had stumbled heavily – was it the drink or simple astonishment? – which gave me my only chance. I hurled myself towards him in a great clatter and crash and as he rose to meet me, blade in right hand, I pirouetted in a half-circle and slammed myself *back-first* against him. I felt the thud, and heard him grunt. A drawer fell out of the burden on my back with a mighty commotion and a spilling of papers, and I hurled myself backwards again, and this time I had him jammed against the wall. The air must have gone out of him, but he was a giant of a man and I could not hold him there. The lamp was still burning and I looked frantically around the room, with all the detritus of his absurd hobby, but he had recovered his wits and I glimpsed the ape hand flash around the corner of the desktop, groping for me, distancing itself for the plunge of the knife into my neck, so I whirled and twisted again and felt the drag of the mahogany and saw the arm slash at me, and I instinctively jerked upwards to fend him off – and felt the searing pain as the blade sliced down my arm, skidding off the wristbone and, with only a faint tremor, severed one of the cords that bound me to the board.

174

Now to retreat. I prayed he had no gun. My right arm was free and I flexed the muscle to check that the damage was only skin-deep, but still I had this great shield strapped to my back as I back-pedalled across the room. He must have realised then that he had me at his mercy, he had forgotten to play games, his blood was up and he was determined to settle with me. We circled each other for a moment, I still backing away, he stalking, cautious. We were both panting with a desperate passion. I had passed before the lamp when my brain sent a last message, reminding me of something I had seen on the wall.

I turned my back on him, sweeping pots and gourds and ironware on to the floor as I went, I reached up and seized the short-handled *assegai* from its place of honour on the wall; I had it in mind to hurl it at him, but I was too slow, he must have guessed at the danger, and he threw himself upon me as I half-turned, and I felt myself go crashing, the desktop splintering under us, and then his giant's body, hairless, sweaty, gasping, crushed me on to the ground, the breath went out of me and, for the third time, I lost consciousness.

Afterwards, I realised I must have lost my senses for only a matter of seconds. My lungs demanded air, my heart kicked into action, and I found I was lying prostrate under the Major's hideous embrace; he had measured his body's length on mine and as I came to I felt him shudder in a long, slow rictus. I was wet, I realised, soaking wet, a warm liquid was pouring on to me, I was drowning in his lifeblood. He was impaled on the *assegai* – I still held the shaft, and over his shoulder I could see the broad blade protruding in the air, gleaming-wet, clean through his great carcase. When he hurled himself upon me I must have defended myself with the spear in some instinctive gesture of defence, jerking the iron erect, and the momentum of his vast weight had done the deed.

With a last effort – it was almost beyond my strength – I rolled him off me, slashed through the belts and ropes, and staggered to the other side of the room. There I vomited. I drank deeply of the bottle, and promptly vomited again. My shirt was a dark and loathsome sticky rag. I tore it off and seized a Native embroidery from the shelf and scrubbed and scraped my chest clean. Then I made myself sit very still for ten minutes. I drank again from the whisky bottle, and this time the nausea left me.

I found the Major's shirt and put it on, but first I made a point of cutting off the epaulettes and ripping off the insignia. I found a key in his pocket and put out the lamp and locked the door behind me and went out through the empty offices into the cool night. I threw the key into the *spruit*. They would find him in the morning, but I did not think they would dare to interrupt his slumbers early. The hotel knew me and would admit me. I reckoned I could risk a bath, and a meal, and a brief sleep. I needed all three.

At seven in the morning the flag was flying on the police post but there was no other sign of activity. I collected my horse from the stable lad and attended to my business. My mission was with the manager of the mining concessions, a nondescript character called Johnson, whom I'd first met in Bulawayo. When we bumped into each other in White River a few months earlier we had exclaimed at the smallness of the world and bought each other beer, but we would never be friends, he was too shifty, too anxious to please – not my totem – and I had deliberately not invited him out to Edenend. Now, I called a boy to hold the horse and made for his office in the clapboard building across from the river. These mining operations don't waste good money on fancy fittings – they keep that sort of thing for Johannesburg – and I had

176

no problem pushing past his clerks and bursting into his inner sanctum. I know this world well. There was a rolltop desk, a tattered carpet, a hefty safe in the corner and a glass cabinet of ore samples. The view from the window was finer than he deserved.

My friend was surprised but affable. He suggested coffee and I reminded myself that I had an urgent appointment on the Berg. I declined, to his evident bewilderment.

I said, "I need a favour, Johnson. Forgive me if I take this rather fast. This is an emergency."

He looked properly concerned.

I said, "You have the records of this operation?"

Mining engineers are all the same – they are punctilious, and also sentimental, and they always keep a history of a mine from its earliest days. A sort of museum.

He looked confused; he said, "Douglas, what on earth are you looking for – ?"

I said, "Do your records include the war? Yes, I know you weren't here yourself. I mean the period when the Boers were running this place."[66]

He was not a Dutchman and he said yes.

"I want some *veldponde*. That's right, the coins – they were stamping them here. I need to borrow some –"

"You must be out of your mind."

He hadn't denied that he had any. I knew he would have kept some specimens for his company collection of specie. It was an indulgence that all his breed subscribed to.

I said, "I can't explain now, but I promise that one day I will tell you a good yarn. The simple fact is that I need to borrow a couple

66 The *Staatsmund te Velde* produced 986 *veldponde*, according to *Valley of Gold* by A.P. Cartwright. Pilgrims Rest produced "payable" gold from 1873 to 1971, which is said to make it the second longest-running gold producing property in the world.

of the things. You will have them back, I guarantee, but I have to borrow them for a few days."

"But why? They're not legal tender any more – I'm not even supposed to have any, you know that."

"Albert," I said, "If you don't deliver – *now, at once* – I'm going to blow your head off." Which may have been when he noticed I was carrying a rifle.

It took three minutes more to secure what I needed. As I say, we would never be friends. "Thank you, Albert," I said. "You're a white man."

Time was surely running out. I forced my horse cruelly, but it was mid-afternoon by the time I was approaching M'Chudi's *kraal*. The children saw me first and scattered, screaming, into their huts or into the surrounding bush. Their mothers and their sisters ran out to gaze at me and put up a babble of consternation, while the old men, squatting in the shadows, perused me silently with the cooler perspective of age. There were very few young men, I noticed – but then I remembered that most of them would be barricading the Lodge. I rode briskly through the huts and stopped in front of the Chief's larger structure, as I had done in happier times before.

M'Chudi emerged, blinking, and his astonishment could not be concealed. I gave him the formal greetings in the kaffir tongue and he responded automatically even as I saw him looking around to rally his men.

I slid down from the pony and, with only the faintest sense of regret and apprehension, held out to him my rifle: I grasped it in my two hands and placed it in his. He looked at me, bewildered yet attempting to assess the situation. He was a fine figure of a man.

"Chief M'Chudi," I said in English, "I have always played

straight with you and I think those of your men who have worked for me have spoken well of me . . ."

He nodded, and still gripped the rifle. I had a sense that the villagers were gathering behind my back.

I said again, "Chief M'Chudi, I have come back to you, to offer you my life –"

The Native gazed at me with furrowed brow. His lips formed the word 'Why?' though no sound came. Now I could hear a ripple of noise from the crowd behind me and knew that they were inching closer.

"Even though I escaped from that house," I said, "and your men were sent to capture me, I have returned. I come in peace. I come to help you. I come to speak privately with you, where no eyes can see us . . ."

"Why do I need to talk with you?" I remember that at that moment the sun slipped behind the crag, its rays splintering to dazzle me for a brief second.

I put my hand in my pocket and then held it open-palmed before him so that only he could see what it contained. I was holding three dull gold *veldponde*. "You and I know what these are," I said, very quietly.

He tried to deny it. There must have been a moment when his instinct was to kill me on that spot.

I said, "Wait, Chief! I found them in the house of the Germans. The old man has discovered a place of treasure . . ."

Chief M'Chudi said, in a quiet and conversational tone though I wonder now what it cost him, "Let us go into my hut. I shall tell my people to return to their work."

He escorted me to a hut (his young men hustled me, but I ignored them) and, to no surprise of mine since it was dark by this time, he asked me, civilly enough, if I would be his guest for the night; he even made some apology in suggesting it. I understood so clearly what he had to do – to explore his waterfall, to check the hiding place – that I did not think of objecting. They gave me some filthy food and secured the door from the outside: again, I was not surprised, I had after all surrendered myself to be his prisoner. From the signs of recent repairs to the grass roof I guessed that this hut had recently been occupied by my colleague. I slept rather better than I had expected.

The consequence can be briskly told. The Chief slipped into the hut early the next morning. He was dishevelled and mud-stained from a journey and did not conceal it; he was wet and unkempt as I had not seen him before, and I have never seen a man make so manifestly painful an effort to control himself. It occurred to me that he would have torn me limb from limb if he had thought me responsible for his discovery, but he was a man of intelligence and on that sweaty climb out of the gorge he must have worked out that I was not the first of his enemies. (Remember, I had been told no detail by my two colleagues. I did not know at this time how the cave lay hidden behind its curtain of water. All I had guessed was that a handful of *veldponde* had been extracted from the treasure by the young lover of M'Chudi's wife.)

On the basis of which mutual misunderstanding, M'Chudi and I had our pow-wow and reached a very villainous agreement. I did not for a moment imagine that he intended to abide by it. I gave him reason to believe that the Germans at the Lodge were in a state of triumph and excitement at a certain recent discovery. I was able to make an obscure reference to a German mercenary soldier and discover that M'Chudi understood me immediately. I made the point that I was concerned for the health of my friend in the Lodge, and he appeared to understand that as well. I explained very carefully that the old man in the Lodge was of a different tribe from mine – and indeed, of a tribe which had a long history of enmity with mine (which was accurate enough), at which the Chief actually laughed. I told him that my concern was to rescue my friend and perhaps keep a few *veldponde* to support my new farm, once the whole treasure had been removed – at which, I recall, he shot me the most furious glare, which baffled me at the time. Most of this must have struck M'Chudi as the ripest idiocy, since he had just visited the cave, and I did not dream that he gave a damn for my future, for my friend or for my farm, but I could see that behind that wall-eye he had taken on board the fundamental and fictitious point, which was that the Professor and his niece had found the gold and the Germans must therefore be stopped. When that had been done, I had no doubt that M'Chudi would dispose of the rest of us – but we would cross that bridge when we came to it.

I had one exchange with him that has lingered in my mind. I must have referred to our English arguments with the Boers and with the Germans. "What have the quarrels of you white men to do with us?" asked the mission-kaffir, and there was venom in his voice. "We shall be here when you are all gone . . ."

"That may well be," I conceded diplomatically. "But the present argument is to do with the Germans discovering some gold."

"And whose gold is that?" asked M'Chudi in a debating tone that tempted me to curse his education. "From whose land was the gold taken? And who were the labourers who did the digging?"

It was not, I thought, a debate to pursue in the circumstances, nor was it the moment to give him a piece of my mind.

We ate our *putu* and a little later the Chief, who had cleaned himself and was wearing the traditional skins instead of his mission shirt, summoned his warriors and addressed them in a delivery too fast for me to catch more than the occasional phrase. He spoke at some length, but he never lost their attention; it was, I guessed, the oratory of a king before his Agincourt. I noticed how he offered them questions which demanded their answer and that he waited for that answer with the timing of a master actor. I knew them to be mere lads, but as they roared their responses their voices deepened to a throaty bass thunder which, had I been their enemy, would have put the fear of God into me. They cheered him, and brandished their spears at me, apparently in greeting, and M'Chudi, to my surprise, gave me back my rifle.

Then I led their charge on the Lodge.

Chapter Thirteen

THAT FIRST MORNING – I resume my own tale – encompassed all the civilised tranquillity of a country house party in a well-ordered Highlands estate, where the revels of the previous evening have been lengthy, the ladies have no intention of descending for breakfast, and – you take my point – the sportsmen have made a discreet and early departure for the slopes. I had, you can imagine, been ready for action as early as the sportsmen but I had heard nothing, except for the single and abruptly silenced bark of a dog, and I prayed that my friends had made a happy exit. Silence, I assumed, spelt success: if M'Chudi's lads had intercepted them, the din would not have escaped us in the Lodge. I cannot claim that I went back to sleep, but I took care not to emerge for another hour or two, when I joined my host at the breakfast table that was laid on the *stoep*. I was suitably vague about the activities of my friends, and by and large put up an accurate impression of a dignified and polite young official who had cause to think he was being detained against his will. There were storm clouds over the Lowveld, I noticed.

Our courtesies across the kedgeree were interrupted by a clatter and a clamour from the direction of the stables and a high-pitched babble; I saw, briefly, a dishevelled Dorando calling for his master from beyond the steps. He was in a lather, his white suit smeared with dust and mud, and when he caught my eye

I reckoned I would be wise to remember that he was not my friend. The Old Man rushed off with the briefest apology, silencing the hysterical Lusitanian and dragging him around the corner so that I could only hear a confused gabble of voices. I concealed my mirth and attacked the eggs. When I looked up Miss Ingeburg was gazing at me from the doorway. She was wearing some sort of flowery gown and I could not read the message in her eyes.

"You will have gathered," I said, "that my friends had to leave. They asked me to apologise for any discourtesy."

"I shall take coffee only," she declared, "and perhaps the guavas . . ." and took her seat, secure in the assumption that I would play the servant. Which of course I did.

There was something unearthly in this. Her uncle joined us a few minutes later, called for fresh tea from the servants, greeted his niece affectionately, and nothing was said. So this, I thought, is our European civilisation: we sit here in beauty and indeed in luxury, and talk of nothings, and yet we are – all of us – on a thin edge: a step beyond this invisible divide and we plunge into barbarity and evil. I looked at my captors. I was not afraid at that moment, I was hardly conscious as yet of the significance of my friends' escape, God willing, to our own world of order and society and decency, I was more conscious of what these people represented. I saw them for what they were: my fellow Europeans who had chosen to live on the other side of that glass frontier.[67]

The Old Man must have been rattled, but I grant that he showed no sign of it. He said, in his usual suave and measured tones, with a hint of a smile on his lips, "My butler is a fool

67 This is a theme which runs throughout Buchan's fiction; almost every book which he wrote can be found to relate or refer to the perilous proximity between the civilised and the barbaric – examples would be too numerous to cite.

and will suffer for it. But you should not imagine that your companions will escape the pursuit of my friend M'Chudi." He gestured, and I could faintly hear the hubbub of wild voices so that I knew the hunt must very soon be under way.

"You forget that I escaped and lived to tell the tale."

"But not in daylight."

"Meanwhile I gather that I am to remain your guest. Shall I repeat, you are detaining a senior officer of the Crown?"

"Come, come, dear boy," said the villain, and actually caressed my sleeve.

I wondered if he were mad: I glanced at Helga, who flashed me another of her smiles. They seemed to have the sort of crazed confidence that would have taken them off on the Jameson Raid.[68]

The Old Man was thinking out loud. "This is so unfortunate," he said, "but I suppose we ought to confine you – lock you in a cellar, put ropes on you – that sort of thing. If you are not to emulate your friends . . ."

"Uncle! I beg you –" breathed Helga.

"But what else can I do? This gentleman has become most precious to us."

There was no need for that sort of nonsense, I thought. I drew the line at being strapped up in some hole while heaven knows what drama was going on out in the fresh air. After all, it had been my choice to stay behind. Schalk and Douglas would by now be on their way to Wheatcroft and I did not doubt their ability to evade their pursuers. My hosts could be persuaded by rational

68 Dr Leander Starr Jameson, a lieutenant of Cecil John Rhodes, in December 1895 led a foolhardy military raid into the Transvaal in support of the *Uitlanders* in Johannesburg. It was easily overcome by Kruger's government. Historians see it as the precursor of the Anglo-Boer War.

argument to understand that their game was over, and no doubt they would soon be considering their own escape route.

I said, "I am prepared to offer you my gentleman's word that I shall not seek to follow my friends. I do not believe that my own departure will be necessary."

"Word of honour?" asked the Old Man, and gave me a candid stare. "*Parole?*"

"My word," I repeated. "I shall not try to escape in these circumstances as we all understand them."

"Then you must have a glass of sherry!" declared Helga, and giggled like the maiden she had long since ceased to be. "I'm so, so happy that you are here . . ." and she leaned forward and squeezed my hand.

It was a curious day because, quite simply, nothing actually happened up there on the Berg while my friends, I trusted, were hot on the road to White River. There was no way of judging the mood of M'Chudi's Natives, though I could observe that there was still activity at the perimeter. No one had entered or left, so far as I could tell, except for the miserable Dorando, whom I later glimpsed trudging across the meadow to the Lodge; he did not see me. When we took luncheon, the Old Man set himself to be civil so I took my opportunity and asked him to his face and in defiance of the courtesies of his table what he wanted of me. He said, "You are being disingenuous, sir."

"No, I imagine that you are seeking something. Something which must be illicit."

He laughed genially and poured more champagne. I said, "It seems that you are looking for gold. Why?"

He looked at me and said nothing: smiled again.

I said, "You have talked to my colleagues about 'waterfall gold'.

What makes you think it exists in actuality?"

He smiled yet again and it irritated me.

"So your military friend in Pilgrims Rest was indiscreet but not very precise," I said, perhaps unwisely.

Yet again, he smiled.

"What I am trying to convey," I said, and put every tone of candour I could muster into it, "is that you may be on to a very minor business. And you are taking appalling liberties in pursuit of what may be – I urge you to consider – a very marginal affair."

He smiled, and shook his head.

"So why are you so sure of yourself?"

The smiles would extend to his dying day. At last he spoke.

"My friend, I *know* that this is no petty business of a couple of *veldponde* in the pocket of a dying kaffir. Grant me a certain intelligence, please. The proof that this affair is worthy of my attention, young man, is – precisely – you! Here we see the noble lord's private secretary, no less, and hot-foot from Johannesburg. Now surely *that* must signify something. He pretends to be a Jew boy, he travels with some dubious Boer hunter, and only in the last resort does he admit to who he is. But is he here on holiday, I wonder, like me? Scarcely! And as I think of these things I begin to remember the rumours. Yes, I am an amateur student of history. I remember that in the last year of the war a lot of gold was said to have disappeared in these parts. That must have been not so very far from here, when *Oom* Paul was departing. I had assumed that it had been swallowed up by these crooked Boers. But first there was the affair of the Native boy down in Pilgrims Rest, when Chief M'Chudi became strangely agitated, and then you arrived with the mysterious hunter who has temporarily disappeared, and bringing with you the estimable Douglas – from whose presence I conclude nothing, I promise you, he is an amiable thickhead who is entranced by my niece . . ." He chuckled. "But *you*, dear sir, are a find. A real treasure!" He raised his glass to me. I was gratified to discover that I did not fear him; rather, I was curious to find out how he and his party would plan their retreat – no doubt to Portuguese East – when Schalk's escape was confirmed. I even wondered whether I would bother to urge Wheatcroft to pursue them.

As he spoke Dorando had been circling the table, clearing glasses and playing the factotum. I must have been the unwitting target of his attention, though I had noticed nothing. Helga suddenly interrupted her uncle, leaned forward abruptly and slammed her fist on the table. She spoke not to me but, over my shoulder, to the Portuguese, whom she must have seen contemplating my figure with a cordial and personal hatred. "You fool!" she snapped. "This is our guest. Without him, all is lost."

The butler vanished. He had a face, I was thinking, the colour of French mustard.[69]

"So you really meant it, Helga, when you promised to look after me?"

"I hope to convince you."

The Old Man had been observing this scene. There was a strength of will in him which made me turn my eyes away from her and face the uncle. Now I could recognise the devilry in his eyes, the evil behind the façade of gentility and scholarship, yet such was their power that I admit I felt the temptation to sue for

---

69 I do not defend this unpleasant expression, merely point out that it was later to appear with reference to the villain Henriques in *Prester John* (ch. 2), who, in addition to his poor complexion, smokes cheroots, wears pointed yellow shoes – and his "skin spoke of the tarbrush". On the other hand, compare Laputa, the great black chief, in the same book, who tells young Crawfurd: "You are too hard on Henriques. You and your friends have treated him as a kaffir, and a kaffir he is in everything but kaffir virtues . . ." (ch. 17).

peace . . . It was at that dangerous moment that he misjudged me. "My dear," he said to the woman, and there was sweetest honey in his tone: he even permitted himself to lay his pale hand on hers in a gesture that had something proprietorial in it. "My dear, would it be wiser to give our manservant the opportunity he so clearly desires and leave it to him to discover what we need to know?"

I tried to mutter something defying him to do his worst, but it was a stuttering effort and was brushed aside by Helga's fury. She snatched her hand away and berated him passionately, in German as well as in English. Her eyes blazed like a veritable Valkyrie's and her protector sank back in his chair and made gestures of apology to both of us. She even turned and seized my hand fiercely in hers.

"My uncle did not mean that. It was his silly joke."

She still held my hand in hers.

"Yes," murmured the Old Man. "A jest."

Time would have hung heavy if she had not set herself to reassure, and so to delight, me. The uncle had retreated to his siesta and Dorando no doubt to lick his wounds. We could not take exercise and I had given my word that I would not try to escape. There was neither sight nor sound of the Natives, though no one doubted that they were there; the longer this curious hiatus, the stronger my hope that my friends would shortly be briefing Wheatcroft. The woman seemed to slip into a more serious mood. For the life of me I would never understand why Douglas was so intimidated by her: true, he had lived a rough sort of life, but I would not have claimed to be a lady's man and yet I confess that I had speedily developed quite an affection for her, though I had not forgotten that there might be an impropriety in her position here. She sat at my feet and talked of her family, of her childhood, of Germany, of Africa. I do not need to repeat what she said. She took me into her confidence and – I now see it – I was flattered.

They brought sundowners before the sun was properly behind the Berg, and when I went to wash and apologised that I could not change for dinner she laughed and admitted that there would be little help for me in her uncle's wardrobe. But she went to change, into a gown that betrayed the sculpted line of her shoulders, and round her long neck she wore a cascade of stones that flickered in the moonlight. Later she called for a shawl to protect her from the evening chill, and required me to arrange the silk beneath her scented hair. The Old Man seemed subdued this evening, almost abstracted, and I decided that he must be concerned for his future. He retired early, pleading the altitude, leaving me to the port and to the company of his niece.

In the morning, as I gazed down into the empty mists of the plains, where the foliage of the bush against the sandy soil was so telescoped that the acacia trees looked like the scrawl of a child on a white page, I had to make a deuce of an effort to remind myself of my duties. Of my dangers, too: Wheatcroft would with luck be mounting his troopers, and their arrival on the Berg would certainly lead to a bit of an affray. I remembered that I had forgotten to tell Schalk that Wheatcroft was on no account to alert Major S. to his movements; somehow I must try to ascertain M'Chudi's own whereabouts; and I had promised myself in the night that I would at least broach with the Germans the wisdom of their retreating to the Portuguese border.

Today it was the Old Man who was full of spirits and Helga who seemed tired. He produced the Transvaal newspapers, only a few days old, and engaged me in a brisk and well-informed discussion of the affairs of the day, with much reference to

Chamberlain's speech in Pretoria. From that he proceeded to an analysis which I found both lucid and impressive of the reasons for the Kaiser's reversal of policy on the matter of the Portuguese role in southern Africa. He observed, I remember, that he had growing fears for the European relationship between our two nations, and briskly added some complimentary remarks about the role that he hoped I and my generation might be able to play in proving his fears misguided.

"Come," he said after luncheon (at which I had noticed, with pleasure, that Dorando was not in his usual attendance), "this summer sun is too fierce for an old man. Let us go to my study to smoke . . ."

The shutters had been half-closed and we sat in cool shade surrounded by books on all sides. The room was exceedingly wide, and was awash with books – they tumbled out of the wall-to-wall shelving into disordered piles on every sidetable and chair. I wondered how he had transported them to this mountaintop, and from where. They reminded me of my own days of scholarly ambition in Oxford, and it occurred to me that one day I might reproduce this room for myself, when I had won the wherewithal, though I doubted that I could ever aspire to the panorama from the windows behind his great oak desk. He observed that he was happy with this room and with this Lodge and hoped to extend his lease from the mining magnate who preferred to spend his days either on the Rand or in Park Lane.

I said, "You live, sir, in a fantasy world."

He allowed an expression of surprise.

I said, "I urge you – take your niece and make your retreat – get back across the border before my people arrive . . ." I knew that my professional position was such that I should not be saying this to him, and he would have known that.

He merely smiled, and I imagine he shook his head. Then he leaned forward out of the shadows that surrounded his chair and gazed steadily into my eyes. I did not understand why, but I thought it discourteous to look aside so I held his gaze for those moments and – I promise I had been sparing with the champagne that lunchtime – I felt myself drift towards some power in him; his eyes were weird and cold, I had not entirely realised the mystery of the man. At that moment I admit I became horribly fascinated by him so that I began to wonder whether I should not reconsider my enmity and – perhaps – consider joining myself to him and to his lady.[70]

Thank God my attention was distracted by the wild scream of an eagle outside the shutters and I suddenly realised that he had been trying to cast a spell over me, to hypnotise me, call it what you like. I glared back into his bright old eyes and I defied them – I think he knew it – then I broke the contact and yawned deliberately and got up to browse along his shelves and make idle chatter about the latest memoir.[71]

When I looked back at him he was once again the genial and scholarly *bon viveur*. "We have so many interests in common," he managed. "You must believe, I ask of you, my passion for Africa."

"That I do," I replied. These passions take us in different ways.

"You have friends, I am sure, in the great mining houses. As I do." I may have nodded. "I sometimes wonder where they differ from me in their motivations."

70 cf. *The Power House* (ch. 3) and *The Thirty-nine Steps* (ch. 6).
71 Buchan's villains try to use hypnotism and drugs against Hannay in both *The Thirty-nine Steps* (ch. 6) and *The Three Hostages* (chs. 5 and 6); in both he discovers he has the will-power to resist them. Hilda von Einem tries to cast a spell on Hannay in *Greenmantle* (ch. 14). There is a hint of hypnotism in *The Power House* (ch. 3).

This facile nonsense irritated me. "They concern themselves with the development of this country," I protested.

"Or rather, the enrichment of their shareholders."

"They give employment to thousands of Natives."

"Our friend Mr Green pays higher wages and gives better terms of employment."

"They have the long-term interests of this country at heart."

"But so do I!"

The conversation had become ridiculous. I said, with weariness undisguised, "Oh come on! You just want the gold."

He said, "So where in that do I differ from your Johannesburg friends?"

"You'll be telling me next that the gold belongs to M'Chudi rather than to the government I represent." (I notice only now as I pen this report that we had both dropped any claim to ignorance about the nature of the treasure.)

"In my considered opinion it belongs as much to Chief M'Chudi, on behalf of his people whose land this is and whose labour extracted it, as to any distant authority. As I suspect, sir, you yourself privately understand. You see, I am a bit of an anarchist . . ."

"Property is theft, you'll be telling me next."

"Ah no! I lack the logic of you young people. 'Theft' is a word I abhor."

And with that he got up briskly, made his apologies, and left me alone in his cool and seductive study. Where I admit that I allowed myself to sleep for an hour, since I had nothing else to distract me.

Let me move on to the next day. My detention had become embarrassing. When I gave my parole I had not thought it would extend more than a few hours. Yet M'Chudi's men were still audible at the perimeter and there was no sign of my friends' return. The Old Man, on those occasions when I encountered him, was courtesy personified. Helga, who was always with me, had turned my imprisonment into a holiday. But I was seized with anxieties. Schalk and Douglas had not been recaptured by Dorando or M'Chudi, of that I could be certain. So where were they? Where was Wheatcroft? How long was I to hold out against the blandishments and the charms of my new German friends before they lost patience? They had attempted all manner of persuasion; I had it in mind that they might be thinking of harsher measures, and I wondered how I would cope with that prospect.[72]

Not that there was any sign of it that next morning, which dawned with the lambent intensity of clear light which is so typical of the Berg in this season. The previous day there had been heavy storms on the slopes below us, but the clouds had been swept away by the night breezes and we had the sense that we could gaze out from the cliff as far as the Indian Ocean (I exaggerate only to make my point). It was the sort of morning when all but the most curmudgeonly character wakes with a sense of revelation and delight.

Helga was full of both, or something approximate, and made

72 At this point I am obliged to refer to the delicate matter of the narrator's relationship with Helga Ingeburg. Not a hint of impropriety enters these pages, but JB was evidently fascinated by this sophisticated and beautiful older woman. We may remember, too, that at this point in the narrative the Germans were using every tactic to extract from the young official the location of Kruger's Gold.

I shall not descend to vulgarity in drawing attention to this opaque passage, but if I were better qualified in psychoanalytical criticism I might wonder whether Helga Ingeburg was a model for the dastardly Hilda von Einem of *Greenmantle*. One might, from the evidence of this chapter, wonder whether, for the young and immature JB, Helga was indeed the "Von Einem" – the first, the "Number One" – of his life. It becomes immediately clear, I need hardly add, that she failed in her efforts to make him betray his trust.

breakfast on the *stoep* into a triumph of the social season. The Old Man joined us rather late and seemed, I thought, preoccupied.

When I look back on those days I realise that I had by this time become ridiculously *disconnected* from the realities that ought to have preoccupied me. I now see that I had accepted the fact of my imprisonment, and also that I had agreed to the indefinite status of my volunteered parole. What had happened, I thought, was that I had abdicated my own proper responsibility for this particular affair of state by the act of handing over to Schalk and Douglas: when I thought of it like this I shuddered because I knew that Lord Milner would not have permitted it. I sat here on the Berg in the morning sunshine, apparently at the greatest of ease and in the lap of luxury, and I tasted wormwood. I knew myself, I knew that I had given up: it was worse than cowardice. I do not say that I ceased to relish my breakfast eggs and bacon, but at that moment I discovered that I could not carry on any longer in this – yes, this *irresponsible* – way. My colleagues had been given their opportunity; now I must re-enter the drama.

As if on cue, the Old Man asked me to join him once more in his study. Helga had already taken her morning constitutional with me along the clifftop, where the mountain breeze tempered the African sun, but the distance was not taxing and she had spoken of her need for a gallop, which, she agreed, was impossible to both of us so long as the perimeter was barred. There was no suggestion that I was to be set free. I repeated, this time to Helga, my most formal complaint at this detention of the High Commissioner's private secretary; she acknowledged it most prettily. "Surely you are happier here than in dreary Johannesburg . . ." and so on.

So there I was in her uncle's splendid study, chatting not unhappily about the latest squabbles in the elegant parliament building in Cape Town. He pressed on me a noontime seltzer and – I write of this in retrospect – from that moment I date my confusion. I see that my description of the previous day's encounter confirms that I have never been sympathetic to hypnosis, which the Old Man may or may not have attempted, but I would not claim to be more immune than the next man to narcotic drugs, and I now believe that that was what, in their desperation and after all their other persuasion, they had decided to subject me to. I can still remember the expression on Dorando's face as he served me a second bubbling glass.

To report the events of the next forty-eight hours is near-impossible: now that I attempt it in these pages there is no one with whom I can check my bemused and disorganised memories. I know that I sat in a deep leather chair (it reminded me of my London club) while my host pottered around the great room, closing the shutters, driving out the sunlight with an explanation that referred to his advancing age. I think that I was smoking, though the taste of the tobacco was dry in my mouth and I stubbed out the weed and drank deeply from my glass. I felt a lethargy unbecoming to my years, and I recollect that I resolved to defy this paralysis. There was one louvre still ajar in the far corner and I remember gazing at the midday sunshine as it slotted through the lathes. Or rather, I gazed at the parallel pattern it projected on to the tribal rugs on the floor beneath. The mathematics of those patterns interested me enormously; I studied them happily and thought I saw where the Native designer had missed her opportunity. Someone had replenished my glass and I made to protest but let the gesture go . . . The pattern on the rug was shifting, but with a delicious hesitation. I hoped they would not close that window too.

Note that I was entirely unafraid.

Nevertheless, I knew that my wits were drifting. "Responsibility!" I had told myself so few minutes ago, and I remembered it. "What would Lord Milner expect of you? Take back your *responsibility*!" That would do well enough for another day. The Lodge was a version of paradise for me, a place of delights beyond the real and its tedious concerns. The lady attended me; her protector was tolerant and hospitable; there were lines running through my head where the poet speaks of Lotus-eating . . .

All things would be solved in due course. My young life, I reckoned, had so far been conducted with too much stress and challenge and haste; here I was set free of these things, I was permitted to take my ease. True, I should one day be called to account, but I could see no urgency. My energy was inadequate to the challenge. I had a sense, accumulated over months, that I had been overworked and unacknowledged for it; here was my chance to relax and recoup at last. I knew that I was dozing – and again I saw no harm in it, it was siesta-time on the Highveld, I had a right to close my eyes for a moment, what else was there to demand my attention? Schalk and Douglas had volunteered for the fray: there was nothing I could do. I was, for once in my Calvinist life, absolved of duty.

Helga was there with me. I knew that she filled my glass and put her hand on my brow. Perhaps I felt her lips touch my cheek. I tried to mutter that I needed to sleep. She chided me for my indolence and comforted me before she disappeared. Then her uncle was with me, somewhere in the shadows of the room. I could not see him but I had a sensation of his presence before I heard him, voice gentle and assuring as I remember my grandfather's late at night in the manse.

He said, "My friend, are you well?"

I tried to say "Certainly!" and gave the word all my concentration though I don't know how it emerged.

His voice, from somewhere behind me, said, "That is excellent. Do you remember where you are?"

I said, "Certainly!" – again and with similar emphasis and, I now suspect, with similar effect.

"That is very good indeed," replied my German enemy. "Then you will know why you are here?"

I said, "Certainly," and this time my brain signalled to me that we were not so lost and hopeless as might appear. Indeed, my keen young brain cells, with the assistance of an undamaged liver and a vigorous digestion, were telling me that I need not be so incapable as the world supposed.

In that moment lay my salvation. For the hours that followed I would be incapable of rational conversation and of autonomous behaviour, but I would never be utterly subject to my interrogator's will. He was able to play his tricks with me, but he had from this beginning failed to control me. And his main problem, he soon discovered, was to keep me awake. I have a memory of a long and drowsy interrogation in which, quite literally, I must have kept falling asleep in the middle of a question: I remember the Old Man shouting at me, shaking my shoulders and (I think, I cannot be certain) I have an image of Helga leaning over me, urging me to try harder. Once, in a moment of lucidity, I heard him cursing Dorando for overdoing the potion.

It must have lasted for many tedious hours. I can with hindsight work out that another night, perhaps two, must somehow have intervened, but I have no memory of it. I admit, to my shame, that I cannot have been altogether hostile to their interrogation. I remember telling them cheerfully about the waterfall. "But we know about a waterfall. *Which* waterfall?", demanded the Old

Man before my attention wandered. I may have told them about a cave, but I doubt whether my slurred speech associated the cave with a waterfall. I know I talked at length about the Major, because in my half-sleep I was having nightmares about a gross Prussian pursuing me over the Berg, but that would hardly have taught them anything they did not know. I probably professed respect for M'Chudi and affection for Douglas and something else for Helga – but I would have tried to suppress the last because I was enough awake to know that I was addressing her uncle.

Once, with Helga's pleading encouragement, I surfaced from this half-world to some minutes of clearer consciousness. I realised that it was night again. That was when I worked out that they had fed me Native drugs to loosen my tongue. "So now you know," I may have mumbled. "Now we know what?" "That Kruger's Gold is only a mile away!" "My dear, is that true?" "Didn't I tell you just now? "Yes, but *where* is it? "At the waterfall. "But *which waterfall?*" she shouted at me, and I realised, in my last moment of lucidity before the herbs dragged me down again, that the Old Man was still with her.

"Will you take us?" said one of them.

"Any time," I replied.

"In the morning? At first light?"

"Why not?"

She said to the other man, I heard her, "But how do we get him past M'Chudi's boys?"

My fuddled brain understood it and I must have chortled as I said, or at least I tried to say, "You are the prisoners here, not me . . ." before I passed out again.

In the morning, or what I guessed was morning, she brought me coffee to my room: large jugs of it, stronger than the usual style in this household and with no offer of milk. I could not say that I was transformed by it. My Johannesburg doctor has since told me that they had taken great risks with certain Native drugs whose impact is far longer-lasting than our familiar European herbs.

"Now you will take us," she declared, as though all was agreed, "to the cave and the waterfall."

I looked blank – or tried to do so.

"What waterfall?"

"The waterfall you told us about last night." For the first time in a week she gazed on me with less than total affection.

I should here confess that my health had secretly improved in the night. I had made myself drink many pints of water and exercised my muscles and attempted to force my sluggish wits to focus on my predicament. I was a very long way from normality – my brain seemed full of smoke and the taste in my mouth was rancid – but I was on the way to becoming master of myself again. Which empowered me to confront the morning.

I repeated, "Which waterfall?"

She said, "My dear, you told us, there's a cave . . ."

"What cave?"

She pleaded with me, and touched me.

"What are you talking about?", I insisted.

The Old Man had appeared unannounced. He was seized, for the first time in our acquaintance, with a violent and untypical rage. "How dare you play these games with me?" he shrieked, or words to that effect; he laid his hand on me and hauled me upright from my bed with a force surprising for a man of his age; it did not hurt me, my body was a sack, impervious to the commands of anyone, including myself.

"You are disgraced, sir! Your master will be told of your behaviour!"

"So be it," I acknowledged this absurd threat.

"We shall go to the waterfall. *The Waterfall*! Do you hear me? Dorando will carry you."

"So be it," I may have said again. I was weak enough to agree to anything.

"Nonsense, he doesn't mean it," snapped Helga, and muttered something in rapid German to her protector. Dorando shrugged, a perfect mime of helplessness.

The Portugoose (as I shall for ever remember him) was standing by the door. I tried to greet him politely, but he would only scowl. Helga said," He is too heavy for you, Dorando, bring a pony –"

"Madame, we take him through those kaffirs?"

"Why not?"

"Madame, they will not allow it."

"Who says they will not allow it?"

"Madame –" – and here I have a bleary image of one grey-faced Portuguese scoundrel within an hour of his death. "They are not our friends any more. Since this morning they have changed. We must not go out there . . ."

We all gazed at him, uncomprehending. The house was bathed in the silence and tranquillity of early morning: daylight was blazing through the half-open windows yet it was still blessedly cool.

I remembered to play my role. I forced myself to giggle, in a horrible and rather effective falsetto. Helga jumped away from my side and glared at me suspiciously. I pretended to galvanise myself into a display of energy. It was time to get out into the open, to discover whatever mischief was brewing.

"Do you want to see this waterfall or don't you?" I essayed, tempting them with my new enthusiasm and pretending that I had decided to make the best of a bad job.

They must have exchanged glances.

"Yes, my dear."

"Then what we are waiting for?"

I stood up and walked, swaying more than was strictly necessary, towards the *stoep* and the terrace. Dorando was called forward to support my arm. We paused, automatically, to look out on the panorama below us. I could not focus properly; I was dazzled by the glare; I knew only too well that I was not in adequate control of my senses. Then we rounded the *stoep*, the four of us, and looked back, across the smooth tongue of land, towards the Berg wall and the exit, the only escape from our belvedere. Their plan must have been to take horses, balance me on one of them, and hope to pass nonchalantly through M'Chudi's men with the casual authority of the white masters going for an excursion. Then to the waterfall – and after that, it would have been the end for me.

Instead, advancing to meet us, there was Douglas Green, intent on my rescue.

Chapter Fourteen

H<small>E WAS WAITING FOR US</small>, with a great crowd of young men. I think I saw him before the others did, perhaps because they were still rational and his presence at the barricade was so supernatural that only someone as delirious as I could have credited the sight of him. But yes, I knew him at once, he was wearing his usual bush kit except that he had no hat. I think I waved to him, spontaneously, happily, as though I had spotted an old acquaintance on the next fairway.

When I say that Douglas and his young friends were waiting for us I am not being strictly accurate because, by an act of God, M'Chudi's warriors had arrived at the barrier and were about to leap over it at the very moment we four emerged from the Lodge. The coincidence did nothing to halt them. On the contrary, our coming into view must have inflamed them, confirmed them in their aggression. As they quick-marched from the *kraal* they had contented themselves with a murmured chant, nothing loud enough for us to hear – a rhythmic reconfirmation, echoed from man to man, of the purpose of their mission. M'Chudi strode next to Douglas, tossing out the sort of questions which elicited a response in unison. No need to understand the lingo, said Douglas afterwards – "Why are we on the warpath?" – that sort of thing – and the answer was "To kill the white bastards!" – or something of that stamp. Douglas said that they did not appear to find his own presence incompatible with all this, and in fact he was being greeted all the time by warriors who reminded him that they had worked in his tobacco fields. They were armed with spears: he alone carried a rifle.

So he felt it natural that he should lead them, with M'Chudi a pace to his right. The Chief had shortened the rhetoric by the time they reached the trim grass of the plateau. He had no further need to remind them of the honour of their ancestors, that had been part of his battle speech at the *kraal*. My point is that there was no blood-slavering hysteria: it was a businesslike assembly and the more effective for that. They had a job to do, which was to clear the Berg of the white man. They were not running, but they were moving fast. Against a single machine-gun it would have been pathetic, but as a charge upon four unarmed Europeans (only Dorando had had the sense to seize a gun) it was bound to be unstoppable.

My own memories, I repeat, are confused. A retreat to the house would have been the only wise course but the others hesitated. The Old Man seemed to want to hail his friend M'Chudi as though to remind him that they were allies; Helga had recognised Douglas and called out to him in a shrill salutation which had a first note of panic in it. They were crossing the open lawn much faster than we credited.

It was the Portugoose who sealed our fate. He, too, now saw Douglas and appeared not to believe the evidence of his eyes: he actually seized my arm to question it. Then he remembered that Douglas was his enemy and – I watched him – he screamed at my friend across the fast-closing enclosure and pulled up his Mauser[73] and made to aim at him. My brain was a sluggish

73 The Mauser was the principal (and very effective) rifle used by the Boer soldiers; before the war Kruger imported 37,000 of them from Germany. The British Army were issued with the Lee Enfield ·303.

creature that morning, but the drama of the moment had attacked me and I managed to hurl myself, more of a fall than a charge – too late! – against his shoulder. I saw the recoil of the rifle even as he tumbled and knew with horror that I had been too slow.

I was on my knees and watched. The drugs were still heavy on me and I had little sense of being a part of this catastrophe. I was watching Douglas, but he did not drop, he paused, saw us, raised his own gun, very grim in face, and fired once. He turned immediately to his right, and I saw that M'Chudi was lying on the turf, his limbs thrashing, and I heard a man scream. Was it M'Chudi? I thought not.

A yard to one side of me, Dorando was dying: the neck artery pumped blood in furious spurts for ten seconds, gushing through his frantic fingers, and then he was gone. Douglas the hunter had chosen the classic neck shot which, if you get it right, brings down all but a rhino. Meantime, I think I must have heard Helga cry out something in German: when I now try to grasp those quick moments of terror and confusion I have a glimpse of the Old Man seizing her arm and dragging her away. I had the wit to confiscate Dorando's Mauser and sling it on my shoulder.

Douglas said, "Can you move? I've lost control of them and M'Chudi is crocked. There'll be terrible mischief done if we can't stop them . . ."

We began to run back towards the house and the terrace. I cannot recall seeing the Germans. The servants had long since fled and inside the Lodge we could hear a monstrous commotion – the smashing of glass, the thunder of up-ended bookcases, an overturning of our elegant European world, a wild and incoherent scream of rage against us. I stumbled as we ran and Douglas paused, concerned to steady me, but I had glimpsed a torn bundle on the *stoep* and the colour of its wrappings reminded me of something and I was turning to look again when I heard a wilder hubbub at the terrace and blundered into Douglas, who had stamped to a halt and was holding his rifle as if he did not know what to do with it. He made as if to aim – his finger was on the trigger – but he could not isolate his target.

Then I focused again and looked out towards the great plains of the African Lowveld, beyond the terrace wall on the very edge of the cliff of the Berg. There were four figures, husky lads. They had discarded their spears for the moment because they were engaged in a curious sport, rather as if they were shaking a heavy eiderdown. It took me a while to realise that each was holding an extremity – an arm or a leg – of the Old Man. They swung him to and fro as in the old game of my Scottish nursery ("*Shake* the bed, *Shake* the bed, and turn the mattress *over* . . ." – is that how it goes?) and he made no sound. I hoped he was dead. No. They swung him gently, to and fro, adjusting their rhythm each to the other, and then they launched him out into space, over the Berg, and I heard him scream, Douglas denies it, but I heard him scream, and scream again. And I shall hear to my dying day the sound of his body bouncing from rock to rock, and the low rumble of the scree as it dragged him away.[74]

But there was also the bundle on the *stoep*. Some instinct revived me and I shouted to Douglas and ran across to it, oblivious of the kaffirs who were turning back from their sport on the terrace.

It was then that I learned, for the first time in my young life,

---

[74] cf. the death of the villain Medina in *The Three Hostages* (ch. 21/IV): " . . . I fell back with a sound in my ears which I pray God I may never hear again – the sound of a body rebounding dully from crag to crag, and then a long soft rumbling of screes like a snowslip . . ." It is interesting to see how Buchan had learned to polish and improve his prose in the years between writing these two similar passages.

that there are few easy deaths. Helga had been so torn and ripped by their spears that a kinder Divinity would have ended it for her, but she lingered, and in torment. There is no dignity in that brand of slaughter, no chance of nobility in suffering such as that: she screamed at us to take away the pain, she cursed us for our indifference in a jumble of German and English, she called out not for me – I noticed it – but for the Old Man. When Douglas lifted her gown to inspect her wounds he became very pale and put it back hastily, his hands scarlet and trembling. We had no drugs. God forgive me, I was tempted to give her the release of a bullet.

She died in an intensity of agony and fury which, I afterwards thought, was a proper conclusion to the violence and passion of her life. She had told me something of herself, and I would not pretend indifference. We attended her as best we could, and then, thank God, she was an empty cloth upon the sodden flagstones. We were, I remember, surrounded by young kaffirs whose clamour seemed to have sobered.

I picked her up. Douglas made to stop me, but I said, "No, I must take her away."

I never knew that anyone could be so light.[75] We walked back, staggering a little, towards M'Chudi. The destruction of the Lodge was proceeding. I said to Douglas, "What do they want?" and he said, "They are looking for the gold."

"What gold?"

"The gold I told them had been taken by the Germans –"

"But –"

"Yes, I know. I made it up. It was the only way I could turn them to our side."

I was soaked in Helga's blood. She was heavier than I had first

75 cf. *Greenmantle*, ch. 21.

thought. There was a smell of smoke, a hint of a crackle of flame. Douglas said, "Let me take her." I ignored him.

He said, "Mark my words, they will now turn on us. I only hope that M'Chudi isn't badly injured . . ."

There we were reassured. M'Chudi had been bandaged in rough rags and managed to acknowledge us. His voice was shaking, but he had his dignity intact. "Thank you, *baas*, for killing that man who shot me." Douglas nodded, and I did not intervene. I had a wild strength in me and I scarcely considered that I would have to lay Helga down.

"Now we must be gone," I said, which was a mistake because it drew M'Chudi's attention.

Remember that I had only seen M'Chudi twice, once as the Jewish Mr Goldstein in all my cosmetics and before that as myself when his young men drove me over the Berg. Now, for the first time since the engagement was joined, he looked at me properly.

It confused him, that was plain. He looked at me, at Douglas, at me again. He called out a question to one of his men and got a negative response. He paused a long time, and we could see his intelligence struggling to overcome the trauma of his injury: to understand, that was his need, and he had the courage to thrust through to the answer.

At last he said, in a conversational tone, "So it is you again, Mister –"

"What does that mean, Chief?"

"You came to my *kraal* with the blanket. Now I understand that it is you who has stolen my gold."

Douglas said, too hastily, "Chief M'Chudi, you are wrong."

"And you, Mr Green, you told me lies. You told me my friends in this great house had taken the gold. I believed you. But we have killed them and we find there is nothing in the house. So now I know that you and your friend are the real thieves."

I said, "I give you my word, Chief, that we do not have your gold. It is in your waterfall cave . . ."

M'Chudi was shaking his head. Douglas had stopped abruptly; I now understand that an ugly thought had occurred to him. The previous night he had given M'Chudi to believe that the Germans knew the secret of the gold. But now the Germans were dead and M'Chudi's secret could be safe again – if these two white men were also dead!

There was no doubting that M'Chudi had worked it out for himself. He glared at us both, as though to confirm his worst fears for the last time, and then he looked around as though to summon his people, but Douglas – whom I would never have credited with a lightning uptake – had acted. The muzzle of his rifle was rammed, painfully (I saw the Chief flinch), into M'Chudi's throat.

Said my friend: "Oh Chief! I hope you can walk. Because we are going to trek away from this place. You will walk in front of me and if you hesitate for one second I shall kill you. You will tell your young men to let us pass. And if they strike at me, even to my heart, my hand will certainly pull this trigger and you will be dead before I am. As for my friend here, he is not well and we shall have to walk slowly. Remember to tell your warriors that my friend's life is as precious as my own, and that you will answer for him."

Chief M'Chudi placed his hand on his bandage and groaned a little, perhaps to try us out. Douglas's gun did not waver.

"On your feet," he said, his voice cool and calm so that I began to appreciate for the first time the true stature of my friend. Then he turned to me and said, "Leave her here! She's dead, leave her be!" I must have protested and I remember him saying, gently, as though he were talking to a child, "We can do nothing for her. Leave her in her own place . . ." So I laid the bundle on the ground.[76]

There was a circle of men around us, edging closer, muttering to each other in consternation. Behind us I could hear the flames taking a hold on the Lodge, but neither of us could risk turning. Douglas leaned forward and seized M'Chudi by the shirt and yanked him to his feet: the man shrieked once with the pain, and gasped again as the gun snuggled into the flesh under his chin. The warriors set up a babble full of dangerous consternation. Douglas barked a series of orders in kitchen kaffir: now he said to M'Chudi, "Tell them, Chief,that you sit on the brink of eternity. If they move, you are dead. If they are wise, I promise that you will be back in your *kraal* by morning."

The Chief glared at him for a long moment, then groaned out loud, whether in pain or in fury. He spoke to his men and they fell back, grumbling. Perhaps they were also afraid: two white men and one white woman lay dead at their hands and they knew that they would not be forgiven. Or perhaps the cleverer amongst them were working out that they would be wise to silence the two surviving white witnesses.

We processed, slowly, in mutual suspicion, away from the belvedere and on to the Berg slopes. I took the lead, but had no idea of where I was headed. Sometimes Douglas called a

---

76 cf. Sandy Arbuthnot of Hilda von Einem's dead body in *Greenmantle* (ch. 21): "Then he came back – walking quite slowly up the last slope, and he was carrying something in his arms. The enemy fired no more; they realised what had happened. He laid his burden down gently in a corner of the castrol. The cap had fallen off, and the hair was breaking loose. The face was very white but there was no wound or bruise on it. 'She was killed at once,' I heard him saying. 'Her back was broken by a shell-fragment. Dick, we must bury her here . . . You see, she . . . she liked me . . .' "

command and I obeyed. He drove M'Chudi savagely, and however the wounded man staggered and stumbled the muzzle was deep in the flesh, the trigger primed. Fifty yards behind us we were shadowed by the Chief's impotent warriors. They would stay with us, we all knew, until nightfall, and then they would take their revenge.

The Lodge, you should remember, was built on the tip of a long, narrow tongue of land, almost flat and covered with smooth turf, that broke from the main Berg massif and protruded out over the eastern plains. It was protected on either side by deep and impassable ravines, dense with ancient indigenous bush. We had passed through the access point, where the Old Man had set up his perimeter defence, and were now climbing back along the slope to the mountain. Gradually the going got rougher. The smooth turf yielded to rough veld, strewn with scraggy and windswept thornbush and thick tufts of sour grass. With a strong Basuto pony it would make for easy going, but on foot it was hard work, and it was going to get steeper.

This was early afternoon. We had neither food nor water. The sun was still high, but a mountain haze, almost a cloud, protected us from the worst of the heat. Douglas was marching as though he intended to outlast the night. I was less confident. My brain was clearing but my physical strength seemed to have been sapped by the kaffir drugs. I was stumbling like an older man and as the sun began to drop towards the horizon line of the Berg above us I started to shudder with something more than physical exhaustion. Not a word passed between us. We remembered that M'Chudi could understand us.

I had no great interest in where Douglas was leading us; I might have guessed that he was aiming for the Lydenburg road, wherever that might be. Our route was deteriorating steadily: the bushes had been replaced by rocks – strangely shaped boulders, fantastical outcrops of limestone, sudden glimpses of mini-*kopjes* above mysterious glens. The mist had thickened rapidly as we climbed higher. It swirled like ether in the hollows and behind the crags, and when I saw that a thicker cloud was building up overhead I wondered whether we might find our escape in this labyrinth – but no, there were just two of us to accompany our wounded hostage, and a hundred warriors kept close to us, shadowing our every turn, treading almost in our footsteps, yet strangely, eerily silent. I wondered if any of them had thought to recover the arsenal of weapons which must have been installed in the Lodge.

M'Chudi was in a bad state by now. The man's dignity was undeniable, but his shattered shoulder was bleeding freely again and three times in ten minutes he tripped and fell, each time to be revived by Douglas with a volley of oaths and obscene abuse. Not once did Douglas remove his muzzle from M'Chudi's head: without that deterrent certainty that their Chief would die instantly, the young men would have overwhelmed us long since. But how long, I wondered, could Douglas continue? How long before M'Chudi collapsed, genuinely, and we had to carry him on our shoulders, just as I had carried Helga? Douglas would have been calculating these odds with all his experience of Damaraland, Matabeleland and points east, and I did not wish to interfere in his judgment.

It was as the sun began to topple over the Berg horizon and the mountain was suddenly covered by a tablecloth of purple cloud that I saw the moment where he took his decision. To our right we had for some time been aware of one of the more grotesque rock formations. It was like a tower, or at least a high cottage, with sheer walls on two sides, and a ledge and stone chimney where the thatch should be.

"We'll take a rest," said Douglas, as though we were strolling on the Coolins on a Whit Monday Bank Holiday, and he cut sharply and suddenly off the notional track and prodded M'Chudi, whose condition now worried me considerably, up the incline and on to an imperfect *krantz*, a sort of flat roof inadequately protected from either enemies or elements. In one respect only was the risk justified: in the flat rocks there was a pool of clear water, still fresh from the latest storm. I knelt at it and drank my fill and then I took a wet cloth and made M'Chudi suck at it again and again. But we were weakening from lack of food.

We were above the heads of our pursuers but not necessarily out of their sight. We sat, or lay, and Douglas kept the barrel very visibly embedded in M'Chudi's neck. After a few minutes the Chief either fainted or went to sleep.

I dared my first exchange. "Can you hold them off all night like this?"

Douglas said, "Our lives depend on him. Without him, we are finished."

"And his life depends on us."

"I hope his lads understand that."

It was a metaphor of South Africa.

So we sat there, defying our fate, as the dusk came down. The warriors squatted on the slope below and raised not a word, either to us or amongst themselves. Nor did they attempt to conceal themselves from us. Did they have a gun? Would they risk a shot? Douglas sat in silhouette against the evening sky, the perfect target, they could hardly miss. Next to him, jumbled askew, unconscious, the barrel of Douglas's rifle seeming to prop him upright, was their Chief, also in silhouette. I lay at their feet and racked my Kindergarten brains.

The mist was now rising all around us, just as the cloud seemed to be drifting lower. The night was unusually quiet. It worried me that I could detect so few of the harmonies of the African evening. I strained my ears to hear what the warriors were up to: they must surely have mounted a cordon around the *krantz*. Would they creep closer and closer, waiting till we dozed, and then make their charge? Or would they depute their most skilled tracker to steal up on us and risk a midnight spear thrust? I looked up and in the faint mulberry light I could see Douglas was alert as on the night he collared me at Edenend – I could even see the whites of his eyes. He spotted me and solemnly raised his thumb in greeting, and I reckoned he would have had a jest for me if we had not been playing dumb.

But no – I had heard something. Not below the *krantz*, where the warriors had last been seen, but behind us, on the higher slope. Had I heard it or sensed it? Certainly I had seen nothing, but at this time of night the senses get easily confused. I strained my eyes and could only see the wisps of misty cloud drifting around us on the evening breeze. Yet still my intuition, normally so clumsy a faculty, persisted in its message. There was something out there in the bush and I was suddenly terrified, convinced that the warriors had lost patience or decided that their Chief's wounds were mortal and had resolved to end the affair. If that was their decision, then our minutes were numbered. The breeze seemed to bring me another message, a more urgent warning, primitive in its instinctive truth, and now I was chill and shaking. I stood up very carefully, taking pains that Douglas was aware of what I was doing, and I looked around.

Still nothing. I became impatient and stepped back to the edge of the *krantz* and leaned over to look for our pursuers. Blackness. But surely there was no need for this utter silence from them? We knew that they were there, they knew of us. Yet it was black as pitch and silent as the tomb. I had an absurd temptation to call out – to shout into the empty bush, to challenge the Berg.

A voice spoke, hushed but clear, from below my feet.

It said, "Beg pardon, sir, but be very careful." The accent was London, south of the river. "There's a gang of hotheads over there, we don't want no trouble. Colonel Wheatcroft always says it's best if they go home to their *kraal* and simmer down . . ."

I said, after my heart had resumed its beat, "And who the bloody hell are you?"

I was relieved to hear that I had immediately resumed the patrician and confident tone, softened with a hint of Scotland, of the man from Oxford and Sunnyside.

The rest is briefly told. We were led half a mile across country by two taciturn corporals whose scouting skills would, as I told them, have been a match for Schalk. They thanked me kindly for the compliment and confided that they were thinking of staying on in this part of the world when they had their papers. We came out on a rough track where the shadows were full of uniformed men and I realised that what I had heard from afar, before still deeper instincts of protection came to my aid, was the jingle of bridles – and no doubt our pursuers had heard it before me. M'Chudi was deposited, none too gently, on a field stretcher and taken away. Douglas and I (Douglas was deferring to me in a ridiculous and unnecessary way) were escorted to an abandoned farmhouse where I introduced myself to a vigorous-looking fellow with prematurely white hair and the insignia of a full colonel. He looked at us with undisguised irritation when we were brought in, which was not at all surprising. We were both filthy to an extreme, but with the special dimension that my clothes were black and stiff with Helga's lifeblood and Douglas was spattered with the equally black stains of M'Chudi's wounds. But our rescuer did not hesitate when he heard my name.

"I've been waiting for you," he said. "My name is Wheatcroft."

"Thank God you got here at last. Why did Schalk tell you to come by this route?"

He looked hard at me in the awkward light of a guttering field lantern.

"What would you mean? Schalk?"

"Yes. Schalk Minnaar. I sent him to ask you for troopers, very urgently."

"Minnaar? If he's the fellow I think you mean, I haven't seen him for three years."

"But he was carrying my message for you! That's why you're here now. Just in time, I might say – you've left it to the last moment, Colonel."

Wheatcroft must have suspected he was being criticised by one of the High Commissioner's puppy dogs. "I'd have you know that you're one of the luckiest young men I've met. I was crossing over from Lydenburg on a routine patrol and my men spotted that a big house on the Berg was in flames. Then they found a gang of kaffirs in warpaint, and I reckon they were looking for you."

"For God's sake!" I cried, "don't you realise that we've found Kruger's Gold?"

In that moment we put our misunderstandings aside. He snapped a series of questions at me. He sent for sergeants and suchlike. He went out on to the track to see for himself when the moon would be up. He despatched his scouts to check that M'Chudi's lads had indeed withdrawn into the night, as we suspected. Order was to be restored; everything would soon be under control. Helga and her uncle had died their terrible deaths, but life must go on – yes, I understood him.

Douglas interrupted us. He may have been intimidated by the way Wheatcroft had turned me into a senior official from Sunnyside, and I grant that he would have been as exhausted as I was, but he was even less coherent than usual and Wheatcroft's responses betrayed his impatience with a Lowveld farmer.

"I think something has happened," said Douglas.

"Like what, Mr Green?"

"No, bear with me a moment, please. I've been trying to sort it out in my head while you two have been talking . . . And I haven't had a chance to tell you what happened in Pilgrims Rest."

"So what is it, Douglas?"

"You know I never trusted Schalk. Not after his stories. Not quite."

"Yes. So?"

"He was supposed to go straight to the Colonel. That's why I let him carry on without me."

"Go on, Douglas."

I felt an awful sense of foreboding, it came straight from the well-spring of my instincts, so recently awoken in the night-time bush.

"You see, Schalk turned up again in Pilgrims Rest, and the Major got us. The Major was in cahoots with the Lodge, of course. I helped Schalk get away – and then he left me behind . . . Or at least, he never came back to get me out. I couldn't be certain what had happened to him, but I guessed he was playing a double game. And then I began to see that he probably hadn't been anywhere near you, Colonel."

Wheatcroft looked baffled, as well he might, and glanced at me for enlightenment, as well he need.

"I told M'Chudi some nonsense about the Germans having found the gold. I made it up. So last night M'Chudi went down by himself to the waterfall to check. I thought that that would finish me, but when he came back in the morning he believed me. And just now he decided that *we* had taken away the gold. He's wrong about us, but he knows that *someone* has taken the gold, because it's clear it isn't there any more . . ."

"Oh Lord!" I said, and my Kindergarten brain began to work so fast that even Ironside would have been impressed. "Colonel, can we have two horses and a supply of torches?"

We found the waterfall more easily than might have seemed possible at that time of night, largely because a trail the width of a wagon had been slashed, crudely but effectively, through the forest and to and fro across the stream since my last visit. Our torches fizzled out when we plunged under the cascade but we managed to light one again and discovered, to the surprise of neither of us, that the cave was empty save for a couple of torn flour sacks.

There was also a note, a folded sheet of paper on which my initials had been scrawled in large letters.

> My friend,
> That you are reading this little letter must mean you have escaped the bad business on the Berg. I rejoice for that. My old travelling companions have helped me rescue what was always ours. One day I think you will understand. My *Volk* have a long trek to make and they will need provisions.
> I am thinking of your Cromwell – you told me

how he said "To be a Seeker is to be of the best sect next to a Finder." You and I are both Seekers. Believe me, one day you will be a Finder too . . .

We shall not meet again. I am sorry for Douglas. Farewell and go well . . .

It was unsigned.

We and Wheatcroft searched for him for a week. In the midst of these confusing times Chief M'Chudi escaped from a field clinic and was not seen again. To my surprise, Captain Ironside had joined us, bruised and limping and offering no explanation; he was not, I thought, in his usual good spirits. Then I went back to Johannesburg to explain to Lord Milner, and to Mr Chamberlain, who I regret to say was still in town, that I had found Kruger's Gold and had thereupon lost it to the Boers.

Chapter Fifteen

THERE IS A GREAT DEAL of deceit and double-dealing in this fragment of autobiography, I can now see: Schalk of me and Douglas, the Native young man of M'Chudi, the Germans of everyone, even Douglas of M'Chudi. None more successful than Schalk of all of us. He had proffered his warning, I suppose – the Boers are the slimmest of the *slim*, Douglas had said, and Schalk had chuckled in agreement – and my masters must at the very least have been guilty of the gravest laxity in trusting him from the beginning (not that that was to help me in the course of the post-mortem in Sunnyside). Douglas, I remembered again, had remarked on a fictitious account of an episode in Matabeleland in 1896; I myself had caught him out in a reference to his own presence in the country in '99 when he was supposed to be in East Africa. Yet in all the recriminations that were to follow my disappointment on the Berg, I never found it in me to blame Schalk personally, so to speak, for my embarrassment.

That may have been because in my final months in South Africa I had become increasingly enamoured of the Boer, our erstwhile enemy.[77] Not necessarily of the typical rural specimen, whose combination of a sluggish intellect with an incurable mendacity had become very familiar to me over long months as

---

77 For this sequence cf. JB's thoughts on the Boer character in *The African Colony* and *Memory Hold-The-Door*.

I trekked throughout their former "republics", but for the general qualities of the race. In fairness I have to set other, more positive qualities against the negative ones I have just cited: a natural generosity, for instance, made evident in their hospitality and their forgiveness of the past; the Boer is naturally law-abiding; he can yet be turned, I am convinced, into a great force for the colonising of the frontier. But what impressed me most of all was the character of their leaders in retreat, seen at its finest in the Boer generals, lean men ragged of dress, bronzed by sun and wind, whom I first encountered after the Vereeniging peace treaty in May '02.[78] Some of them I became proud to consider my friends, which can only mean that they must have ceased to hold my position at Sunnyside against me.

This preamble serves to explain the surprising fact that in October of the same year I found myself visiting Menton, that particularly respectable resort on the coast of Southern France immediately adjacent to the Italian frontier. I had left South Africa in August, and in the circumstances I was not so distressed as I might have expected to be. The reason I was in Menton was because one of my new Boer friends, Jan-Christian Smuts, had suggested it. He had proposed that I, of all people, should call on none other than the former Transvaal President, *Oom* Paul Kruger, who was then living in defeat and lifelong exile in a climate benevolent to his great age, and suffering a state of health which, as we were well-informed in Sunnyside, made it impossible for him ever to consider returning to his homeland even if Lord Milner, by some inconceivable and dangerous charity, would have permitted it.

78 The war ended when the Boers, meeting at Vereeniging on May 31, 1902, voted to accept British peace terms. See *Memory Hold-The-Door*, ch. 5. The terms of surrender were actually signed in Pretoria late that night.

But Smuts, whom I had rapidly learned to admire for the charm of his personality as much as for his wisdom and philosophical intellect, had taken it into his mind that I ought to meet his one-time leader.[79]

"You are beginning to know your enemy," he said to me in his perky manner. "It may be too late for us, but I perceive a new – what shall I say? – a new sympathy – or perhaps I mean a new understanding – for us Boers. I shall regret your departure. I trust that it is not connected with your recent acquaintance with myself and my colleagues."

I hastened to assure him on that point.

"You tell me that you are planning to write a book about your experiences here.[80] That means you will seek to write an analysis of us Dutch – who were your enemies, and perhaps one day will be your friends. So! I think you must meet *Oom* Paul."

I did not conceal my astonishment.

"Why not, why not? He is no longer in Utrecht, he has moved to the Riviera this summer for his health – as you may know."

I tried to conceal a smile and must have failed.

"So be it. Yes, I know that the British must still be spying on his every move, you will even know where he finds his rusks for breakfast. But I am serious, if you write about us you must know us. And *Oom* Paul cannot be of this world for much longer. His health is failing. And, as you can imagine, his heart is heavy . . ."

It appeared that Jannie was serious. He intended to give me

79 Smuts had led the delegation that called on Lord Milner on January 8, 1903. Lawyer, philosopher and soldier, he had been one of the Boer generals in the war and was to become not only Prime Minister of South Africa for many years but also an international statesman. His electoral defeat in 1948 opened the way for the official introduction of *apartheid* by the (largely Afrikaner) National Party.
80 This would be *The African Colony*, 1903.

a letter of introduction, offering an absolute assurance of my integrity, which would carry me past Kruger's protectors (though who, I wondered, would bother any longer to threaten the life of this tragic old man?) We conceded only one deception, and it was Smuts's decision, not mine: the former president could not be expected to admit a member of Lord Milner's private staff. I would therefore present myself not in that capacity (which, we agreed, was in any case inaccurate since I would no longer be employed in Sunnyside by that time), but rather as a young author who was preparing a book on the future of the Transvaal – and that would be incontrovertible. On those terms Smuts thereupon made his farewells and shortly afterwards sent me a letter of introduction which I was to present on my arrival in Menton.[81]

The villa of the exiled leader, as I discovered it on a blustery autumn day, was considerably more elegant than the simple bungalow in Pretoria from whose *stoep Oom* Paul had governed his Transvaal Republic. It was what the French would have considered a suitable retirement home for a successful member of the *haute bourgeoisie*. There could hardly have been a less appropriate final address, it occurred to me, as I paced the corniche, for a simple boy from the Highveld, who now lingered on in the sickness of old age, the sadness of defeat and the loneliness of recent widowerhood. I would have hesitated to approach him except that Jan-Christian had said, "Go on – he's sad and lonely, he needs to see visitors." But consider, he had added, that some days the old man was better than on others. I found that I was disinclined to impose myself under false

81 The friendship between JB and Smuts was to endure: e.g. "In the Great War I was much with the South African Infantry Brigade and at the request of General Smuts I wrote its history . . ." *Memory Hold-The-Door*, ch. 5.

colours; and yet the prospect of meeting the man fascinated me. So I sent up Smuts's letter from my hotel and with mixed feelings received the reply that I was to present myself, for a necessarily brief meeting, the next morning.

The villa was situated in a quiet avenue lined with aromatic eucalyptus and pine trees. Beyond the iron gates the front garden was paved and formal, the stone stairway to the front door lined with miniature pine trees set in a variety of dusty terracotta pots. No specimen, I noticed, of the proteas or aloes of the old man's native land, which would surely thrive in this climate.

There was no evidence that the house was occupied: no sign of servants, nor of carriages, nor of medical attendance. But I had my invitation, a simple card, in my hand. I rang the bell and waited for a long time. I imagined that I had glimpsed a figure behind the curtains in an upper window.

Eventually, when I had begun to debate my retreat, the door was opened by some sort of retainer. He was a dried-up figure of a man, stooped, dressed in grey drabs, and afflicted with an asthmatic cough. He gazed at me blankly, as I did him, whereupon he uttered a few words of execrable French. I had the wit to make a bold guess and switched into the *taal*, of which I once had a modest command. The trick was done, I proffered my pasteboard invitation, and I was bowed inside with much wheezing respect and old-fashioned Free State courtesy. Then I was left alone, standing in the inhospitable hall of what was evidently a residence empty of warmth or character or intimacy. I confess that I felt for the old devil; I even wondered whether Lord Milner would have wished his enemy to have fallen so low.

These charitable emotions were interrupted by the retainer. I gathered that my host was frail that morning – at which I hastily offered, in a dialect which I discovered I was fast forgetting,

224

to depart. But no, the great man would esteem it a favour if I would call on him in his bedroom.

So we ascended the dusty stairway, surrounded by the anonymous furnishings of a style you would expect to find in a superior but not distinguished hotel, until I was led into a larger room which was somehow different. I guessed that it looked out to sea – I wondered, incongruously and fleetingly, whether Kruger still held to his lifelong belief that the world was flat – but I had not anticipated the simplicity, the rightness, of this, his last *laager*. There was no High European clutter to this place, only a high bed, a stinkwood wardrobe that glowed gently with generations of wax polish, a great chair with an embroidered stool. And in the corner I noticed, hanging like an ancient battle emblem, a tattered *Vierkleur*.

The man in the bed, raised on linen pillows, was very old. He gazed at me as I entered and I could not be sure that he realised who I was or what I represented. I recognised him at once from his whiskers and his heavy jowls. I had a quick sense that I was playing an unworthy game, that Smuts had erred in insisting that I intrude on what was surely a deathbed. Yet Jannie had wanted it, and the retainer had permitted it, so I need feel no guilt.

The servant was fussing over the bed, proffering syrups, smoothing sheets and another pillow, muttering the while into the old man's ear. He beckoned me forward and brought out another chair on which I was intended to sit: then he withdrew, though only as far as the window, where he stood looking out towards the sea, his face in shadow, constant in attendance.

I have in my youth, as a son of the manse, done my share of attendance at the bedsides of the sick and the dying, and I think I realised at once that there was no possibility that this was to be a candid dialogue with the old President. Jan Smuts had been

225

too optimistic, I saw with regret. I might have wished to record the occasion for posterity, but I could see that there would be no profit in it, so I remembered how my father would comfort his parishioners with cordial chatter and I launched into that peculiar one-way dialogue which consists of a cheerful sentence, a brief pause to give the possibility of a response, and a resumption of generality and benevolence, all of which is to conceal the sad fact that no response is going to be forthcoming, not now nor ever. I was attending, I realised with a pang of surprising sadness and distress, the deathbed of a great leader.

Did the old man understand any of my platitudes? I was struggling to speak the *taal*, attempting to reminisce about the places I had so recently visited, the men – his lieutenants – I had met, Smuts, Botha, De La Rey. I think I tried to repeat De La Rey's offer to me of employment, the jest which had fallen so flat at the High Commission dinner those few months ago, but I cannot say that the heavy, pockmarked features against the pillows showed more than a confused courtesy.

We must all respect the old and the dying: we feel we owe them our consolation, our confidences. Is it therefore absurd that in this monologue I found myself seeking to offer comfort to him, to search for things to say that – if only he could grasp the simplest message – would comfort him in his last days? That I of all people, Lord Milner's right-hand and private political secretary, could be searching for words to console his arch-enemy?[82] What could I report? That the Republics were overturned? His followers dead or laid low? That the cause of the *Uitlanders*, his hated

82 cf. JB's assessment of Kruger nearly forty years later: "There was a gnarled magnificence to the old Transvaal President, but [Lord Milner] saw only a snuffy, mendacious savage . . . [They were] men deeply in earnest who were striving for things wholly incompatible, an Old Testament patriarchal regime and a modern democracy . . ." *Memory Hold-The-Door*, ch. 5.

foreigners, had triumphed? That we British were planning the establishment of a future Union of South Africa? No, there was so little of actuality that I wished on him that I found myself, without conscious decision, resorting to one small part of the truth.

"Excellency," I said, struggling still to find the words in this absurd dialogue with a mute, "do you remember that, when you went to Komatipoort, your people sent the gold reserves after you? They called it 'Kruger's Gold'. . ."

Was it my imagination that spotted a flicker in those dull eyes?

I said, and must have leaned closer to the pillow, "They tell me the gold was intercepted. Perhaps by the kaffirs – yes, it was by the kaffirs, not by the British Army. But now – please try to understand me, sir – it has been recaptured by the *Volk* . . . Your own men have taken it back. Now they call it Kruger's Millions, and it is hidden again, safe from Milner and his soldiers . . ."

It was futile, his eyes had closed. I could scarcely have credited that he was still living.

A voice interrupted me.

It was quiet, and conversational in tone, it was accented, but it spoke in English.

"It's no good, *basie*, he cannot understand you. You are too late."

It was the voice of Schalk Minnaar, I recognised it as I would the voice of my mother, and after a brief moment of panic and consternation I forgot the body in the bed and crossed the room in a bound and – well, I half-struck, half-embraced, the grinning retainer, who had suddenly become upright and slender and much, much younger.

"Schalk!" I found myself saying, and I still don't know how I can have forgiven him, despite everything that had happened to me that year, "Schalk, you scoundrel, it's so very good to see you . . . You bastard!"

* * *

It all proved, he pointed out, his Theory of Disguise. I had not looked at *Oom* Paul's servant in the hallway in more than the most cursory way because I had assumed that someone, some retainer, would be in attendance. This meant that Schalk merely had to remain short of my conscious attention in order to be safe; he would be my "blind spot". Now that I could scrutinise him, behind the servant's anonymous uniform, I marvelled that I could have failed to recognise him.

The old man seemed to have drifted into sleep, but because this room had a peace and simplicity denied in the bourgeois clutter of the rest of the house, or perhaps because I was the old man's guest and Schalk his nurse, we did not think to leave. "Is the end near?" I murmured, nodding towards the bed, and Schalk shook his head firmly. "He is old and frail, but with good care he can make a fine old age." It seemed that the great hunter had dedicated himself to that sedentary task.[83]

He smiled at me. If we had not been in a sickroom he would have been lighting the great bowl of his pipe. He said, "Have you come to hunt me down, *baas*? I warn you, I shall not come quietly – I have more pressing business, here in this strange *kraal* so far from home."

"Schalk," I said, "you bamboozled us all the way. I am not the most popular servant of the Crown these days. Douglas has gone back to his farm – he's in a great rage with you – and Wheatcroft is still looking for the gold . . ."

He grinned, without any sign of repentance. "He will not find it."

"Because the gold is here?"

---

83 Minnaar was wrong. Kruger was to die quite soon, in Clarens, Switzerland, in July 1904 (he spent the winter months in Menton). His house in Clarens was purchased by the South African Government in 1954 and turned into a Museum.

228

There must have been too much curiosity in my voice, although I had long since accepted that we would never see the treasure again. Schalk frowned a little and, ridiculously, I found myself reassuring him; *no, of course not*, I promised, I was now a private citizen. I had taken his defection hard at the time, but now I understood that he had been in the service of his own cause: that was why Smuts had vouched for me.

"*Of course not*," echoed Schalk, and I knew that he was saying, we don't need the gold here, we need it, one day, down in the very place where it was created.

Since that day in Menton I have often wondered why Schalk's seizure of the gold had distressed me so little. The explanation, I think, is that throughout this episode – this footnote of history – all of us, all the parties involved, thought that the gold belonged to *them*. Lord Milner did not for a moment doubt that it was the rightful property of his Administration. M'Chudi was certain that the gold belonged to the Natives as the product of their land and of their labour. The Boer exiles knew that it remained theirs, and that one day they would recapture their authority in their own land. True, the gold had originally been Kruger's. M'Chudi had seized it from him. Schalk had repossessed it and hidden it, who knows where, to await the revival of his people. And I, and Douglas, and Wheatcroft, had tried to assert Milner's will, and failed. The outcome was not good for me, nor, I suspected, for my masters – but I discovered that I liked it better that the treasure should be in the Boers' hands rather than M'Chudi's. That was why I forgave Schalk the harm he had done me.

But all I said was, "Make sure it's hidden properly this time."

He answered easily, "We know the Berg, and you allowed me enough time to reach a safe place. Not even M'Chudi's wives will discover it this time –".

"We allowed you nothing."

"It was touch and go. Fortunately, I managed to delay Douglas for a few hours when my friends in the Lowveld gave him two dud horses in succession so he didn't have time to get back on the Berg that night. And then I was able to divert him, with Ironside, to Rooi Rand, which took him another day. That was before I had gathered my friends to return to the waterfall." It occurred to me that M'Chudi must have arrived at his waterfall to discover his loss only hours after Schalk and his transport-riders had finished. I also observed that Schalk seemed to have forgotten that he had deserted Douglas in Pilgrims Rest. Come to think of it, he had consigned me to my own oblivion up on the Berg.

"He's a good man is Douglas. Did he tell you he and I nearly handed in our cards together in a fire in the bush? But I needed to get away from him. I was sorry about that."

"And before that, after you and I had found the cave, you persuaded us to hang around and have lunch with the Germans and all that nonsense rather than rush off at once to Wheatcroft."

"You spotted that?"

"Only afterwards, Schalk."

"I thought you were happy to spend more time with the German *meisie*."

The joke turned stale. I began to say, "But Helga is dead, Schalk" – and then I realised he would not know of their fate at the hands of M'Chudi's young men; at the moment of their death he would have been burying the gold in another secret hideaway.

"The Portugoose was killed," I began. "Then Helga, and then her protector. Never mind the detail. He was thrown over the Berg. Thank God Douglas managed to get back even after you had sent him off in the other direction. He saved me by a whisker – but that was no thanks to you. Then Wheatcroft arrived – again no thanks to you . . . For God's sake, Schalk, take the gold if it meant so much to you, but you could have warned Wheatcroft that we were in one hell of a mess up on that mountain."

I told him more of the tale and it occupied a quarter-hour. Did he look abashed? He had broken faith with me and with Douglas. He had deceived Douglas twice and abandoned him in cold blood. If Wheatcroft had not turned up on the Lydenburg road by accident, and if Douglas were not the man he was, the lives of both of us would have been on his conscience. Would that have threatened his Mediterranean sleep, I wondered?

"You left us in the lurch, Schalk. Or rather, you left me to my deserts – and you abandoned Douglas and left him to the mercy of that Prussian murderer. Yes, of course you did – you had to get him out of the way. First of all, you tried to send him off with Ironside on a wild goose chase – if he hadn't been loyal enough, or brave enough, to come back to rescue me, I wouldn't be here now. And when you had the bad luck to bump into him in Pilgrims Rest, you used him to help you to escape – and left him behind so as to give you a clear ride to the waterfall." (I sometimes wonder whether, when I ordered Douglas to accompany Schalk on his escape from the Lodge, at an unconscious level I did not trust Schalk to operate by himself.)

He said, very low, and even then he glanced over his shoulder at the old man, "The war is not over, you must remember that. You and I have fought our battle and now I hope we can be friends. But do not think that the *Volk* has been defeated."

"For God's sake, Schalk, your *Volk* was defeated at Vereeniging. Smuts and the others will tell you I am right. You are talking about a few bars of gold which you have hidden in a mineshaft for the sake of a handful of your people."

But it occurred to me as I spoke that this gold represented

a power, a future, and that Schalk had been right to bury it, to bide time; that the gold was something inchoate, assuming a symbolic importance for a future Boer revival; that one day the descendants of *Oom* Paul and Schalk would mine that treasure and do with it God knows what; that therein lay my defeat, and M'Chudi's too; it was the Boers', to do with it what they chose, so long as they had the patience and the wisdom to bide their time.

Schalk might have been reading my thoughts. All he said was, "*Ja*, it is well-hidden. We do not need it now, but the day will come . . ." and we turned back towards the invalid on the bed. Schalk added, as though to seek a painful precision, "For us – or rather, for me and for my generation – you can say that it is too late. But the struggle continues, have no doubt of that."

I said, "Schalk, we should have spotted you. How did you get away with it for so long?"

"Because your bosses were so happy to have a *waar Boer* working for them. They are very innocent, you must know that."

"But you made those stupid mistakes! You told a silly story about being with Rhodes in Matabeleland, which Douglas spotted. And you told me a tale about '99 when you were supposed to be in East Africa."

"And I persuaded you to go back to the Lodge, to eat and to drink, when we ought to have run off to White River with our discovery . . . *That* was the moment I began to win. *You* found the gold for me, remember. Then all I needed was time. I needed more time to round up my men, so I had to delay you, or rather, Douglas. You must see that. And then I sent a telegram to Sunnyside, as soon as I left him, so that Douglas would waste more time with Captain Ironside."

"You stranded Douglas in the Lowveld, then left him to the

Major, and at the same time delivered me to the Germans and then to M'Chudi. That's quite a record, Schalk."

"I told you, my friend, the war is not over. I promise you that I regretted it then and I regret it now. But can you imagine how long I had been assigned to this venture? You came so late to it, I promise you . . ."

"And why did you do it? Did your mother die in our camps?"

"No, only a *tante* or two – but let us not joke about the camps! Listen to me, I know you too well. I know that you understand us. You have stolen my country – you are unlike your companions, *you* know what I am saying, and that is why you are here today.[84] That is why I shall allow you to enjoy your temporary victory, my friend . . ."

We were standing over the body of the exiled President. I glanced down at the heavy flesh of his features and discovered, with a start, that the old man had awoken, his pale eyes were gazing up at me. I felt myself shudder: they were cold and weird and devilish, they were like the eyes of a snake, they chilled me just like the eyes of the Old Man from the Lodge. Perhaps that last phrase of Schalk's – we had been speaking in English – had penetrated his failing consciousness. I saw him react, and reject what he had heard Schalk admit. Then the eyelids fluttered and fell over those cold, old eyes: those eyes, I saw, were hooded like a hawk's. Then he seemed to drift back into sleep, and I shivered again and hoped that Schalk had seen nothing, and decided that I must leave.[85]

84 In *Greenmantle* Hannay in an early chapter posing as a Boer: "England has stolen my country and corrupted my people and made me an exile. We Afrikanders do not forget. We may be slow but we win in the end . . ." (ch. 3).
85 cf. *The Thirty-nine Steps*, ch. 6, for the moment when Hannay spots that he has walked into the enemy lair. It is the Old Man, Hannay's most intimidating enemy in the whole canon, who is revealed by his habit of hooding his eyes like a hawk.

"Don't forget, Schalk, the words of the Good Book – the words that led me back to the waterfall with you that morning: 'Lay not up for yourselves treasure upon earth . . .'"

Yes, I was taunting him.

He burst out laughing, like a boy, and took up the reference. "'For where your treasure is, there will your heart be also!' So *that's* how you made the link between the kaffir girl and the gold behind the waterfall. You are very clever, *baas*. So that's how we found the waterfall! My nation is grateful to you!"

That sounded a bit too smug for my taste. The Boers might have got their gold back, but I didn't want them to think that this was the end of the story.

"Remember Cromwell – and he would have got on well with you people. I told you about Seekers being next to Finders, and you had the nerve to repeat it in the letter you left at the cave, but I didn't finish the quotation –"

"Which says?"

"'To be a Seeker is to be of the best sect next to a Finder, *and such a one shall every faithful, humble Seeker be at the end . . .'* Which means, don't underestimate us, Schalk."

"That's very good," said Schalk, and I could see him memorise it. "That sums up everything." He punched me on the arm as a token of appreciation.[86]

And a gruff voice from the bed said, "*Amen!*" and launched into a disordered speech. Though whether the President spoke in Dutch or in English or in a half-remembered tongue from the

86 cf. *A Prince of the Captivity*, ch. II/2: "I call myself a Seeker. You remember Cromwell's words? 'The best sect next to a Finder . . .'" etc, as above. In this same book there is a group calling itself "The Seekers". See also the final pages of *Memory Hold-The-Door* (1940) ch. XII/4. In *The Path of the King* (1921) the mother of Abraham Lincoln "was assured that the day of the Seekers had passed and that the Finder had come . . ." (ch. 13).

days before Majuba and Blood River I do not know. I left the pair of them to their victorious exile, for I must be off to London and the rescue of my fortune.

Editor's Epilogue

I HAVE ALREADY RECORDED the brief letter to "Lionel" [Phillips] which, it seems, would have accompanied this manuscript. (I find myself wondering what the bold and unconventional Randlord had made of this thank-you for the loan of his Hampshire mansion to the honeymoon couple.)[87]

I have also already quoted in my Foreword the curious passage from Buchan's autobiography in which he refers to "an unpleasant and rather dangerous business, *for which I was not to blame but the burden of which I was compelled to shoulder . . .*" (my italics). Let me at this concluding stage take up my initial challenge to my readers to consider the editorial comments which follow, and the footnotes throughout the text, and then to form their own judgment on my thesis. We may assume today, I think, that after so many years, one-half of which have passed under Afrikaner (i.e. Boer) rule, no further evidence is likely to emerge from official sources (that is, in Pretoria or in London) or from private archives. Hence the importance of this document, which I have entitled *The Buchan Papers*.

---

87 After his period in South Africa, Buchan's first two "shockers", as he called them, were extremely slim – *The Power House* has fewer than 35,000 words, no more than a novella in today's terms, and *The Thirty-nine Steps* is about 40,000 words. After that Buchan got into his stride and with *Mr Standfast* (120,000) and later books like *A Prince of the Captivity* he was allowing himself to exceed the norm by a very large margin.

I shall depart from the conventional caution of my academic discipline and suggest, first, that this narrative, if we assume its general accuracy (and I see no reason to doubt that, now that I have had the opportunity to edit and cross-check the text), goes far to explain one of the minor mysteries of Buchan's career.

What I mean by this is that when the ambitious twenty-seven-year-old returned to London in August 1903 his career did *not* blossom as he might have hoped, and as his friends expected, after several years at the heart of imperial affairs as the protégé of the great Milner. To be specific, it had been thought he would next go out to a senior financial post with Lord Cromer in the Egyptian administration. He did not get it, although he continued to hope for it until the spring of 1904. In his memoirs, published in 1940, Buchan – by then Lord Tweedsmuir, Governor-General of Canada – was on the face of things candid: "the home authorities declined to ratify his [Cromer's] choice, no doubt rightly, on the grounds of my youth and inexperience . . ."

This sentence, on first reading, is rather surprising: on second reading it becomes unconvincing. I suggest that this narrative of events on the South African Berg in January 1903 offers another explanation: in short, that Buchan was considered to have failed in a mission of supreme importance. The Secretary of State himself would presumably have been furious, not just because Buchan had failed to recover the gold as he was charged, but – the worst imaginable result – because it had instead fallen into the hands of the Boer rebels.

Buchan can hardly have hoped to remain the "blue-eyed boy" and his career might have been expected to suffer – *as it did*. If we now re-read his autobiography with this insight, a different story emerges: "So I was compelled to go back to the Bar where, with much restlessness and distaste, I continued for the next three years . . . Those years were not the pleasantest of my life. South Africa had completely unsettled me . . ."[88]

Only his closest intimates might have known the truth of the matter and they are long since dead, nor would I expect him to have confided this embarrassing setback to his family or to his sons. Certainly his pursuit of success and of the recognition of the British ruling classes in the years ahead was to be energetic and unflagging; he was an example of what has sometimes been called a "driven man". (It is only proper to add that Buchan rapidly overcame any black mark and became a most honoured, distinguished and respected public servant.)

Secondly, I suggest that, if these revelations are true, the acquisition by Kruger's "friends in exile" (the words "party" or "government" would be too strong) of a very substantial treasure is likely to have played an incalculable part in the slow revival of the Boer nation's cause in the years before the Second World War. (President Kruger died in July 1904; his health was such that he would have been able to play no role in the disposition of the gold, presumably hidden by Schalk Minnaar somewhere in the Eastern Transvaal.) As Minnaar's brief comments in Menton to Buchan indicate, he and his transport-riders would not have risked moving the treasure far with the efficient Wheatcroft in pursuit; and Minnaar must have had his own associates who had learned the lessons of the war, one of which was that they would have to lie low for many years. I am utterly unqualified to discuss, let alone research, this area, and I am happy to hand over these suggestions to my colleagues in the Afrikaans universities.

Thirdly, I want to raise – though again I admit my lack of qualifications – the question of the impact on the young Buchan's

88 *Memory Hold-The-Door*, ch. 6.

character and (I make a close association) his career as a writer, of so serious a professional setback at a point in a man's youth when high-flyers feel the need to achieve rapid success or promotion.[89]

I ventured into this line of enquiry when I found myself wondering why he had felt the compulsion – and no doubt breached all official and binding oaths of confidentiality – to write down the detail of the fiasco, even if he was to entrust the record to a close friend. (Did anyone else see the manuscript, one wonders, apart from Lionel Phillips?) My tentative answer – and I am not qualified in psychoanalytical interpretation – is that he needed to *do* something, to *write it out* of himself, to explain, to justify to the world (whose judgment he so much respected) why the mission had gone wrong. *Tout comprendre, c'est tout pardonner*, and I suppose something like that formed a part of his motivation. Only then – to change a modest metaphor – can you wipe your slate clean.

But it occurred to me that this might not be enough, and that he might continue for years to come to need to compensate for so traumatic an experience; but because his professional career was committed to, and confined by, the conventions and rules of Edwardian society, it might be interesting to look for this process of compensation in his fiction rather than in the public achievements. When you think of it this way, at the simplest level of discussion – the plotting of his novels, for instance – the traumatic events described above surely had an undeniable influence on his mature writing. To mention only the most obvious and dramatic examples, he used the Old Man's death (reworked) in the climax of *The Three Hostages*; Helga's death (significantly changed) in

89 "I learned a good deal in South Africa, and the chief lesson was that I had still much to learn about the material world and about human nature . . ." (*Memory Hold-The-Door*, ch. 5/VII).

Greenmantle; Green's rescue of JB at the end is symbolically developed in the scene where Hannay carries Launcelot Wake over the Schwarzsteinhor in *Mr Standfast* (and, later, Adam Melfort carries the dubious Warren Creevey over a similar ordeal in *A Prince of the Captivity*); the whole sequence was originally picked over in *Prester John*.[90]

But it seems to me that the "compensation" factor works at a deeper level. Here again I am unqualified to hold forth, but I very diffidently offer the briefest of comments on various aspects and personalities of the Buchan *œuvre* as they might be reconsidered in the light of these new autobiographical facts – after which I trust that my colleagues in the literature departments will take over . . .

For example, let us take Buchan's famous and utterly sympathetic creation of Peter Pienaar (*Greenmantle*, *Mr Standfast*, *The Island of Sheep* and, peripherally, *The Thirty-nine Steps*). Here, surely, is Buchan's "revenge" on Schalk Minnaar who, from the British point of view, is the principal *villain* of *The Buchan Papers*, who totally deceives and outmanœuvres Buchan, betrays Douglas Green several times, and vanishes with the gold. His reward, in fiction and indeed in history, is to be transformed into the faithful British loyalist, the dearest friend of Richard Hannay (of all ironies!), the scourge of the Boer patriots, who is first crippled in the British cause and then, in *Mr Standfast*, gives his life for the Empire; Hannay (Douglas) would collect Pienaar's posthumous Victoria Cross.[91]

Or take Helga Ingeburg. After terrifying, enchanting and bamboozling the young and virginal Buchan, she is adroitly turned into the diabolical Hilda von Einem, the only really memorable

90 See *Mr Standfast*, ch. 17 and *A Prince of the Captivity*, ch. III/3.
91 Hannay of Pienaar: "He was the man who taught me all I ever knew of *veldcraft*, and a good deal about human nature besides . . ." (*Greenmantle*, ch. 3).

female in Buchan's fiction, who is so villainous and at the same time so irresistible that Buchan's ultra-hero Sandy Arbuthnot is captivated by her, while Hannay (a.k.a. D. Green) discovers that he hates and also fears her. She dies, too, in a violent way, but Sandy carries her body gently through the bursting shells outside Erzerum. The mercenary and probably criminal Helga has become the aristocratic Hilda and they all dig her grave: is that a gesture of forgiveness? Or just the burial of an unfortunate and afterwards regretted infatuation? Interestingly, while Helga dies in bloody agony, Hilda is allowed to leave without smudging her lipstick. As has been frequently noted by the commentators, all the rest of Buchan's women are slim, boyish, splendid, rather indistinguishable, and not at all sexy: not at all like Helga/Hilda, slim though she may be.

Her co-villain in *Greenmantle* is the beastly, effeminate, grotesque but very dangerous Colonel von Stumm, who is eventually worsted by Hannay after giving him a very hard time. He is extremely evil, although, as is not uncommon in Buchan, he is given a positive quality as well – "he was that vile thing – but also a patriot . . ." – and he can only stem from Buchan's memory of the torturer and mercenary German thug, Major S. in Pilgrims Rest. JB. was determined to deal with Major S.: he seems to have done it twice, once in fact (Major S. vanished from the records) and once in fiction. The reason for this transformation of a British officer into a Prussian monster seems very obvious. Buchan in the real world had to live with the fact that the British used torture to impose their rule, and in that were no different from all occupying powers. He preferred to forget this and fictionalise the man responsible.[92]

92 cf. Hannay of von Stumm: "I began to see the queer other side to my host, that evil side which gossip had spoken of as not unknown in the German army . . ."

Then there is the more complicated matter of Douglas Green. He has the physique and some of the personality of Buchan's most famous fictional hero, Richard Hannay (*The Thirty-nine Steps, Mr Standfast, The Three Hostages, The Island of Sheep*, and brief appearances in *The Courts of the Morning* and many of the short stories), together with a remarkably similar background in Rhodesia, South-West Africa and, briefly, in the Boer War, in Delagoa Bay, plus mining, hunting, languages, Natives (tricks of), and, of course, he has "made his pile". (He is also bored, which will one day years later take him in Buchan's imagination to London and, via a circuitous and perilous route, to the thirty-nine steps and thereafter to international fame.) In this affray in the Eastern Transvaal Douglas Green may be slow and unsophisticated, but he saves JB's life and, equally important, gives him loyalty in a crisis. Green is a youngish, decent, bluff, undeveloped and unintellectual Rhodesian mining engineer. His return to the rescue, after surviving Minnaar's treachery and worsting the Major, swings the balance, rescues JB and gets a fictional reward. These qualities of courage, strength, decency, endurance, so impressed themselves on the young Buchan that Green was rewarded by being turned into one of the most *parfit* knights that fiction has ever known. He also became more intelligent, more rich, and got himself a teenage upper-class wife and a country house in the Cotswolds. (In Hannay, Buchan suppressed Green's evident liking for a drink.)[93]

I could go on in this academic vein, but shall resist the temptation. The influence of Dorando on Buchan's work is almost too obvious to mention – his books have a number of "Portugoose" villains (e.g. Henriques in *Prester John*) who are

93 In *The Thirty-nine Steps*, Hannay takes a whisky-soda for breakfast.

portrayed in near-racist terms. Colonel Wheatcroft, who saved them all, was thanked when he became Captain Arcoll in *Prester John* (Arcoll also figures, as a good chap, in *The Island of Sheep*: he is the only character who links *Prester John* with the Hannay books – no mean immortality. I wonder if the actual Wheatcroft ever knew.) As for Chief M'Chudi, about whom JB here seems ambivalent, the young author settled scores by using the chief's name in his next novel.[94]

Finally, the Old Man became, I suggest, an identifiable element in a variety of Buchan's villains in the earlier novels, such was the young man's need to heal the psyche. He is spotted most clearly in *The Thirty-nine Steps*, in "the benevolent old gentleman" who turns out to be Hannay's arch-enemy. He betrays himself to Hannay by hooding his eyes like a hawk at a critical moment, just as Buchan had observed President Kruger do in Menton in these pages; he is also weird, devilish, cold, malignant, unearthly, hellishly clever, with the eyes of a snake, and so on and so forth. The Old Man is certainly the model for the suave exponent of pre-war anarchy, Andrew Lumley, in *The Power House*. He may also be somewhere behind the younger Dominick Medina of *The Three Hostages*, though I am influenced by the hypnotism scenes, as I would be if I also referred to Ivery in *Mr Standfast*. But my most startling discovery, which came to me only as I was completing this edition, is that the Old Man in these pages is remarkably close in physical appearance to Dickson McCunn – Buchan's lovable Glasgow grocer, retired senior citizen, royalist and "incurable romantic", patron of the Gorbals Diehards, the affluent and innocent hero of *Huntingtower*, *Castle Gay* and *The*

94 "Machudi (*sic*) was a blackguard chief whom the Boers long ago smashed in one of their native wars . . . A Boer farmer on the plateau had his skull and used to drink whisky out of it when he was merry . . ." *Prester John*, ch. 15.

House of the Four Winds. Here is the true revenge. You turn your most feared and hated adversary in the real and difficult world into a grandfatherly sage and saint in the world of your imagination; and then, I believe the theory goes, you have exorcised the nightmares.[95]

I am therefore suggesting – with the real diffidence of a professional historian meddling beyond his field – that Buchan in his middle years used his fantasy-fiction as a way of enabling himself to come to terms with his failures as a younger man in the real world. This may well have been an effective therapeutic tactic; the universal agreement of his many friends and admirers, before and after his death in 1940, as to his wisdom, confidence, authority, distinction, kindness, etc., all appear to confirm this. Of course, this psychological stratagem would also have been crucial to the achievement of his mature literary art – though that is an area I shall not venture into. I shall merely note that, in doing this, his necessary process of self-delusion paralleled the late-Imperial

---

95 These pages raise some questions about the actual ages of the protagonists as compared with the ages that Buchan was to give to the fictitious characters which he created out of them.

JB was born in August 1875 and is therefore twenty-seven at the time of this episode. "Richard Hannay", according to *The Thirty-nine Steps*, was thirty-seven in 1914, and therefore would have been twenty-six in 1903. In this manuscript Douglas Green says that he did duty in Rhodesia in 1897, in the rebellions; he must surely have been older than twenty at that time. But it is understandable that Buchan, in launching Hannay on a magnificent military career in 1914 at the desperately late age of thirty-seven, needed to lose a few of Green's years. I suggest Douglas Green was probably about thirty at the time of these events.

Peter Pienaar in the canon is dated only once, in *Greenmantle*, where he turns out to be fifty-six in 1916, i.e. he was born in 1860. This manuscript, with its implication that he had been active all over Southern Africa throughout the 1890s, offers nothing to contradict that Schalk Minnaar was a fit and trim forty-three in 1903.

Finally, Buchan was a gentleman and, perhaps because of his particular feelings for the lady, it is not remotely surprising that we never get a hint of the age of Helga Ingeburg – nor, for that matter, of Hilda von Einem – except that it seems clear that both of them are "older women".

Britain's confusion between fact and fantasy, a self-deluding dialogue which was to involve many of Buchan's Kindergarten colleagues who came together in what became known as the "Round Table", which features in all the histories of British politics in the first half of this century.

But this is not the place for such a discussion. Buchan was not "re-writing history" since this particular history was fated never to be "written" for public scrutiny; it was intended to remain hidden for ever in the secret world of affairs which has so preoccupied Britain's subsequent political, diplomatic and also literary life. However, it helped Buchan to cope with the setback, and so to play a full role in the later dramas of his distinguished career.

After the bland pomposities of *The African Colony* in 1903 he did not write at length about these things again, except in his autobiography and, famously, in *Prester John* (1910). This was indeed his first full fiction following his return to London, after the unhappy years that preceded his happy marriage into the English aristocracy. It is only superficially a boys' story: his theme is the young white man who is caught between black and white ambition in South Africa, between Laputa, the charismatic black leader, and a mixed bunch of Europeans; the prize is not just Sheba's jewels but the future of the sub-continent, and the young Scots boy is at the heart of the drama.

There is no doubt at all from *The Buchan Papers* that the young JB, if he had to fail in his mission, would have preferred the gold to go to Schalk Minnaar and his people rather than to M'Chudi and his. This is surely evident in his reported visit to Menton. Buchan later also admitted to sympathetic feelings for the Boers; he did not record much feeling for the Natives; he was a man of his time and we cannot guess at his response if he had lived longer and had known of what was to come when the heirs of Oom Paul Kruger and Schalk Minnaar came to power in 1948. All I can offer is the diffident suggestion that, in its symbolic meaning, the legacy of "Kruger's Gold" was to be the story of South Africa for the rest of this century.

Editor's Postscript

I am grateful to my publisher for agreeing to allow a final comment as this book goes to press.

In deference to the rigorous codes of Academe, I feel I have to record a final qualification of the pages above. To explain: my brother-in-law, who happens to be South African by birth and no mean authority on the history of his homeland, has been reading these page-proofs and has offered me what is on the face of it an alarming interpretation. He suggests, with his usual eloquence, that the entire manuscript represents a fantasy by the young John Buchan, written for his private amusement as he travelled the Transvaal in early 1903 on the dull business of land settlement. Buchan's lively imagination, my friend proposes, was fired by the landscape, by the talk in the Kindergarten of Kruger and his gang, by the well-known and teasing rumours of the hidden gold treasure of "Kruger's Millions", by the frustrating drama of Chamberlain's visit in which Buchan felt himself to be largely ignored. Buchan – continues my brother-in-law – was before all else a novelist, a fantasist. His defence from the world, as his career was to demonstrate, lay in fiction. So, his imagination aflame, he created these fancies. He sent the manuscript to Lionel Phillips as a private jest, which he signalled when he said that he was rehearsing his future career as a writer of "shockers": that was why Phillips paid it no further attention.

I am told that it is too late to withdraw these pages from the press so I shall merely record, as is my professional duty, this footnote. The reader must form his own judgment.

Glossary

The reader may be helped by the following list of Afrikaans words which appear in this book

agter, behind

baas, master, sir (diminutive: *basie*)

bittereinders, those Boers who fought the war to the bitter end

bobotie, traditional Boer dish of curried meat

boerewors, traditional local sausage

bo, *bowe*, above

braaivleis, traditional local style of barbecue

dankie, thanks, thank you

dominee, clergyman, minister

dorp, small town

duiker, species of small buck

Godsverdomp, 'God damn it!'

goeie nag (Nag), good night

ja, yes

jakkals, jackal

koeksister, traditional local syrup cake

konfyt, jam

kopje, small hill

laager, traditional defensive alignment of wagons

mampoer, homemade brandy

meisie, girl, lass

Meneer, mister, sir

oder, under

ons, onse, we, our

oom, uncle

skelm, rogue, knave

skerm, screen, shield

slim, clever, smart, sharp

spoor, track, trace (today = railway)

spruit, stream, tributary

Staatsbank, State Bank

stoep, verandah

taal, the Afrikaans language

tante, aunt

tot siens, goodbye

tronk, prison

uitlander, foreigner

veld, field, open land

veldpond, literally: field-pound or sovereign

velskoen, traditional homemade shoe

vierkleur, flag of the Transvaal Republic

vlei, valley, bog

volk, nation, people

Volksraad, house of assembly

vrou, woman, wife (*Mevrou*: Mrs, madam)